Trystin S. Bailey
Eternia

Eternia (Book 3 of the Reverie series)
Copyright © 2020 by Trystin Steven Bailey

To you.

Prologue

Nihilo stood in the endless white expanse that was Origin Point, thinking of nothing. Nothing, after all, was his domain. His obsession. The manifestation and co-ruler of Eternia, the spirit realm, longed for nothing more than the end of existence. Nihilo's physical form, a depthless cut-out of a massive man, existed in great contrast to the white void of Origin Point. Against the pristine backdrop he was an aberration. Something that simply did not belong.

Yet here he was, in a rare moment alone and free of the judgement and company of the five other manifestations whom he loathed. Even Mortem, manifestation of decline.

This solitude at Origin was the closest to nothingness he could achieve, for now.

With a mere thought, Nihilo conjured a window that offered him sight into any corner of the three realms...

First he gazed upon a jungle, but not like any of Earth. For this was the dream realm Reverie. The trees were impossibly tall and twisted, contorted, entwined more and more as they reached upward until they created a thick canopy that allowed in very little light. On the jungle floor was a collection of creatures built to survive in the darkness. These creatures were led by a thing worshipped by many and feared by many more. A monster that prepared for its part in a scheme further-reaching than it could imagine. A monster that understood more than most the true power of darkness: in the absence of light you could truly become anything.

In the physical realm, Cosmos— Earth specifically —there

was a prison. One reserved for criminals of a truly horrific nature. Amongst the hundreds that called this place home, Ezekiel Christopher Clark was the worst of them all. Even he didn't know how many he had killed. He lost count years ago. Currently, Ezekiel was held in solitary confinement, separated from a world that he seemed hell bent on destroying. Fortunately for him (and unfortunately for many others), Ezekiel's reign of terror was not constrained by a single realm. He was a gifted Lucid, able to slip into Reverie and wreak his devastating and widespread brand of havoc each night when he went to sleep. He, too, was ready for the task at hand.

Over a thousand miles away a man stood in an open field under the hot summer sun. He was dressed in a three-piece gray suit and held a full white styrofoam cup. To pass him on a busy street you would think nothing of him. But with great passion and authority he launched into a sermon on hope and hellfire to the nearly one hundred loyal followers that made up his congregation. When he completed his declaration, some cheered, some were in tears, but all had made up their minds. At the preacher's word, the congregation drank the contents of their cups. Five minutes later, they were dead; their corpses strewn across the grass. The preacher tossed his cup to the ground, a smile on his face. "Nihilo's will be done," he said. "More soldiers are on their way to Eternia."

PART 1
BROS.

1

Jamal Anderson pulled his dreadlocks back into a ponytail, revealing his dark brown face glistening with sweat. His hair was always the first thing he toyed with whenever he was nervous or frustrated. He was currently experiencing a level of both that he had never felt before.

"We're in Reverie," said Vic for the tenth time, dark eyes observing the area. This time he said it in response to Jamal searching for the portal that had disappeared only a few minutes before. Vic's lean, muscular figure was completely naked, but he was unfazed by it. Pieces of ceramic were clinging to his tan skin.

"No shit," said Jamal. Vic had after all just transformed from a pile of ashes in an urn to a fully alive young man. Not to mention that they had just passed through a portal. Or that the grass beneath their feet was blue. Or that the sky was an unearthly magenta.

"Dude…" Max, Jamal's best friend, was poking something with a stick. His bright green eyes shone innocently from a freckled face through scraggly red hair. "Look what I found…"

The dead animal wasn't much larger than a raccoon. It was cream-colored with massive ears and a long tail. It had the sharp, blocky features of something from an old video game. Pixelated blood was still seeping from its wounds.

"Whoa." Max noticed something else part way down the small hill on which the three boys stood. Jamal followed Max's line of sight to find a considerably larger creature, also dead. It was roughly twenty feet long, a dark blue color, and lined with thick centipede-like legs.

"What happened here?" Jamal wondered aloud, a chill moving up his spine.

"Doesn't matter." Vic's response was quick. "We've got work to do. For starters, I need clothes."

"No." Jamal stepped up to Vic. He was a few inches taller than his naked companion. "We're not going anywhere until you tell us what's going on."

Vic threw his hands into the air. "How am I supposed to know? Up until a few minutes ago I was a pile of dust!"

"The white man. Er...the man in white," said Max. "Do you think he knew this would happen? Vic coming back? I mean, he had to, right?"

Vic's eyes widened. "The man in white?"

Jamal shot Max a look, then he rolled his eyes and turned to Vic. "There was this...thing. Shaped like a man, but didn't have a face or anything. All white. Like, paper white. Not Max white. It convinced me that the only way to help Claire was to steal your urn and...and go to the portal we'd discovered in your journals."

Vic smiled. "My journals...? You mean I was right? Of course I was right! Ha ha! Did the man in white tell you anything else?"

Jamal shrugged. "Nothing. I assumed that since you're here maybe you'd have something in mind."

"Oh I do. I do indeed." Vic began pacing. "You see, while in Harvard— before my untimely demise —I was trying to uncover the secrets of Reverie so that I might tap into its power. As you know, I've got this handy deus ex machina sort of gift where I can summon the knowledge to answer any question. What you may not know is that the information I can tap into is limited to the realm I'm in. But...through your desperate love for Claire and this man in white, I'm here. Which means you can ask me the one question I've been dying to answer since I learned of this chaotic, wild place. So, boys, I need one of you to repeat after me: How does one take complete and utter control of Reverie?"

2

Vic marched ahead as Jamal and Max walked side by side in silence. Just a few days ago they were enjoying a life of small town high school popularity and basketball practice. They were still wearing their red and white Addley High Osprey uniforms.

Max, though, was never one to keep quiet for long. "Jamal," he began, "since we're in Reverie do you think there's a chance of seeing Mindy?"

Jamal halted his thoughts of Claire to think back to a simpler time when he was a simple teenager with simpler needs. A time when his best friend Max pined for Mindy Sparks, never finding the strength to ask her out. That is, until the Spring Fling when he asked her to be his date...and she said yes. It was the happiest Jamal had ever seen Max. In an unfortunate twist, the night of the fling was the night Mindy disappeared to Reverie. That was almost a year ago. In all the drama and war and confusion that happened since, Max never brought up his feelings about Mindy. And Jamal had been too caught up in Claire's drama to ask.

"Dude," began Jamal, "remember what Claire told us? How Reverie's so much bigger than Addley?" Max lowered his head, nodding. "But look. If there's anything we've learned this past year, it's that pretty much anything is possible. So, yeah. Totally! There's totally a chance of seeing Mindy."

Max smiled his trademark genuine smile. "Thanks, man."

"Anytime, dude."

"Excuse me!" Vic's voice was sharp and loud. "We're almost there. In order to be effective in the task at hand we're going to need armor. And this," Vic gestured ahead to what seemed to be a thick, dark jungle, "is where my instincts tell me we can procure some."

"Your instincts," Jamal said. "You mean your creepy powers."

"Obviously, yes." Vic grinned. "Now come with me."

Max whispered to Jamal, "I don't trust this dude."

"Understatement of the year," said Jamal.

They followed Vic into the jungle. The bright sky gave way to deep shadow, the sun blotted out by the near-impenetrable canopy above. Chirps, screeches, and howls permeated the place. Jamal could not help but feel like they were being watched. The large green orbs that shone from the blackness all but verified the feeling.

"What are those?" asked Max. As Vic began to answer a pair of enormous purple eyes opened from the shadow, dwarfing the other orbs.

"Oh my, oh my what have we here?" rang a voice like a 1920's radio host. "A trio of trespassing boys, it appears." The eyes changed from purple to turquoise, then merged into one even larger eye. Then separated into three.

"We don't mean you any harm," said Vic. "Honestly, we couldn't care less who you are or what you're doing here. We just need to pick up some armor and weapons, then we're on our way."

The three turquoise eyes turned red and the hundreds of green orbs went black. The once loud jungle turned dead silent.

Max leaned over to Jamal. "If we survive this Vic is not allowed to do the talking anymore."

The voice returned, louder this time. Angrier. "Your rudeness is crude, yes, you insolent turd. Let's test now how good you truly are with words. I'm known as Estralus, the lord of this land. And many men greater have died at my hand." A huge white sharp-toothed smile opened up beneath the three eyes. The eyes merged back into one.

Suddenly, dark purple tendrils emerged from the darkness and wrapped around Max and Jamal, immobilizing them.

"I shift my shape and know your soul. Submit, my pets, to my control. Out of fairness I'll give you one chance to be free. You need only slay these riddles three."

"Riddles?" A sly smirk crept across Vic's face.

Estralus' eye glimmered gold. "Get them right and my treasures are yours. Fail even one and-"

"Alright. I get it." Vic sighed. "Let's keep this moving."

Estralus' eye flickered red. "I look forward to tearing you limb from limb," he grumbled.

"Yeah. Yeah."

"First riddle!" Estralus' voice boomed. "You can see me in water, but I never get wet. What am I?"

"A reflection. Next!"

Estralus' eye disappeared and its mouth grew larger. Its teeth became longer, sharper, dripping with gray-green saliva.

"One makes it, but has no need for it. One buys it, but has no use for it. One uses it but can neither see nor feel it. What is it?"

Vic feigned a yawn. "A coffin. How about a challenge next time?"

The entire jungle quaked. In the shadow behind Estralus' large open mouth one could see something squirming and shifting. "A challenge you want, then a challenge you'll receive. With this last riddle from you I'll at last...um...be...relieved?" It let loose a ferocious roar then spoke rapidly. "Four obnoxious little friends need to cross through a dark, terrifying jungle in the dead of night. Thing is, the fools only have one torch between them and the jungle is way too dangerous to traverse without one. Due to the density of the jungle only two people can go through at once. For various reasons each friend takes a different amount of time to pass through the jungle. One can do it in one minute, another in two, the third in seven, and the last one can do it in ten. What is the shortest time needed for all four of them to make it through the jungle."

Vic remained silent.

"Ha!" Estralus laughed. "Looks like victory is-"

"Seventeen minutes," said Vic. "The one- and two- minute fools cross together. Two minute fool comes back. Seven and ten cross. One comes back. One and two go across. Bam."

Estralus' smile dropped into a deep frown then disappeared. The jungle sounds and the green orbs returned. The tendrils that had ensnared Max and Jamal slithered back into the darkness. "Proceed," Estralus said, sounding farther away with each word.

A moment of relative silence passed.

"We certainly lucked out with that challenge, didn't we?" said Max.

Jamal marched past his friend and smacked Vic in the back of the head. "Why do you always have to be such a dick?"

Vic shrugged and walked deeper into the jungle. "Dicks get results," he said. "Now hurry up. Let's get the goods."

3

Jamal carefully stepped over a root that Max had just tripped on. They had been following Vic through the thick trees for at least an hour. The journey had been oddly free of danger.

"Our objective," Vic had said, "is to find the appropriate protection to allow us safe passage into the lower levels of Reverie. Obviously my current nude state and your flimsy sports outfits won't do the trick."

"Hold up," Jamal grabbed Vic by the arm. "What exactly are we up against?"

"Monsters." Vic pried Jamal's fingers from his bicep. "That fool Victor once spoke of an island where vicious feline beasts emerged from the ground to torment a young version of Claire's mother. Their point of entry onto the island is our best bet to get deeper into this world. We've got to get to the center of this world so we can stabilize Reverie."

"And how exactly does that help my Claire?" Jamal asked.

Vic flung his hands into the air. "I don't know! I don't care! Ask your man in white the next time he shows-"

Jamal swung his fist at Vic, but Vic caught it in his hand and brought him to the ground. "Save your tantrums for someone else," said Vic. "We don't have the-"

Before Vic could react, he was tackled to the cool, jagged jungle floor. Max had pinned him to the ground. "We're not your henchmen, dude. Let's make that clear, okay?"

"We're not here to enact some evil plan," Jamal added, brushing the dirt from his knees as he stood up. "We're here to make things better for the woman I love. We're here—you're here —because of choices *I* made."

Vic took a moment to appreciate the seriousness of Max's green eyes looking back at him. "Okay, okay, fine." Vic said, "Get off of me and I promise I'll be more of...of a team player." Max turned to Jamal who nodded, then backed off from Vic. "Claire, the Claire of this world, doesn't belong on Earth. As much as I hate to say it neither do I. If you want her to be happy then we need to get her back here. If you want her to be safe, we need to keep moving. It's that simple."

Their walk was mostly quiet after that.

The thick jungle eventually opened to a great clearing, faintly lit by the ever-present distant green orbs. Jamal's foot made contact with something. He thought it was another root at first, but it was too soft. Looking down he saw that his foot had made contact with a corpse; a body more bone than skin wearing camouflage and pieces of plated armor over his torso and shoulders. A soldier.

Jamal jumped at the sight, then realized the body was not alone. Similar corpses were strewn across the entire jungle clearing. Hundreds, maybe more, men and women both. They littered the ground and were slumped over the scattered remains of ancient stone buildings.

"Whoa." Max felt his heart pounding in his chest. "What happened here?"

Vic reached down to a corpse and wrestled a large weapon from a skeletal hand. "Well, I'd guess they couldn't answer the riddle." Before Jamal could comprehend all the death surrounding them, Vic said, "Search the bodies. Take whatever weapons, clothing, or armor you can find."

Jamal and Max weren't too keen on taking clothing off of the dead, but it still was the fastest way of getting out of that dreadful place. Jamal and his best friend grabbed a knee pad here, a chest guard there. Max even found a fully functioning flamethrower. Within fifteen minutes all three were armored head-to-toe in the sort of suits you'd find in some futuristic war video game; bulky, strong, but surprisingly flexible and light. Each also held an oversized and intricate weapon.

"That's more like it," said Vic. "Let's-"

The green orbs, there were hundreds now, brightened. Small black dots emerged from each one. Pupils. A low growl joined the noise of the jungle. Hundreds of growls, actually, sounding as one. The creatures came from the forest depths. It happened so fast that they had already closed half the distance between them by the time Max screamed, "RUN!"

All three moved as quickly as they could out of the clearing and into the trees and vines and streams and darkness.

"Just keep straight," shouted Vic, whose figure would peek in and out behind the trees as they dashed. "Even if we get separated all you have to do is keep going straight. The jungle ends right- Ah!"

"What happened?!" Max asked. "Vic sounded like-"

"Doesn't matter." Jamal was running alongside him. "You heard him. Keep going straight."

The sound of a hundred snarls and growls was all the motivation Jamal and Max needed to keep moving. After some time a yellow light shone ahead between the trees.

"Freedom!" Max announced.

Something landed on Jamal's shoulder and began clawing at his armor. Jamal swung his weapon and knocked it off. Max noticed a few pairs of green eyes come into view at his side.

"Faster!" Jamal shouted.

As they got closer to the light, Max caught his first glimpse of the creatures. Furry, mangy things with matted brown fur and sharp white fangs. Fortunately, his first glimpse would be the last as he and Jamal charged out of the dense jungle and into a field of golden grass.

They continued to run as their eyes adjusted to the warm yellow sun.

"Wait," said Jamal. "Look." He came to a halt and pointed to the jungle. The creatures had stopped chasing them, as if afraid to step into the light.

Max removed his helmet and wiped the sweat from his brow. "Well, that's convenient. But what about Vic...?"

"I'm sure he's f-"

A beam of red light let loose from the trees. Then another. Vic emerged, gun blazing. One of the creatures was gnawing at his forearm, but he deftly tossed it back where it came from.

"Boys," said Vic, spotting Max and Jamal, "we've got a reality to rewrite."

4

"I feel like I'm in real-life Halo right now," exclaimed Max, taking in this armor for the thousandth time. "Do you think this is bulletproof?"

"Bullet-proof: definitely," said Vic as he took in the surroundings. A ruinous city of black. Buildings in disarray, broken robots of all sizes littering the streets. "Estralus-proof: not so much."

"Too soon, man. Too soon," said Max. Vic cracked a small smile at that.

Max lowered his voice and turned to Jamal. "Is it me or is Vic becoming more bearable?"

Jamal shrugged. "I'd be bearable, too, if I was getting everything I wanted out of this trip." Louder, he asked, "Where are we anyway?"

"Futara," Vic responded. "Once a bustling metropolis led by an evil artificial intelligence it was one of the places most affected by the flood. Speaking of…" When the three young men rounded a massive skyscraper, a mountain came into view. It was a few miles away, far beyond the limits of the destroyed city, narrow and quite tall. "That mountain was actually covered in water almost to the top. It was an island surrounded on all sides by a storm-prone ocean. When the walls that separated dreams went down, the ocean was unleashed on Reverie, causing the great flood that killed so many. Sucks." Vic pointed to the top of the mountain. "We'll climb to the top and enter from there."

They walked for a while to the edge of Futara, which happened to be an eighty-foot drop to the sand-covered floor of the next world.

Max scratched his head. "Um...how are we supposed to get down there?"

"Jump," Vic replied.

Jamal stepped up to Vic, "Are you out of your damn mind, man? That's-"

Vic pressed a button on his chest plate and his entire suit surrounded itself in a faint blue light. He then leaped into the air, only to descend slowly and softly to the ground. "Anti-gravity field, my friend. Jamal, you've got one, as well. Just press your chest." Jamal touched his hand to his chest and a light surrounded him as well. "Max, simply touch any part of your suit to Jamal's or my own and we'll safely float to the former ocean floor."

Vic walked to the edge and extended his arms to Max. Max looked to Jamal, who stepped between both of them. "Nah, man. Both of you are taking my hand. If we go down, we're going down together."

Vic rolled his eyes and shrugged. "Fine." He pressed his chest and the blue light faded. "Though, I technically could have known you were going to do this and that very moment could be part of my plan as well."

"Not helping, dude," said Max.

Vic sighed. "Perhaps you are right."

Jamal clenched his teeth and extended his hands to the others. "Now, before I change my mind."

Max and Vic took Jamal's hands in theirs. Upon contact, the

blue light spread to cover all three of them. "If we fall," Jamal said to Vic, "I'm going to find some way to kill you before we hit the bottom."

With a smirk, Vic leapt from the edge, leaving Futara behind and pulling Max and Jamal with him. Down they went, descending quickly. A couple minutes later and they touched the sandy ground below.

"That was definitely one of the cooler experiences of my seventeen years on Earth," Max said. "Or Reverie."

"Why is there no water here?" Jamal asked. "I get that the walls came down, but this is below the surface of the surrounding worlds."

Vic sighed. "There's an old woman who lives on the mountain and punishes herself by isolating from the rest of the world. When the walls came down and freedom became real, she removed the water to make sure that, even if she tried to escape, she would fall and die on the dry ground below."

"Dark," said Max.

They traversed the flat terrain, trudging through the sand, until they reached the base of the mountain. Jamal touched his finger to it and a chunk of hard sand broke off and tumbled to his feet. "There's no way we can climb this. It's too unstable. Unless these suits have jetpacks, too."

"Hmm…" Vic scratched his chin. He then shrugged and toyed with a few knobs and buttons on his gun. "Stand back." Before Max or Jamal could respond, he unleashed a wide arc of hot red light at the mountain. The force of the impact kicked up a miniature sandstorm. A cloud swirled upward, cancelling out all visibility except for the light of the beam itself. A crumbling sound was heard. Then a crash. Then...something else.

Max, Vic, and Jamal found themselves up to their shins in sand when the cloud began to dissipate. Before them was a hole just big enough for a person to crouch through burned into the mountainside. They caught a glimpse of the mountain's interior, rocky and lit up with yellows and oranges, before a creature crawled into view. It was feline, but much, much larger than any cats from Earth. Its appearance was demonic, with round dark eyes and pink, wrinkled, hairless skin. Its claws were long and sharp, as were its teeth. And from its mouth protruded a long, wet purple tongue.

5

"FIRE!" cried Vic.

Jamal, who had only just begun to free himself from the
sand, aimed his massive weapon at the creature and pulled
the trigger. A blue orb of light launched into the air and
landed on the creature's back, searing and lodging into its
pink flesh. The orb glowed brighter and brighter until it was
white and then- BAM -the creature exploded into a mess of
blood and guts.

"Let's move." Vic pulled his leg from the sand and marched
toward the opening he had blown into the mountain. "We
have to assume more of those things are on their way."

Jamal watched as Vic entered the mountain. The moment he
stepped inside, growls and hisses echoed from within. He let
loose a series of red beams at unseen enemies. Jamal and
Max shared a knowing look, nodded, and followed Vic.

Once inside, they were hit with a wall of heat as if they'd just
entered a furnace. The mountain's interior was crudely
designed. A crumbling staircase so worn it was more a
bumpy path carved from the mountain itself, stretched
upward to the peak and downward into the widening depths.
There were at least a dozen creatures coming at them from
above. Far more from below.

Max took aim at the ones descending upon them and
unleashed a torrent of flame from his gun. The two creatures
leading the charge caught fire, one stumbling backwards and
taking itself and another over the edge, falling into the
orange glowing depths. Jamal launched an orb at one of the
creatures ascending the stone stairs. The resulting explosion
took it out along with three others, sending an additional two

over the edge. Vic picked off some of the others one by one. His aim was flawless.

The threat from above was handled quickly enough so they fought their way down, deeper and deeper underground. It was a near-painless journey except for the intensifying heat and the time Max nearly slipped. He would have gone over the edge if not for Jamal's quick reflexes.

The path ended with the boys standing before a hole in the wall, much like the one they had entered, but large enough for an elephant. They stood only a foot or two above a pool of bubbling magma that made up the base of the cavern.

Vic led the others through the opening into an open space roughly the size of a small city block, with a domed ceiling. Nearly half of the space was taken up by a craggy boulder that rested against the far wall.

"Are we done?" Max removed his helmet and sweat poured down his face. His red hair was matted against his forehead.

Vic removed his helmet as well. "We've got to to go deeper. Jamal, I'll weaken a spot on the floor. Then I'll need you to place a few of those explosives-"

The ground began to rumble. Rocks fell from the ceiling.

"Put your damn helmets back on," said Jamal. Max did as he was told. Vic seemed unfazed.

It took very little time for the three of them to discover the source of the tremors. The enormous boulder that practically filled the room was no boulder at all. The beast uncurled, revealing its pink and wrinkled underbelly. It resembled the creatures they'd slaughtered on their journey, but it was thicker, more muscular, the majority of its body covered in rocky armor. Not to mention it was nearly twenty feet tall. On all fours, its head practically brushed the ceiling.

Before Jamal could lift his weapon, a clawed hand nearly the size of him whacked him into the wall. Max let loose a stream of fire, but it seemed to have no effect. Vic used the monster's focus on the other two to circle behind and let loose a few rounds of laser beams. The beams fizzled into puffs of smoke.

"We gotta aim for its belly," said Jamal. "It's the only thing that's not protected!" Jamal launched a pair of explosives. The monster was quick enough to evade one, but the other lodged on the inside of one of its hindlegs. The explosion broke skin on the underside of the creature, but not much more. "Shit!"

"Guys," Max called. "I don't think we can-" Just like that, Max was caught in the monster's jaws, its sharp teeth closing tight. "Help!"

"Max!" Jamal raced for his friend, who was dangling ten feet from the ground, fangs pressing into his armor.

Vic switched the settings of his gun and launched a rapid-fire laser barrage at the monster's stomach. Irritated, it spat Max out and charged Vic. Vic tried to get out of the way but found himself being crushed under one of the monster's large palms.

Jamal knelt by Max's side. "Dude, you okay?"

Max, dazed, nodded. "This is some really great armor. Halo wishes it had this armor."

"Look," Jamal whispered. "I know this is a shitty thing to do, but that thing is distracted with Vic."

"Dude…"

"Let's get out of here." Jamal took Max's hand in his and helped him to his feet. "We can make a run for it. Figure out stuff on our own. Make our-"

"AAARGGHHH!" Vic's shout from the other end of the cave silenced them. "I've had enough of this," he said as eight dark purple tentacles leapt from his body, snaking between the monster's claws and up its arm. The tentacles tightened and pulled the monster forward before hurling the monster back, off of Vic and into the nearest wall with an earth-shaking thud.

Vic climbed to his feet and turned to Max and Jamal with a large sharp-toothed smile. His eyes were big with glowing red pupils. Vic's smile grew larger as he said, "The time has come to move ahead. This foul beast will be soon made dead."

Interlude I:
Olokun

Olokun's history stretched back millennia. Worshipped since ancient times as a goddess of the ocean depths, the unknown, of dreams and secrets lost to the darkness. One of the oldest of the gods, she was also one of the most powerful and one of the most intelligent.

When the gods of the ancient world were exerting power over humanity for their own designs, Olokun also saw value in learning from them. Humanity's propensity for creativity, innovation, the arts and sciences, intrigued her. She would alter her form, her gender or race, in order to learn under such great minds as Archimedes and Sheba, then Sun Tzu, Da Vinci and countless others.

While her time with humanity had granted her knowledge unsurpassed by man or immortal, it also formed within her a deep resentment for the mortal creatures many thought her kind were meant to protect. Their pettiness, racism, selfishness, sexism. Their inability to see the beauty in the world, always longing for more, for a power that would never satisfy, but would time and time again cause them to take advantage of others. Ingrates unappreciative of the paradise given to them.

She saw firsthand the most gruesome wars of god and man, both on the battlefield and in the countless underworlds she'd traversed. Rape. Murder. Slavery. She wanted to end it all. And in attempting to heal, she created myriad solutions in her lab in the depths of the sea. All failed in the face of the innate corruptibility of god and man.

Most of the gods died when they began warring with each

other. Some went into hiding. The gods had essentially wiped themselves from the earth. One less problem for Olokun to solve. And humans could only cause so much damage, she thought. That is, until the Industrial Age and all that followed. Steam and iron, petroleum and steel, electricity and nuclear power. Humanity's memory of the gods before them had become little more than myth, but they succeeded in surpassing them all in cruelty and capacity for destruction.

What began as a genuine hunger to learn so that she might help to heal the world twisted into a deepening belief that it could not be healed at all. That, instead, it must be remade.

Olokun stood in her laboratory, a massive facility nestled in a cavern beneath the darkest depths of the ocean somewhere off the coast of Mozambique. Despite its size, the lab was so cluttered and packed with items of science and spiritualism spanning millennia - bookshelves that reached to the high ceiling full of tomes and tablets long forgotten - that it felt much smaller.

She had spent the better part of eight hundred years constructing the latest addition to her lab. The dark space was lit by the eerie green light given off by thirty large cylindrical tubes, each one roughly ten feet tall. If one looked close enough one would see suspended shapes within the tubes. The majority of those shapes looked human.

From the tops of each cylinder was a smaller tube pumping a glowing green liquid to an old copper machine in the center of the room. Olokun approached the machine and placed her finger under a small spigot. The tiniest blue droplet fell onto her finger. She brought her finger to her mouth and tasted it. Her dark eyes flickered a brilliant blue.

Suddenly she felt that she was not alone. Olokun turned her head and saw him, an average-sized man without a face. His skin, his clothing, all paper white. His entire appearance was blurred, so much so that one could not tell where his skin ended and the clothing that covered it began. He said nothing, but Olokun understood his intention better than anyone.

She sighed. "Just because I do not agree with Nihilo does not automatically mean I will side with you. You're an accident. A miscalculation. But this..." She gestured toward the green glowing tubes and the living or once living things they held. "This is my great victory. This is how it all begins."

PART II
FAMILY TIES

6

In the past year, Claire Ashford had experienced more than most would in a hundred lives. This could be summed up by the fact that having a baby at seventeen was one of the least stressful bits of it. Her recent history was littered with goblins and killer robots, homicidal dream-siblings and a baby-stealing alien monster; all-powerful manifestations of core human concepts, and a talking velociraptor for good measure. Still, none of that was stranger than the situation she currently found herself in.

Claire, Victor, and their baby girl had returned to Earth through a portal in a forest miles away. Nearly one day later following a ton of walking and a ride by a very kind elderly couple, they had made it to Claire's house. Exhausted and starved they entered the home of Karen Ashford and Claire was still finding it hard to process who was waiting inside.

She entered the large, exquisitely decorated living room holding a plate of crackers, grapes, and assorted cheeses; her third serving since arriving there. Seated on a soft white couch on the other end of the room was Victor Soto, the father of her child and awkward high school loner she'd drunkenly slept with a year ago leading to everything that happened next. They were a team now, whether she liked it or not. And more often than not these days, she liked him. A lot. She didn't think a person could look at anyone the way she would catch him looking at her. In fact, Claire felt most distant from Victor when she was guilty that she might never love him the way he did her.

In Victor's arms was Anza, their child. She was a fragile, squirming thing barely four months old. She had her father's tan skin and dark brown hair; her mother's green eyes and button nose. Though Claire would not say she loved being a mother, she would do anything for her child. She found herself increasingly irritated by forces claiming her sweet Anza was destined to save humanity when all Claire wanted was to keep her safe.

Seated beside Victor and stroking Anza's tiny hands was Claire's mom, Karen Ashford. The last conversation Claire had with her mother before being transported to Reverie was a heated argument about how Claire should use a better moisturizer and put a little thought into her overall style choices while she was at it. Their relationship was strained at best. But when Claire returned a few hours ago, she was met with tears and joy, appreciation and gratitude the likes of which she didn't think her mother was capable. Oh, Karen had also been blinded and gifted with ominous visions of the future, granted to her by an old African goddess. Truth be told, Claire was quite happy to be reunited with her mother.

Hovering above Victor and Karen was a near-transparent young man in a bomber jacket, with curious green eyes and a dashing smile. This was Patrick Ashford, her brother who had died two years before in a car accident. He had been drinking with friends the day he got behind the wheel. He killed one person in addition to himself and put another, Jack, in a coma. Claire had encountered a dark, vile version of her brother in Reverie which soured this reunion with the real thing. After what she had been through, she had very little trouble accepting the reality of ghosts and was quietly warming up to the spirit of her beloved older brother.

There was one other person in the room; one Claire had the hardest time accepting. She could barely even look at her. This person was Claire, a different Claire born in Reverie; a version of herself that she had wished to be once upon a time. She was a little taller, a little curvier, with full lips and a fuller chest. Her nose was a lot less button-y. She was dressed to perfection. This other Claire was basically the

Claire that Karen had always wished her actual daughter was...which is why this Claire existed at all. Much like the Claire of Earth, Reverie's Claire stood off in a corner, grumpily assessing the situation they found themselves in. There was a strange energy between the two of them. As if they were drawn to one another despite both doing everything in their power to remain apart.

Karen shrieked, clutching the arm of the couch and breaking Claire from her daze. Startled, Victor leaped to his feet, clutching Anza in his arms. Anza started to cry.

"You okay, Mom?" Patrick asked, his voice sounding strangely distant.

"She's fine," said the Claire of Reverie, rolling her eyes. "You'll get used to this."

"Anza..." The word left Karen's lips like a whisper. Horror was written all over her face. "Something...something's coming for my grandbaby. You can't take my grandbaby!"

There was a knock at the door.

7

Everyone froze.

"Don't answer it," said Karen, trembling.

There was another knock. This one louder, faster.

Victor, with Anza squirming quietly in his arms, stepped from away from the couch, from the door, and moved closer to Claire.

"Hello?" A woman's voice, muffled through the door. "Is anyone home?"

Victor gasped. In all the excitement of the reunion he had forgotten about the one that hadn't happened yet.

He walked to the door and paused with his hand clutching the knob. Beads of sweat were already forming on his brow. He turned the knob and slowly pulled. On the other side of the door, sharing identical expressions, was a man of middle age and average size, wearing an old suit and a thick brown mustache, and a plump woman in a floral dress with her black hair in a bun. It was Carlos and Ornella Soto, Victor's parents.

Ornella fainted.

She came to a few minutes later on the couch next to her husband, son, and grandchild. For the hour or so that followed, Victor and the others tried their best to explain to his parents the strange series of events that led them to be speaking with a son they thought they'd buried less than a week earlier. They described everything once again, from Jack and the flood to the manifestations that started this whole mess: Somni and Timor, manifestations of desire and fear, the rulers of Reverie. The pregnant Initia, manifestation of growth and her love and manifestation of decline, Mortem, rulers of Cosmos. And lastly, the rulers of Eternia, Nihilo, manifestation of nothingness and his eternal foe Vita, manifestation of existence. Carlos and Ornella listened as best they could, but they were mostly just happy that they had their son back.

"Lo sentimos," said Ornella in a particularly emotional moment. "Your... reemplazo... your, uh, doppelganger, we should have known it wasn't you. He was just so… We were just so proud, you know, and…" She began to cry and Carlos put a loving arm around her. It was clear in his expression that he shared the shame of failing to realize the son they'd accepted was not truly their own.

"It's fine," said Victor, concealing his own sadness. "Es loco. All of it. How could anyone assume their kid was body-swapped with their dream self? And, honestly, I wasn't the best so I can only imagine how relieved you were when that other me…" He took a moment to halt his swelling tears. "We're together. That's what matters. We're a whole family. You're grandparents."

Ornella's face lit up. Victor offered Anza and his mother took the baby in her arms.

"I'm really sorry to interrupt all of this." Patrick materialized in the center of the spacious living room. There was an unmistakable look of concern on the ghost's face. "But... I can't wait anymore." He turned to Claire and smiled. Then to Victor. Then Anza. He extended a translucent arm, pointing to the baby. "I've been trying to reach you guys for a while now, but my connection to Cosmos- to Earth - wasn't strong enough." He glanced at Claire of Reverie who remained quiet in her corner. To Earth's Claire he continued,

"But your arrival, it allowed me to fully push through, I think. It gave me a true anchor. And so now I have a mission to fulfill."

"What are you talking about?" asked Claire.

Patrick bit his lower lip, then said, "It's no news that the walls of Reverie have fallen. We think that there are forces at play trying to weaken the barriers between all worlds. If the barriers between Reverie and Earth are destroyed, it will be the end of our world as we know it. Imagine if every monster that's ever been in someone's nightmare were set loose on Earth. And if any of these prophesies are even a little true it's only a matter of time before those forces start sending things after the one destined to stop them...my niece. Your daughter. And trust me when I say that Cosmos is the realm least capable of protecting her from the evils of this existence."

Claire stepped to her brother. "Wait. What are you saying? Who is this 'we'?"

Patrick grinned. "Guillelmina. She found me in Eternia which, trust me, was not easy after what I did." A wave of melancholy fell over him. "Guilly taught me how to pass parts of myself between realms. To concentrate so hard on you, Claire, that I could reach you. And," he hesitated, "so I can take Anza back with me to Eternia where she'll be kept safe until she's old enough to-"

Another knock at the door, this time hard and sharp.

Again, everyone froze. Everyone except for Claire of Reverie.

"Oh God, I'll get it." She pushed the perfect blonde hair from her eyes and took a perfect stroll on perfect legs to the door. "Trust me, no otherworldly monster is going to knock."

Claire of Reverie flung the door open, revealing a young woman. She was tall and thin, with round pretty brown eyes that were warm and welcoming in contrast to her thin, serious lips. She had flawless copper skin and wore her straight black hair in a ponytail. Her navy blue blazer matched her skirt and heels. Somewhat out of place was the bright green T-shirt she wore with a cute anime kitten and penguin eating ice cream on it. In one hand she held a pen and the other a reporter's notepad. "Hi," she began. Her words were quick, energized. "My name is Satya Shirazi, journalism intern at TheNeedle.com. I'm researching some strange occurrences in Addley for my thesis, starting with the disappearance of cheerleader Mindy Sparks. Do you have a moment to answer a few questions, Ms…"

"Ashford," said the Claire of Reverie after a healthy eye roll. "Claire Ashford 2.0: The *Much* Improved version. Good day." Claire attempted to slam the door closed in a moment of bitchy triumph, but Satya stopped it with her arm and slipped inside.

An instant later her eyes opened wide and her hands were trembling as if she'd seen a ghost…which was likely in that household…but she was actually looking directly at… "Victor…V-Victor Soto? How- how are you…alive?"

Before anyone could answer the lights in the living room began to flicker and the front door slammed shut. A chorus of moaning sounds arose, louder and louder, as the ground began to quake.

8

"An earthquake," said Satya, stating the obvious.

"I don't think this is your regular earthquake," Patrick said. He noticed Satya's surprise at noticing him for the first time.

"Tenemos que salir," Carlos, Victor's dad, shouted as he helped his wife, who still held Anza, up from the couch. Karen grasped wildly for something to hold onto, eventually grabbing Carlos' free arm.

"My papa's right." Victor took Claire by the hand and signalled for his parents to join him. "We have to get outside."

Claire nodded and led them out of the living room, down the hall toward the front door. The tremors increased. Pictures fell from the walls and an expensive vase crashed to the ground. As they passed the door to the basement, it rattled and seemed to fling itself open. Claire was startled to see something staring at her from the dimly lit staircase. It was roughly the size and shape of a man, but it had small shiny black orbs in place of eyes and its body was comprised of concrete and dirt and even patches of the off-white carpet that covered the basement floor. The creature let loose a deep moan from a cavernous mouth and charged up the stairs. Claire gasped and slammed the door close. She took a step back just as the thing tore through the door, reducing it to splinters.

"Oh God," Karen exclaimed. "What's happening?!"

"Outside!" Claire shouted. "Turn around. We have to get out of here!"

Claire rounded the corner from the kitchen into the hall, the creature right behind her. She watched as Satya and the Claire of Reverie headed for the front door ahead. Satya opened it and Claire of Reverie tried to slip around her, but stumbled back. In walked a similar creature, this one comprised mostly of dirt, grass, and stone. A few flowers from the front yard stuck out from its earthy hide.

Ornella let out a mighty scream, startling Anza into crying.

The first creature raised its concrete arm and swung it at Claire. Fortunately, Patrick was there to stop it from making contact. His translucent form was stronger than it looked.

Victor grabbed a butcher knife from the kitchen and made it down the hall, past Anza, his parents, and Karen, to the living room. Claire of Reverie flew through the air right past him, landing hard on a coffee table, the glass cracking beneath her as she rolled to the floor on the other side. As he started to return to the hall he noticed something vaguely human-shaped emerging from the far wall.

"Ah!" Satya grabbed Victor's arm so hard he could feel her fingernails digging into his skin. "Is this real? What's happening? I should be writing this down! I should be-"

The third creature, all rock and wood and wallpaper, moaned loudly in Satya's face, silencing her.

Victor tried stabbing the creature, but, as it was mostly rock, there was very little effect. He then pulled himself and Satya away from the thing and to the group of terrified people currently huddled in the hallway.

"Give me Anza," Patrick said, his voice deadly serious. "The only way to make this stop is to let me have her!"

Ornella screamed as a fourth creature stepped into the hall from the dining room. It had taken on some of the attributes of Karen's long mahogany dinner table.

Claire took her daughter from Ornella's arms and held her close. "I'm not just giving you my baby! I...I don't know what you are!"

The creature that had come through the door took Victor by the neck and tossed him aside like he was nothing, moving deeper into the hall. Another shoved Satya into a nearby wall and trudged forward.

Even though he was barely visible, one could see Patrick's face turn red. "It's me, Claire! Your brother! The brother who used to let you paint his nails, every one a different color except green because it reminded you of asparagus!" The creature from the dining room swiped at Patrick, its rugged arm passing right through him. "The brother who missed your eighth grade graduation because I got too drunk at the park and tried to make it up to you by writing you that terrible apology rap." Claire stepped away from the creature, only to open herself up to the first. "The brother who was way too stupid and left you way too soon and hurt way too many people." Carlos stepped between Claire and Anza and the creature. The creature lurched forward and broke Carlos' arm with a forceful punch.

"I've seen it, sweet girl," Karen said. "The future. This is the only way. I know I haven't given you a lot of reason to in this life, but you have to trust me. Give him the baby."

The four creatures tightened their circle around them. Claire saw Victor bruised on the ground and Satya with blood on the back of her head. Carlos was in agony, clutching his broken arm and Ornella was out of her mind with terror. She saw her mother's eerie black eyes pleading without a word. And she saw that look mirrored and intensified in the eyes of the young man she now thought of as her brother. Tears swelling in her eyes and body shaking, she offered her daughter to Patrick, never loving her more than she did in that moment. Patrick smiled a sad smile and took Anza from her. There was a quiet "pop" and both he and the baby were gone.

All four creatures stopped. The earthquake stopped. The creatures looked around, confused, almost as if they no longer knew where they were or how they got there. After surveying the area they left one by one, returning to the earth.

9

Satya climbed to her feet and wiped the blood on her hands against her navy blue blazer. She had arrived in Addley two nights before. Following a few leads, she had a few interesting interviews so far, but never expected anything like this. How could anyone have expected anything like this?

Satya pushed her pen to her reporter's notepad. To no one in particular she asked, "What. The. Heck. Just. Happened?! What were those monsters? Were they monsters? Who was that baby? Who was the ghost? How are there ghosts?!"

"Who is this girl," Karen said, gesturing toward Satya's voice. "Does anybody understand why she is here?"

Satya paused and took a look around the room. Everyone there seemed just as confused as she was.

"Forget about her right now. Necesitamos un hospital!" exclaimed Ornella. She held Carlos tight. He groaned, his right forearm dangling awkwardly from his elbow. "Call nine-one-one."

"No," said Karen, "there'll be none of that. The last thing any of us needs is to draw more attention to this house. That is, if that slut Maria Banksford next door hasn't called the cops already. Might I add that I have never been more happy to be blind than I am now. I'm sure if I saw the state my beautiful home is in right now I'd surely kill myself."

"His arm is broken!" shouted Ornella. "We can't just-"

Karen sighed. "You can drive, can't you?"

Ornella mumbled something in Spanish. She helped Carlos

to his feet then turned to Victor. "Mi Monito, help me walk your papa to the car."

Victor remained on the floor in the hall, staring blankly forward, his mouth hanging slightly open. His voice soft and void of emotion he said, "You gave away our baby."

Claire's eyes widened. Her heartbeat increased. She turned to him. "What?"

"How could you give our baby away?" he asked. "After all we've been through…"

"To save her," she said through clenched teeth. Her face was turning red. "I did it so those *things* wouldn't tear her apart."

Tears began to pour from Victor's eyes, but his eyes remained fixed forward, his voice tempered. "So, after all this, after all we've made it through *together*, you decide to just give our daughter aw-"

"You heard what Patrick and Mom said!" Claire snapped. "I didn't have a choice! And I didn't give her away. Her uncle will keep her safe. Isn't that the most important thing?"

Victor's eyes met hers. "Well, it didn't look like a struggle for you. But, hey, she's safe. And you're finally free of h-"

Claire slapped Victor hard across the face. Her eyes, too, were wet with tears. "I love her just as much as-" She looked away. "I love her."

"Anza would have died, you idiot," said Karen. "What kind of grandmother would I be if I wasn't cursed with visions of the future to keep my family safe? A terrible grandmother, that's what. So how about you don't speak to my daughter and mother of your child that way?"

Ornella stepped in. "How about you don't talk to my son that way?"

Karen groaned. "Ugh, I forgot you were here. Don't you have a broken husband to get fixed?"

Victor paused. He took a deep breath and wiped his eyes. He reached for Claire, who pulled away instantly. "Claire," he began. His tone was pure. Apologetic. "I don't- I shouldn't've- " He climbed to his feet. "I never thought- I never wanted to not be near her or to feel like there was something that I- that the both of us- couldn't give her...which is stupid."

"Very stupid," Karen added.

Claire shook her head, a mix of sadness and bewilderment. "I was excited to be back here. For things to be normal for us again. But...there's no more normal…"

"Um, guys?" Satya had been feverishly jotting things down in her notepad, but was now searching the living room as if looking for something specific. She pointed to Claire and asked, "Did anyone see what happened to that other girl who kinda looked like you?"

10

The Claire of Reverie was nowhere in sight. They searched the house, called her cell, and eventually added her absence to a large pile of questions in need of answers. Her car was gone so chances were she left of her own volition anyway.

Once Carlos and Ornella were off to the hospital, Claire, Victor, Karen, and Satya sat around the island in Karen's kitchen to discuss their next move. Victor had just finished sweeping the wood splinters from the destroyed basement door and Claire had just finished pouring her mother a second glass of Chardonnay.

"Do you all really think it's safe to be here?" asked Satya. "I mean, just because your baby is gone doesn't mean all the monsters know your baby is gone." She added, "Wow, there's a sentence I never thought I'd say."

The others agreed while Karen chugged her wine. They all piled into Satya's rusty green Chevy and made their way to Eddie-O's Diner.

Karen groaned, uncomfortable in the loud vehicle. "So, now's as good a time as any to ask, who are you, Satya? Why are you here?"

Satya seemed a little hurt by that, but shook it off. "I'm...I was Vic's girlfriend in Harvard. He was obsessed with dreams and stuff and so I continued his work as some sort of morbid way to cope with his...death? Or whatever. This is all so strange. Anyway, I started researching the disappearances of Mindy and Jamal and Max and thought this would be a great story for class and here I am! I could not have been more right."

The rest of the ride was silent.

"What is that abhorrent aroma?" Karen pinched her nostrils shut as she entered the eatery which wasn't too crowded that weekday afternoon. Eddie-O's was a classic example of a 1950s American diner...except for the fact that it had been purchased by a big-bellied and jolly man named Basu who decided to infuse the very American diner menu with a few favorite Indian dishes from his home country.

Satya gave the air a good sniff. "If I had to guess, I'd say beef keema."

"You've got a good nose," said Basu in his deep, friendly voice and thick accent. He appeared behind them, towering over them all. "Your parents make you that as a little girl?"

"Nah." Satya shrugged. "I'm actually adopted and my moms suck at cooking, but they were all about giving me the authentic cultural restaurant experience."

Basu didn't quite know what to do with that information so he smiled and asked, "Table for four?"

Satya nodded. "Somewhere private-ish, please." Basu offered all four of them a strange look this time, but proceeded to lead them to a secluded table in the back corner of the diner.

"I'll give you all a minute to-"

"We're ready." Satya scanned the large laminated menu. "We'll have four waters, a side of fries, a side of samosas, an order of chicken fingers, and an order of tandoori masala with tofu, and your finest dinner white for the lady to my right. All of it delivered together, got that?"

Basu scribbled the order as fast as he could. "I-I think so."

"Awesome, thank you!" The moment Basu walked away, Satya leaned forward to Victor and Claire and said, "All right, now tell me everything."

This was the third time they had to share their story since returning home and it came out of them quite easily. They'd even remembered a few more details than they had when they'd told Karen and Patrick. Somewhere during their story the food arrived. They paused then, but picked up again once Basu was out of earshot.

Upon completion Satya was speechless. All this talk of Reverie and Lucids and goblins and machines and manifestations was a level of unbelievable she wasn't sure she could get anyone to accept as truth. She cursed herself for not taking pictures of the rock creatures. Or of both Claires side by side. Or the ghost...if he would have even photographed. Still, she knew two things. The first being that the story was far from over. And the second, this was going to guarantee her an A.

"Hm." Satya scratched her chin. "I guess I could take a picture of you, Victor, holding your own obituary. Yes. That's a good start, but still not enough to ground the full scope of this thing in reality."

"Yeah, about that," Victor said, looking down awkwardly at his plate. "I'm not really sure how I feel about this being a research project for you."

"Well," Karen said, playing with the empty wine glass, "you dragged me from my home and made me drink what I can only assume was toilet water. The least you could do is ask me about *my* part in this tale."

Satya sat up and turned to Karen. "Oh, I'm sorry! I didn't

know you were in Reverie, too!"

Karen groaned. "I wasn't, girl, but while my baby and this boy were galavanting about in a dreamworld, I was suffering my own woeful series of events. I wasn't always blind, you know."

"Yes, I was going to ask-"

"Don't interrupt, dear. I received this handicap while going through my dear and recently departed friend Guillelmina's house in search of some sort of token of memory when a dark-skinned menace put a curse on me!"

"A curse?" Satya was writing away.

"Oh yes." Karen touched her hand to her chest. "From what that Jason Baker boy told me, she's an ancient goddess named Olokun."

"A goddess?"

"Am I stuttering, dear?" Karen frowned.

"Hm." Victor was chewing on a chicken finger. "The manifestations did say that they created gods to keep humanity in line...but it all went wrong and most of them killed each other, so...I guess that makes sense."

To Karen, Satya said, "Do you know why Olokun was there? Any idea what she was looking for?"

"Aside from disabling me, I have no idea what that bitch was doing. All I know is that she was at Guilly's funeral, as well."

"Curious." Satya shouted across the diner, "Check please!" To Karen and the others she said. "Then that's where we'll start. Victor, you and I will go to Guillelmina's house and search for clues as to what else is going on here. As for you, Claire. When I first came to Addley it was to learn more about the disappearance of Mindy Sparks last year...which you have now shined a light on...but since then there's also been a strange break in at the high school as well as the disappearances of star basketball players Max Grayson and Jamal Anderson. Your other self was dating Jamal, if my sources are correct, Claire. I wasn't very welcome at his parents' house, but if you could maybe drop by and see if there are *any* clues about where he might have gone, that'd be great."

"What about me?" asked Karen.

Satya shrugged. "I'll buy you a couple of bottles of wine-sorry *toilet water*. We won't be gone long."

11

In their short time together in Reverie, Victor had grown quite close to Guillelmina. Her death was difficult for him to process and, as he rounded the corner onto the block of cracked sidewalks and dilapidated townhouses that defined Guillelmina's former home, the emotions of longing swelling inside him made him realize that he had not truly processed them at all. Which in turn made him realize that he may not have fully processed his daughter's recent departure. And he certainly hadn't thought all that much about the sweet strangeness of his daughter being rocked in the arms of Guillelmina herself in Eternia. It was enough to make anyone's head spin, but as long as thing after thing after thing kept happening, Victor feared he would have to put the processing off for another day.

"There it is," said Satya after double-checking Google Maps on her phone. Unlike the other rowhomes on the block with their three stories and small front yards, Guillelmina's house was only two floors tall and set at the end of a long yard, stretching deep within the block. An outdoor staircase led to a balcony and separate door on its second floor. The last hints of the purple paint that once covered the house were fading and all the windows and doors were boarded shut.

Satya and Victor walked through the front yard, through grass, weeds, and wildflowers reaching up to their waists. When they reached the door they noticed a bright orange sign stapled to it that read, "DANGER: This house is declared unsafe. It is unlawful to occupy this building."

Satya smirked, "Challenge accepted." She and Victor climbed the rickety old wooden stairs to the second floor. Satya reached into her purse and pulled out the hammer she had grabbed from the toolbox in her car. Nail by nail, she began to remove the wooden planks that covered the door. Victor kept watch, but this part of Addley was old and mostly abandoned. A single car went by in the fifteen minutes it took Satya to clear the way.

Satya turned on her cell phone's flashlight and stepped into the dark, small, cluttered room with Victor behind her, all of a sudden wishing he'd brought his sword. An overturned table, hundreds of papers, shattered glass, and dishes littered the floor. Old bookshelves covered in cobwebs lined the walls.

"As interesting as this Guillelmina was," Satya thought aloud, "what could she have possibly had that was of any interest to a goddess?" She pointed her flashlight to the papers on the floor, most of them pages torn from books or articles from newspapers or magazines. "I don't even know where to begin."

They moved to the next room, just as small and crowded, but with less natural light. Satya was on her tip-toes reaching for something, anything on the top of the bookshelves while Victor was on his hands and knees sorting through strange trinkets and scraps on the floor.

"These are notes from her journeys to Reverie," he said, "or articles about dreams and stuff. I don't know if-" He noticed something catching light under one of the bookshelves. Reaching his arm as far as he could, he grabbed it and pulled out a dust-covered picture frame. He used his sleeve to wipe the dust away, revealing an image of two women and a boy not much younger than Victor, blonde with big green eyes. They were standing in front of the fountain at John C. Addley Park. "I think I found something…"

Satya turned her light to Victor and joined him on the ground. She examined the first lady, short and cute and possibly in her thirties or forties. She had black hair and was dressed in a wild, colorful patchwork of thick wool shawls. Beside her was a tall, beautiful woman with dark skin and high cheekbones and a bald head. She wore an elegant blue gown.

"Guilly was beautiful, wasn't she?" The voice belonged to neither Victor or Satya. It was deep, but feminine. Powerful. Alluring. "I told her, 'Guilly, love, if you would slip out of those rags and into something a little more fashionable, maybe these humans would have a deeper respect for your craft. Humans are petty that way,' I'd say."

Satya shined her light in the direction of the voice, but it was as though the light refused to cooperate. A shape did begin to take form, though. Tall, but fluid, like a drop of black dye mixing with water. Every other moment it would take on a human-like form, then dissipate immediately after.

"Who are you?" asked Victor. "What do you want with us?"

"Victor," said the voice. "What I want, young man, is to give you the one thing that only I can...the truth."

And with that everything went cold. Wet. Black. Like the depths of the sea.

Interlude II:
Lester Wilkes

Lester was a good man for just about all forty-eight years of his life on Earth. He kept a respectable job at a jewelry shop for twenty-two of those years. Had a nice house, three dogs. Still, it wasn't strange for him to think of what it would be like to have a wife to come home to or little children pitter-pattering across the floor. He'd tried, of course, for that sort of thing but it just never worked out for one reason or another. That's why Ben Burnham's offer seemed so very welcoming.

Almost two years ago Burnham showed up at Lester's doorstep wearing a gray three-piece suit. He had a bit of a belly and always wore a red bowtie and a big white smile. His strawberry blond hair was combed over a prominent bald spot and looked as if it had been caught in a strong gust of wind. Burnham had a lot to say to Lester about higher callings and overcoming life's many challenges. But the part Lester liked the most was the part about an end to loneliness.

Six months later Lester left his job and his house and moved to the forty-eight acre compound about three hundred miles north. It was a community of two hundred; people who, like he did, felt alone or like they didn't belong. Everyone had their part to play: cooking, farming, cleaning, teaching... It was a sort of paradise with Burnham in charge of all of it.

Burnham only asked for two things in exchange for giving so many people the lives they'd always wanted. The first was allegiance to the Church of Nihilo, which was founded on the belief that the concept of nothing is to be embraced. That when you stop fearing nothingness you can finally have everything. The second was to give themselves to Nihilo when he called for it. A portion of Lester's day- of everyone's day -was spent training for that very moment.

"And on that blessed day when Nihilo calls to us, his faithful children," preached Burnham, "we will drink of his bounty and be transported to a new world. And in this world we will use the information that Nihilo has bestowed upon us to further his will. Truly embrace the nothingness within us all."

Lester thought this trade was more than worth it so when the day came, he drank from his styrofoam cup and felt his muscles tighten and his throat close up. The end came swiftly and painlessly as promised. He then experienced the strange sensation of watching his own lifeless body drop into the grass as his translucent spirit rose up and up.

Shortly after, everything went white.

The next thing Lester knew he was on a crystal conveyor belt, moving upward through a cavernous world that sparkled with iridescent blues and purples and greens. Both in front and behind him were the others who had given their lives for Nihilo. In the sky were creatures that looked vaguely human, but larger and more slender with skin that glistened like pearls, gliding through the air smoothly and confidently on magnificent wings. Some wore crystal armor and others white togas. All held massive golden swords or axes or spears.

"You'll find yourself on a moving platform meant to transport you to the Court of Judgement," Burnham had said. "You'll only have a few minutes before being sorted so you'll have to act fast…"

Lester noticed a person not too far ahead of him jump off the edge of the conveyor belt into the white abyss below.

"The abyss is not to be feared," Burnham had said. "It is free will, a chance to escape Vita's sinful judgement in Nihilo's blessed name. He allows us to judge ourselves."

Lester was warned time and time again: "As soon as they realize what you're up to they'll come after you. All of them."

One more, then two more, then three hurled themselves into the white nothingness. The creatures, angelic things, took action, scooping them up mid-fall at an alarming speed and disappearing into flashes of light.

Dozens dropped at once, Lester included. A creature's hand barely missed Lester's leg as the former jewelry shop owner fell into the cosmic abyss, black and blue and magenta like a photo of a galaxy from a telescope.

As Lester and the others fortunate enough to evade the winged ones descended, seven portals into seven crystal cities opened up before them.

"And for those few Chosen Ones of our Lord, Nihilo," echoed Ben's voice in Lester's mind, "you will be met with windows into the seven planes of Eternia itself. Each a home for sinners and saints as defined by Vita, our mortal foe. You need only envision yourself entering one of these windows-based on the number you each have been given -and Nihilo's will will be done through you, my brothers and sisters."

The portals appeared just as Ben had described them in his holy napkin sketches. Lester cleared his thoughts and focused only on his designated portal. Almost instantly, he felt his body being pulled toward it.

Then he blacked out. Something grabbed his arms, plucking him from his freefall. A few moments later he crashed against something hard. Lester's sight returned and he found himself in a small, dark room. What little light that crept in through the door revealed the floor, walls, and ceiling were made of iridescent crystal. A tall, thin figure stood with Lester. The silhouette of its wings filled much of the space.

"Human," said the winged one. "Welcome to your destiny." The winged one then thrust its fist into Lester's chest. A feeling of pure power, pure oneness, coursed through the man, followed by intense, unimaginable pain as Lester Wilkes burst into an explosion of liberating light.

Nihilo be praised.

PART III
THE MARCH

12

Agalfia Tirk sat under the shade of a weeping willow tree, propped against the trunk as she whittled a piece of wood with her hunting knife. Not too far away were two boys, each with a full head of wild blond hair like her own, swinging and sliding and climbing and hanging in a complex and colorful tangle of rubber and metal tubes and platforms. A playground, she was told.

In the distance hundreds of others talked and relaxed and milled about.

"Osip! Oleg!" she called to her brothers. "Be-" One stopped, causing the second to crash into him, both tumbling onto the bedding of small black rubber chunks. "Careful."

"Okay, Aggie!" They giggled as they hopped to their feet and made their way to something called a jungle gym.

Agalfia, or Aggie as almost everyone called her, promised to never let her brothers out of her sight again. They were all the family she had left, after all. And they had been through enough under her watch: Kidnapping. Nearly being transformed into mindless cyborgs. The war. And now, especially now, she had to protect them from the many threats lurking in the shadows and those walking in broad daylight.

It had been three weeks since they left the Valley of Hope. "What a stupid name," she thought. The Dark Valley is what she had called the village in which she spent all eighteen years of her life. It was a fitting name for a place ravaged by an evil ruler; a monster who ordered the death of her parents, leaving her with two eight year-old brothers to raise. Changing the name of a place doesn't change its history, she thought. And just because one leaves the Dark Valley doesn't mean the darkness won't follow.

"Credcoin for your thoughts?" Eliza approached Aggie from behind. Aggie, a skilled tracker and hunter, had heard her coming for some time. Eliza wore a skintight black, one-piece uniform that covered her from neck to ankles. Black fingerless gloves covered her hands and large clunky black military boots her feet. Aggie had worn something similar during the war, but opted after to return to her hunter's gear of leather and cotton.

"Huh?" said Aggie.

"Oh right." Eliza rolled her eyes and adjusted a belt that held a silver futuristic gun and other high-tech weapons. "Credcoin for your thoughts. It's a saying that means 'You look like you've got a lot on your zagging mind, girl. Now share it so we can bear it together." Almost a month had passed since the war and Aggie still found the sight of Eliza jarring. An explosion that would have decimated any normal human left the right side of Eliza's face, well, exposed. What was once a full round brown face with curious brown eyes and a black afro, had been blown away to reveal half of a cold, robotic face with a glowing green eye. Eliza was the most advanced AI in her homeland of Futara- a concept difficult for tech neophyte Aggie to grasp.

Aggie sighed. She trusted Eliza. Since Rumi's death they had become fast friends. "It's all of this," Aggie began. "Terrible decisions are constantly being made that put us all in danger."

"Then make your opinions known," Eliza said, gears shifting on the left side of her face to facilitate the moving of her mouth. "You do have a seat at the table, you know."

Aggie brushed the thought aside. "Please. My voice is outnumbered by those fools. Each one licking the hand of their fragile usurper. And I must focus on protecting my brothers. Everything else is a distraction."

Eliza leaned against the willow tree, shoulder to shoulder with Aggie. "Mindy's not that bad…" She stopped mid-sentence.

"Not that bad? Not that bad?!" Aggie's nostrils flared. "She is an inexperienced child who plays at being queen! And what has that amounted to? She seeks counsel from Del, an old, opportunistic blowhard, and Peeps, a goblin who once made it his mission to ensure my people remained poor and starving. Not to mention Aemon, the greatest evil this world has known, murderer of my dearest family and friends, is now always at her side. She led us into a doomed war and instead of showing the humility to admit failure and step down so we might rebuild, she uprooted us from the only home we've known and forced us on this journey to some mysterious, promised land."

"Then why do you stay?" Eliza asked, hands on her hips. They'd had this conversation dozens of times, but Eliza had never asked this question.

"Because," said Aggie, "this Reverie is a wild, untamed land and there is strength in numbers, even numbers as questionable as these. Besides, my people, the natives of my village, are still here and I will need to protect them when our inevitable betrayal comes."

Eliza shrugged. "Fair enough, Aggz, though I really hope you're wrong. About the betrayal."

The two sat in silence for a while as Osip and Oleg raced to see who could make it to the bottom of the bright orange spiral slide first. Other children, some of them human, joined the boys. Aggie watched them with an eagle eye.

"Where is Pasqual?" Aggie asked, never taking her gaze from her brothers.

Eliza smirked. "Taking advantage of his seat at the table. You know Pasqual. You can always find him where the most work needs do-"

The sound was faint. Any normal person wouldn't be able to hear it, but Eliza's enhanced aural processors and Aggie's keen senses had no problem picking up the light 'pop' that heralded the arrival of someone not of this world.

Aggie groaned before she even saw him.

"Ag- Aggie…" His voice trembled. His words had a pronounced slur. Jack wobbled back and forth as if standing upright was a chore. While his light brown skin and buzzed black hair remained fixed, everything else about him was in a strange flux. He would flicker between tall and muscular and short and scrawny. From a full perfect smile to teeth that were oversized and crooked. From a skintight black uniform like Eliza's to sweatpants and a dirty white T-shirt. From eyes that glistened purple like amethyst to a dull chocolate brown. Glasses with lenses that almost cartoonishly magnified his eyes would leave his face as quickly as they appeared.

Jack took a step toward Aggie, tripped and fell forward, forcing her to catch him in her muscular arms.

"I missed you." he said.

"It is the middle of the day," she replied. "Shouldn't you be awake?"

"I don't... I don't wanna be awake." His eyes rolled back. He could no longer stand on his own. Eliza helped prop him up. "It's stupid, Aggie. I hate it. I hate that stupid, stupid world…"

"Well, Jack, that is your world. Your home." Aggie tried hard to fight back her own tears as Jack's eyes began to water. Of all the things she'd lost recently, this was the worst. She once loved him and counted him among the only people she could always rely on; her hero. Now she dreaded his visits. The only solace is that in his current, fragile state he could only ever maintain brief visits.

Very few things could have made the situation worse, but when Mindy arrived dressed like a queen and wielding her beautiful staff, Aggie clenched her teeth and cursed her gods.

"Jack!" Mindy exclaimed. Her bright green eyes had too much life after what she'd put everyone through. "I heard you were here and we could really use your-" Mindy stopped, allowing herself to inspect Jack's unfortunate state. Her attention moved to Aggie who only glared back, then to Eliza who shook her head and shrugged.

"Mindy?" Jack welcomed her with a dopey, drooling grin. "Min- Mindy, what can I help you w-" And he disappeared.

A spell of tense, awkward silence passed between the three young women before Aggie spat on the ground and turned to face Mindy. "At least he visits me," she said, a comment specifically designed to cause Mindy maximum pain.

Mindy's eyes began to water. She puffed out her chest to feign strength, but her growing sadness was betraying her at every turn. Without a word she turned and marched away.

Eliza ran her hand through her half-fro. "Aggz, you're my girl, but that was cold. You know she hasn't heard from Jason since the war."

13

Mindy Sparks wiped the dust from the clear orb. It was fixed atop a long wooden staff, a true work of art made of multiple intertwined branches covered in elaborate etchings. It was the gift of a friend, the centaur Nikkylos, who had abandoned her. One of the many things lost at the end of the war.

Mindy sat on a stone bench facing a sculpture of cherubs and giant wide-eyed fish facing upward, their lips pursed. It had been a long time since the fountain functioned, by the looks of it. The area acted as a central point from which seven paths snaked outward to the empty pool, the playground, and the five large block white buildings that made up the perimeter; the abandoned apartment complex she'd decided would be their home until the next morning.

A hand landed gently on her shoulder. She tensed, and the orb glowed a fiery orange.

"Mindy." His voice was soft, soothing. She looked to the dark blue, almost indigo hand and rested her head against it, taking in his warmth. An arm wrapped gently around her waist and she felt his chin rest atop her other shoulder. "We have to be nearing three hundred."

"Three twenty-six, actually." She grinned and turned to him, met with his glacier blue eyes and inviting smile, despite the fangs. "Miles and some of the other scouts found a couple of families hiding in that building over there. After the initial shock of a talking velociraptor, they convinced them that we were the good guys and that they'd be safer with us."

Even as the words came out of Mindy's mouth she had a hard time believing them. It wasn't a month ago that she promised sanctuary to the lost and displaced of Reverie only to watch as most of them were decimated by the Nexis and his cyborg army. The death and destruction haunted her every day. As did the moments that followed. Combing the battleground for anyone still alive. The agony when the final body count was determined. Nikkylos and the centaurs' decision to leave her, regardless of her pleas that Aemon was a different man than the one who ravaged their land. And yet she persisted. She opted to remain their leader despite every ounce of her seventeen-year-old mind telling her otherwise. All because of a deep need to maintain control in a crazed situation. And a best friend who, until recently, had been there to support her.

Jason.

"You miss him," said Aemon, as if reading her mind.

Mindy rose from the bench and faced him. His pointy ears protruded from a head of straight black hair that reached down past his shoulders. He was a beautiful monster. "It's not just that," she said. "I mean, of course I miss him. I just- I don't know if he's okay. I mean, I do know because he's my best friend and if he was okay he'd *be* here! Like, did something happen at home? Or maybe he's stuck somewhere in Reverie!"

Aemon took Mindy in his arms. Other than Jason, he was the only person who was allowed to see her cry.

Wiping the tears from her eyes, she pulled away from him and cleared her throat. "I need to say something to them. It's been a while and we've collected a lot of new faces. Will you gather the council?"

Aemon nodded, kissed her hand, and walked off.

Twenty minutes later, the old fountain was encircled by hundreds of humans and other assorted creatures, all colors and shapes and sizes. Mindy stood upon a small raised platform at the center of the fountain. Standing in the empty pool at the fountain's base were Del, a wrinkled old man with a hunched back and a hard look, Peeps, a tall lanky goblin with thick tufts of tan hair and eyes large as plates, Pasqual, a young, handsome man with thick black hair in a skintight, black uniform, Eliza, and, of course, Aemon.

Mindy clutched her staff for strength as she studied the faces looking to her for guidance. She took a deep breath. "Hello, everyone. For those of you I haven't had the chance to meet yet, let me introduce myself. My name is Mindy Sparks and I, along with the council standing at my side, wish to welcome you to our family: The Alliance of Hope." A few claps and cheers went up, quickly banished to silence. "We'll spend the rest of the day here and then continue forward in the morning. According to my calculations- Jason's calculations - we'll reach our destination in five or six-"

Mindy noticed Aggie then, glaring at her from a distance. She felt a myriad of emotions coming from her audience (fear, joy, anxiety, exhaustion, relief), but none was so strong as the pure hatred Aggie directed at her. A hatred that, as much as she tried to deny it, was brewing within her toward Aggie as well. In Aggie Mindy saw all of her doubts, failures, weaknesses made tangible.

Mindy felt a hand reach up to hold hers. Aemon smiled at her and her insecurity waned enough for her to continue. "In five or six days we'll reach our final destination," she continued to the masses, with a smile. "Our new home."

"Why?" Aggie's voice cut through the calm. "Why will this place be safer than the one we have abandoned along with our memories and our livelihoods?"

"No one's taking your memories, Aggie," said Mindy, perhaps a bit too abruptly. Her grip on Aemon's hand tightened. She didn't even care that the orb atop her staff was taking on a reddish glow. "And whatever work you, any of you, enjoyed doing, we'll do everything we can to replicate it." She took notice of her irritation and exhaled. The orb became clear again and she returned her attention to the crowd. "As some of you know, I'm not from this realm. I'm from a place called Cosmos- Earth. The people there created a lot of what you see around you. It sounds crazy, I know, and I'm happy to explain further later, but for now just know that we're heading to a slice of this world that *I* created. My own personal piece of Reverie. And if there's anywhere I can keep you all safe...it's there."

14

The sun was just beginning to set.

Osip pulled the spear out of the ground. A dead squirrel with yellowish fur dangled from its end. "I did it!" he exclaimed, his eyes, one blue and one green, rife with excitement.

"So?" Oleg, identical to him in every way except his blue eye was on the right, dangling his own yellowish squirrel by its tail. "I got one, too. And it's bigger. And I got it faster."

"Did not!" Osip waved his squirrel-tipped spear in Oleg's face.

"Both of you, stop!" Aggie barked. She squatted atop the corpse of a massive black bear with faint blue stripes, carving into its hide with a hunting knife. Her face and clothing were drenched in blood. "Weapons are not playthings. You use them to hunt. And you use them to protect. Understood?"

"Yes, Aggie," they said in unison.

"Good," said Aggie. "Now go find Eliza and tell her to help me load this into the cart." Her brothers ran off toward their latest camp. "And avoid any strange plants! Remember what I have taught you!"

Every day Aggie led a troop of skilled and unskilled hunters, foragers, and fishers into whatever strange land they found themselves in to gather food and water to feed the others. She used the opportunity to teach her brothers about the hunt, about survival. In case anything happened to her, in case she was imprisoned again, she wanted to make sure they were as capable as she was of staying alive. At the same time she instilled in them her natural distrust of Mindy and the others, instructing them to believe only her, Eliza and, if absolutely necessary, Pasqual.

"Not bad," teased Eliza as she pulled a wooden cart piled high with oddly-colored foxes and deer and other dead woodland creatures with inhuman ease.

Aggie pulled her own cart beside Eliza, albeit with more of a struggle. Her cart carried the bear and two squirrels. She smiled. "Thank you. And I obtained my prey without cheating," she said, indicating Eliza's array of laser blasting weapons.

Others followed them out of the forest carrying fruits and nuts and vegetables and fish. They entered the clearing that would act as camp for the night. Hundreds of faces perked up, excited for dinner. The fires had already been set and the prep crews approached the hunters, ready to skin and slice and test for general edibility. (Pasqual had retooled one of his scanners to identify certain deadly toxins.)

Aggie woke up in the middle of the night, a bolt of fear rushing through her. Immediately she turned to her brothers, who were wrapped in the same woolen blanket, soundly asleep beside her. She looked around. Aside from a few whispers and snores, there was silence amidst the slumbering masses. Guards surrounded the camp's perimeter making sure nothing unsavory crept in from the outside. Aggie's primary concerns were the unsavory things that remained within.

She scanned the area with a keen eye. The guards were evenly spaced around most of the clearing's edge except for one area to the east where there was a substantial opening. *Odd*, Aggie thought. Upon further inspection, she realized the opening was closest to where Mindy and her minions slept. Even stranger, the guards on either side of the opening were Peeps and a hulking red creature covered in spikes: both she knew to be staunch Aemon loyalists.

Aggie gathered her best hunting knives and a couple vials of poison, just in case. A master of stealth, she slipped from under her blanket and began to rise when-

"Where...where are you going?" asked a small, sleepy voice. Osip.

Aggie put her finger to her lips. "Quiet." She leaned to him and whispered, "I must leave for a short while. It is for the safety of you and my people. If I do not return, run. Take care of your brother. Assume it was Aemon's doing."

Aggie deftly crept over the sleeping and out of the clearing into the woods. Fortunately, Eliza and a familiar man from her village were on guard, allowing her an easy escape.

Through the starlit darkness she moved, making her way over twisted roots and thorny bushes to the forest near the opening in the perimeter.

Footsteps, fresh ones, leading from the clearing. Of course. She tracked them for an hour, maybe two. The instant she heard voices she climbed up a tree, opting then to move across the canopy, from branch to branch, until she spotted the source of the sound: A conversation between a dozen goblins, each one a familiar face from her recent past. How stupid she was to think they had all been wiped out. The cowardly bullies, brutish tormentors of her people, would have run the second they realized the tides of battle had turned against them.

She moved closer, hiding above them among the leaves. That's when she saw him. Aemon. Standing in the center of the monsters, handing them the fruit and the meat that she and her hunters had collected.

"Here you go," said Aemon to a particularly sickly looking goblin. "Eat up. Once we reach Mindy's home our time will come."

15

Mindy smiled as she led over three hundred followers into the next world. This was the third version of Addley they had set foot upon in the past five days. It made sense that Addley's dreamers would often dream of their hometown but she loved how each Addley she'd seen was unique. Sometimes the colors of the houses were different, the general layout of the town, the prominence of one building or neighborhood or park based on how important it was to the one who dreamed it. This particular version of Addley was small. Specific. It only contained the town square and the surrounding brick buildings and cobblestone streets. And everything was decorated for the Fourth of July. From the courthouse to the bank and the statue of John C. Addley, the town's founder, it was all draped in ribbons and banners of red, white, and blue. People crowded the area, grabbing hot dogs at the hotdog stand or listening to the big band playing patriotic tunes. Mindy was amused by the normalness of it all. This was the first realm she had seen since their walk that was so lively, so unaffected by the war or the flood which had ravaged so much of Reverie.

It was a child who first spotted Mindy and her massive, motley crew as they entered the square. A hush fell over the milling crowd. Even the instruments fell silent as all eyes were on the newcomers.

"I am Mindy Sparks," she said, sensing the need for an explanation. "Together, my people and I make up the Alliance of Hope, a collection of displaced people in pursuit of a new home. We're just passing through. We mean you no harm."

A hundred pairs of eyes were locked on her, on Aemon by her side, and the rest of her strange companions. None dared reply until, "Mindy…?"

The crowd parted, revealing a large, round Indian man with kind eyes and a thick moustache. He wore a royal blue three-piece suit and a white sash that read "MAYOR" in big black letters. "Mindy Sparks?" he said in disbelief. "Is that you?"

Mindy's mouth hung open. "Basu?" She approached the man. Basu, the kindly owner of the diner she frequented with her friends, was standing in front of her. "You…you're you?"

"As me as I can be!" He unleashed a thick belly laugh. She had missed that laugh. "So, I'm dreaming, I guess. And here you are. My oh my, I heard the rumors about you disappearing to this place, but they were too ridiculous to believe. And, yet, here you are. In *my* dream!" His big, toothy smile faded to a frown. "Here you are," he said again, suddenly distant. Then, with a sense of urgency, "You must go. You all must go now."

"Wait," Mindy said, confused. "I don't understand, I-"

Basu took Mindy by the arms so quickly that she almost dropped her staff. "This dream. My dream. It always ends the same. You have to go before-"

"O-oh say can you see…"

The song, an echoing chorus, rose up from nowhere, everywhere at once.

"…by the dawn's early light…"

Suddenly, hundreds, maybe thousands, of men in blue blazers and red and white-striped pants, wearing plastic Uncle Sam masks, appeared marching down the cobblestone streets toward the town square, singing in unison.

"What so proudly we hail'd…"

They were holding weapons, from pitchforks and baseball bats to crowbars and the rare but unmistakable automatic rifle.

"…at the twilight's last gleaming…"

"These guys here to hurt you?" asked Mindy.

"Almost every night," said Basu, voice trembling.

"I see." The orb atop Mindy's staff took on a fiery orange light. She turned to her people and shouted, "Destroy them!"

Mindy pointed her staff down one of the stone streets, sending a torrent of fire that reduced twenty Uncle Sams to ash. With a thought, Aemon flung fifty more into the air and out of sight. Miles the velociraptor bit into an arm holding a particularly large firearm. Beams of light tore through the enemy, fired by Eliza and others armed with Futaran weaponry. Not to mention dozens more of Mindy's fighters armed with swords, magic, and brute strength.

Within twenty minutes the battle was won. Mindy, covered in sweat, placed a hand on Basu's broad shoulder. She grinned. "Mind if we spend the night?"

The rooms in the mayor's mansion were considered historic sites, so the furniture and decor retained its late-nineteenth century elegance. Floral prints, ornate mirrors, and lace curtains dominated the bedroom…just like in the real Addley.

"Take off your shirt," said Mindy as she entered the room, a warm, wet washcloth in her hand. "These decorations are so overwhelming, huh?"

"Oh, I don't know," Aemon said as he unbuttoned his bloodstained shirt. "I kind of like it."

Mindy rolled her eyes and sat down on the bed beside him. "Wow," she said as she examined the wound on his chest. A small, circular dent. "Either that bullet was super weak or you're super durable in addition to being a telekinetic and, ya know, handsome." Mindy leaned in to kiss him only to realize his mouth was full. "Oh God, really?!" Aemon shrugged. "Where were you even hiding those?!"

Aemon swallowed and reached for another barbecue chicken wing, one of many in a bowl resting on the bed behind him. "I've never tasted something with such flavor!"

"Ha, yeah." Mindy placed her hand on his thigh. "There's really no food like good old American cookout food. Basu's people threw us quite the party."

Aemon nodded. "And gave us quite the accommodations."

Mindy took her warm cloth to the wound, which was already healing. "Yeah. Four walls. A roof. A comfy bed...I feel like we should maybe make the best of it?"

Aemon's big smile mirrored hers as he moved his bowl of chicken wings off the bed, taking just one more before he did.

Mindy pushed him back onto the bed as he chewed. And climbed on top of him. "It's been a while since we've been alone, huh?"

"Too long," he mumbled.

"Too long." She leaned forward, bringing her face to his face, her lips to his lips.

Then Aemon let loose a sharp cough. And another. His eyes widened and his hands clutched his chest.

"Oh my God!" Mindy exclaimed. "Are you choking? You're choking!"

Aemon began to convulse. His eyes rolled back into his head. And, as Mindy ran out of the room for help, a green, foamy substance poured out of his mouth.

16

Aggie couldn't sleep. And even if she was tired she wouldn't spend a night in those fancy rooms the natives offered her. No. She would sleep under the stars when the time came.

She sat at a long wooden table covered in the scraps from the feast that had been laid for them hours before. Others wandered around, getting drunk or recounting the battle they'd just won. Aggie was plotting her next move as she watched Osip and Oleg play fight with a crowbar and tiki torch the Uncle Sams dropped. Would she tell the others what she saw or just run for it now?

A scream rose from within the largest building facing the square. An hour or so later, a handful of people emerged from the building, whispering to each other. One ran off into another building. All of this went unnoticed by the other people in the square.

"Yo, Aggz." Aggie was so distracted by the goings on that she didn't notice Eliza approach her from behind. The streetlights reflected off the metal half of her face. "Something's gone down in the mayor's mansion."

"What is it?" Aggie scanned the windows of the mansion for any clue, any sign.

"It's Aemon," said Eliza. "He's been poisoned. Pasqual's scanning him now, but-"

"Will he survive?" Aggie stood perfectly still, offering no emotion. "Will he die?"

Eliza threw her arms into the air. "Will he-? Ha. Of course he won't die. That man is zagging indestructible. Pasqual says the amount of poison he ingested could've taken down a bear- twelve bears -but his system's already fighting it. He'll be weak, but only for a few days."

"A few days…" Aggie's mind was spinning. She did her best to plot a response, a suitable reaction, a-

"Agalfia Tirk." Mindy stood at the foot of the statue of John C. Addley. The staff in her hand was glowing red. "I know it was you."

Aggie's brow lowered. "Mindy."

"That's right." Mindy took a single step toward Aggie. "It's me. Mindy Sparks. The person you have continuously gone out of your way to disrespect, to belittle. But this. This is unacceptable."

"You don't know I did it." Aggie's fists clenched.

"Ha." Mindy's laugh was all venom. She moved closer. "But I do. Pasqual's tech is fast and it's accurate. The poison used to murder my- Aemon, was from a flower native to the Black Forest. A flower that he in all his obsessive cataloguing has not encountered again. And let's be honest. You've made your hatred of Aemon far from a secret."

Del, the crazy old man, stepped into the light. "No one brews a poison like you, little lady."

Osip and Oleg dashed for their sister's side but a sharp, "Stay back," from her clenched teeth, kept them away. Aggie stood eye to eye with Mindy now. "You are weak," Aggie said. "A stupid little girl who cannot tell a wolf from a lamb, playing queen with your little stick, good for nothing aside from ensuring the deaths of those foolish enough to trust in-" Her speech was cut short by a hard fist to her face.

Mindy pulled her hand back, then tossed her staff to the ground, eyes never leaving Aggie. "Is this what you want, you animal? A fight? Is this the only language you speak? Fine."

Aggie's pink lips curled into a grimace and she pounced.

Mindy planted her feet, took Aggie by the arm and used Aggie's momentum to take her to the ground. Mindy pinned her in seconds, holding Aggie's arm firmly behind her back. Osip and Oleg started to charge.

"Get off our sister!" they shouted, but Eliza easily held them back.

"There was a guy named Zen," said Mindy. "He was the main character in some video game, I think. Zen was strong and he was kind...he was my knight, you know? He believed in me. And one of the many things he taught me in my months at the Black Rock was how to fight. We trained in the Black Forest. Me against him, at first. But I graduated to bears and then trolls...even a fire golem once."

"Months." Aggie scoffed. She tensed her core and rolled so hard to the right that Mindy was forced off of her. "Congratulations. You learned a juvenile takedown and a simple hold." She hopped to her feet and, in a blur, had Mindy pinned to the ground. "But instincts, survival, basic intelligence…" Aggie landed a swift kick to Mindy's stomach then placed the blade of a hunting knife against her neck. "These skills require years to hone."

"Aggz…" Eliza's human eye exhibited worry.

"No, Eliza." Aggie pressed her foot into Mindy's thigh. "She must learn." A deep breath and then, "Three nights ago I saw Aemon sneak into the woods. He was conspiring with goblins. The same goblins that tormented my people. He was planning an assault. He has not chan-"

"He has changed!" Mindy shouted, the fear in her voice highlighting just how young she was. "He saved us! What more proof do you need than that if it wasn't for him we'd all be dead?! You need to let go!"

"Let go?" Aggie applied more pressure to Mindy's neck. Any sudden move from either and blood would be shed. "So you expect me to simply forgive the deceit? You expect me to extend a warm welcome to goblins...not *other* goblins, but the *same* goblins who slaughtered, who *raped* my family and friends?"

Mindy closed her eyes. Exhaled. "Aggie," she said softly. "I'm not your enemy. Please take this knife away from my neck." Aggie hesitated, then did as she was told.

Mindy sat up and leaned against the base of John C. Addley's statue. It was an aged but beautiful sculpture of a portly man who enjoyed tailored suits and top hats. Aggie returned the knife to her belt and squatted low to the ground.

"I hate it, too," said Mindy. "The goblin thing. I know about it, but I hate it. Before Reverie, before all of this, someone who was supposed to protect me did things to me, terrible things that more than justified my hate. It's just that Aemon- God, he's, like, too good...good and stupid, you know? And he keeps saying 'If *I* can change then anyone can change,' but it's different and he doesn't get that and I don't want to tell him about my stuff because- I dunno, if there's anything truly good that's come from my relocation to Reverie it's that I can leave that dark mess literally in another universe."

Aggie frowned. "The darkness, Mindy Sparks, is the only

thing we can never escape. It is a part of us. And it will drive or destroy us."

Mindy wiped a tear from her eye. "Despite what you may think, I like you, Agalfia Tirk. If I was half as strong as you I'd- Well I'd hate myself a lot less right now, that's for sure." She climbed to her feet, dusting herself off. "You have to go, Aggie. I respect you, but you can't be trusted. You don't belong here. You have to understand that, right?"

Aggie stood tall. "I do," she said. She turned to her brothers. "Osip. Oleg. Gather your things. We're leaving."

Eliza took Aggie by the arm. "Aggz, what are you doing?"

"What I should have done from the start. She's right. I don't belong here. I don't believe in this. These..." Aggie gestured to the onlookers. "These aren't my people."

Osip and Oleg scurried to Aggie's side carrying a bag of their clothes and things. "We're ready," they said in unison.

"Let's go." Aggie started to walk away, but once again, Eliza grabbed her arm.

"Rumi saw you as one of us," Eliza said. "And that's enough for me. I'm coming with you."

Eliza turned to the handsome, stoic man by Mindy's side. "Come on, Pasqual, let's go." Pasqual remained silent. He pulled his clipboard close to his chest. "So that's how it's going to be...after all these years? After Rumi?" Pasqual said nothing. He only bowed his head and look one step closer to Mindy. "Fine then. All the best, bud."

Aggie, with Osip, Oleg, and Eliza in tow, left the town square, into the comfort of the unknown.

Mindy stood in the doorway for a while, delaying what she felt she had to do. Aemon was resting in bed, as pale and frail as he was when she first met him- *this* version of him -in the cave. Mindy laid down on the bed beside him, eyes wide and fixed on the ceiling. He turned his head to her, slowly. Coughed a little.

"What's wrong?" he asked.

"Nothing," she replied. "Something." She took his hand in hers and faced him with those lovely green eyes. "There's something I have to tell you. Something that happened to me a long time ago, but it's important now. It'll always be important…"

Aggie and the others walked in silence along a moonlit beach in the dead of night. The sound of waves crashing against the sand filled the salty air, the lights from town square were faint but visible far behind them.

Aggie came to a sudden stop. For a moment she did nothing, staring blankly into the blue-blackness ahead.

"You all right, girl?" asked Eliza.

Aggie turned and faced her brothers. She lowered herself on her knees so that she could look them in the eye. "How did you do it?" she asked.

At first they feigned ignorance. Then, falling victim to her continued gaze, they began to fidget. Then pout.

"When everyone was sleeping," said Osip. "And…and you

snuck away. You told me to protect Oleg in case...in case…"

"Then he took some of your poison," Oleg said. "And he told me the next morning. And we said we would save everyone like you saved us. Before he could hurt anyone else."

Osip continued, "So we waited for the perfect time."

"The party," said Eliza. "Everyone was so busy getting drunk and you two little monsters saw Aemon losing his mind over those chicken wings…"

"We saw a situation and took advantage!" Osip chirped.

"Just like you taught us, Aggie," said Oleg.

Aggie said nothing. She simply frowned, rose up, and started walking forward. Ever forward. Knowing that no matter where she went the darkness would follow.

Interlude III:
Patrick Ashford

A gentle "pop" and Patrick appeared in a place altogether new.

He adjusted his grip on Anza as she squirmed in his arm. A calm came over her and she grinned.

They stood in the middle of a large garden, alive with various plants small and large, thick and tangled. The garden took up nearly the entire area of the backyard of a modest cottage, all of it surrounded with a picket fence. The cottage and the yard were a curiosity all their own, dwarfed and in stark contrast to the giant hulking buildings that surrounded them. And everything, from the soil to the cottage's shingled roof to the ornate carvings on the skyscrapers' window sills, was made of a beautiful crystalline substance; white and clear with dancing hints of iridescence. Even after three years, Patrick could not help but be in awe of Eternia.

In the garden a small old woman was hunched over a plant and worked her shovel into the ground. Like Patrick, she was translucent and had the crystal glow of the rest of the realm that in no way overpowered her multi-colored shawl or body-length braided salt and pepper hair. His glow, though, was a bit darker.

"He's back," said the old woman through a toothless smile. She yanked a carrot out of the ground, examined it closely. It had the subtlest hint of orange. "Will you look at that?" Her thick Mexican accent was soft. "The best one yet." She then stood up on her skinny legs and walked with bare feet to Patrick. "Anza. Finally, I get to meet you in person." The baby cooed. "You don't know me, but I know your parents.

81

You can call me Guillelmina. May I?" Patrick nodded and handed Anza to Guillelmina. "Ah, such a sweetheart. She looks just like them, doesn't she?" With a sly grin she added, "And she's got a bit of your knack for trouble. I can tell."

"Guilly," said Patrick, abruptly. "It's already starting. On Cosmos. On Earth. Creatures, monsters came out of the ground and tried to take her. God, I hope Claire and the others are okay…"

"They are a formidable crew," said Guillelmina. "But, yes, we must move." A wave of her hand and a bright white portal opened before her. Slowly the whiteness faded into a scene, not unlike the one they found themselves in currently. "Come. Quickly." She stepped into the portal, Anza nestled in her arms. Patrick followed.

———

This new place was one Patrick had never seen before. He didn't think it was possible, but it was even more magnificent than the one he'd just left. Instead of skyscrapers there were beautiful castles and towers of all styles, adorned with banners and flags and sculptures. People conversed merrily and openly with the winged yazata; the angelic creatures that policed all of Eternia.

He found himself on a tower balcony overlooking the glorious land below. A tall, slender woman in a dress that fit tightly against her body stood and sparkled like a diamond, her back facing them as they took in the view. Her hair, sparkling white like the dress, was full in the pompadour style. She turned her head to catch a glimpse of her visitors. Her eyes, like the rest of her honestly, sparkled like diamonds.

"Well, this is unusual, darling," she said, her words mellow, seductive. "And I see you brought...others."

Guillelmina began, "Vita, this is-"

"Anza, the savior of Reverie," Vita interrupted as she rolled her eyes. "I know, darling. I was there when the creature was born." Her eyes then darted to Patrick, who stood eyes wide and mouth hanging open at the splendor all around him. "And you're another rule breaker…"

Patrick's heart sunk. "No! I mean- I stayed within the Laws of Visitation! I never revealed my name or...or any clues as to who I was or-... I mean, until recently...but the rules are breaking and they were in danger and-!"

"It's beautiful isn't it, darling?" Vita had returned her attention to the vast, glistening world below, no longer interested in his yammering. "Eternia. My precious, perfect domain. The oldest of the three realms, you know. Unlike the utter chaos of Cosmos and the, well, even greater chaos of Reverie, my sweet Eternia is a paradise of structure and regulation split ingeniously across six distinct planes of existence. When people die, their bodies decompose in Cosmos, but their core substance, their essense returns to Eternia, intact. It is placed on a pathway where my lovely, winged yazata examine it, rating each based on a simple system of lives ruined versus lives improved and then place it in the appropriate plane."

Patrick had of course heard all of this before from Guilly. His plane was a little darker, more crudely put together. Things like pain and anger and fear and doubt were more common there. But Guilly rescued him. Her ability to exist between Cosmos and Reverie seemed to transfer quite well to Eternia, allowing her to move between the six planes.

"Speaking of appropriate planes," Vita turned her attention

to Guillelimina. "I know that you were accustomed to do and go wherever you pleased on those *other* realms, but I insist you stay in your place, old woman." Then, gesturing to Patrick, she added, "And I simply cannot abide dragging in this foul trash to a plane so many levels above his proper place."

Patrick half expected Guillelmina to cower at that. A number of chills had already gone through him. But old Guilly's brow lowered and the small woman confidently stepped toward the towering entity before her.

"Vita," she said, "with all respect due to you as co-ruler of Eternia, as the manifestation of existence itself, unstoppable monsters roam freely through Reverie. And in Cosmos, gods and beasts we thought were long gone are waging war on Addley. And *you*, you and the other manifestations brought this baby, these children, into the middle of all of it. You've made them targets. You're practically the cause of all of this mess."

Vita bared her perfect white teeth and clenched her thin fingers into fists. "Says the one who we purposely elected to keep them safe."

"I died!"

"Whose fault is *that*, darling?" Then, as if suddenly appalled by her own behavior, Vita inhaled and composed herself, a cool smile returning to her face. "Garbage aside," she said, gesturing to Patrick, "you were smart coming here. I am quite curious about this child's fate and, loath as I am to admit it, am beginning to experience a twinge of *potential* guilt that this chaos might partially be the doing of my kind." Under her breath, she added, "One in particular."

"Nihilo," said Guillelmina.

Vita offered a subdued nod. "Initia and Mortem suspected it. I always thought his obsession with the destruction of, well, everything to be an ignorant joke. I mean, how could there ever be nothingness so long as I, the proof of existence itself, exist? But it seems he has been preying on Reverie and Cosmos for years, manipulating those who crave nothing but, well, nihilism, darlings. I am repulsed to say it, but his agreeing to lend his power in the creation of Anza might be a part of his plan as well." Vita laughed nervously, a terrifying thing to behold in itself. She then swiftly shifted to Patrick. "Who are you?"

"P-Patrick."

"Ah." Vita examined him. "You reek of, what, level three?" She turned to Guilly for validation. "Yes. Level three, and for someone who left his mortal coil so young... You must have done something awful."

Patrick felt like someone punched him in the chest. Not a day, not an hour, went by that he didn't think about what landed him in Eternia at the age of nineteen, nearly three years ago. The look on the face of the boy driving the other car, of his little brother in the passenger seat, when he lost control and rammed into them head on, killing himself and the driver.

"He's sorry," said Guilly, brave enough for the both of them.

"Sorry doesn't bring people back from the dead, darling." Vita again gazed out beyond the balcony. "And if he truly feels remorse, he should follow protocol, alert a yazata, and express desire to be reincarnated in hopes of returning to Eternia at a higher pla-"

"Vita, enough." Guilly patted Patrick on the back. "This is

Patrick Ashford. Claire's brother. You know the connection between relatives is strong, even across the realms, and I- we may need that in order to...to stop whatever's coming."

Vita scoffed. "A feeble attempt at convincing me, darling, but I grow tired of all this dialogue. You may have sanctuary in this tower while I figure out what's going on. Don't do or touch anything. Don't make yourselves known. And if the yazata find you and take you away...that's on you." A pause and then she added, "You were right coming here, darlings. In an existence marred by confusion and pandemonium, Eternia, the first and greatest of the three realms, will always be a bastion of stabili-"

BOOM! An explosion echoed from the distance. They all peered over the balcony to see a large dark crater far below, nearby buildings were slowly crumbling into it. Shrapnel from the buildings caught in the blast crashed into the surrounding land.

BOOM! Another explosion in the same place deepened the crater.

BOOM! And another.

Patrick heard a fourth explosion, faint, almost a whisper. He thought he'd imagined it until, from out of nowhere, enormous, mountain-sized chunks of crystal began to fall from the sky...

PART IV
A FRIEND IN NEED

17

"Heel. Toe. Heel. Toe."

Jack hardly paid attention to the woman with the iPad and the head full of messy strawberry blonde curls as she excitedly mused over the coming milestones in his physical therapy. Every day she approached him bright-eyed, repeating that mantra: "My goodness, the way you're progressing, I've never seen anything like it in all my years. It's downright miraculous!"

He'd heard similar statements from a number of white-haired doctors. He hadn't been out of his coma for more than a week and he was already speaking in complete sentences (the slurring lessened a little each day). His muscle deterioration was minimal for having been in a vegetative state for so long, they said. And not a single doctor, scientist, nurse, or therapist could explain how such a thing was possible.

But he could. Reverie. Jack wasn't sure of the science behind it, but he knew it had something to do with his deep connections with the dreamworld; his powerful, capable other self. And perhaps a little Guillelmina. Or whatever Aggie and Dion had done to wake him up.

Miracle or not, he found no joy, no reason for celebration, in his current state. For almost three years he spent his days fighting goblins and robots, exploring new worlds on a futuristic motorcycle, falling in love. Now he was back on Earth, in Addley, a mere mortal imprisoned in an electric wheelchair that he was barely strong enough to steer. He could barely walk; barely feed himself sometimes. In Reverie he had dreamed himself to be tall and handsome and fit. Here he was, as he had been before, small, scrawny, weak.

His mother picked him up from therapy, helped him into her van. He was happy to see her. He really was. And happy that he was able to give her the gift of one of her sons returning from the dead. But this feeling of such crippling powerlessness after having taken down a dragon, after *flying*...it was almost too much to bear.

Jack sat on the recliner and watched TV as his mother prepared dinner. There was a knock at the front door and a wave of dread went through him.

"It's Anne," his mother said, verifying his dread.

The mousy girl with oversized glasses and buck teeth walked into the living room, already removing her backpack and slipping out of her shoes. She planned on staying for a while.

Jack didn't hate Anne. Far from it, in fact. In Reverie, sleeping wasn't necessary for him to survive, but he'd do it sometimes because when he did he occasionally heard bits from the other side: his mother's heartfelt prayers, nurses bickering out in the hall, and, more recently, Anne, reading poems and stories and recounting her day. It was nice. It was appreciated. It offered him a glimpse of a world that he missed. What bothered Jack about Anne is that her relentless and selfless interest in his well-being was in stark contrast to the anger he so desperately wanted to sit with.

"So, how was therapy today?" she asked, all smiles and concern.

"Fine."

She plopped on the part of the couch closest to his recliner. "Any milestones?"

"Nope."

Jack sensed her chewing on the next question before she asked. "How's Reverie?"

His whole body tensed. Through clenched teeth, he said, "I don't know."

Anne didn't respond. Her silence was somehow worse.

"How was school?" Jack asked.

"Good," she said. "Same stuff." A stretch of quiet filled by the TV, then, "Maybe it's stress." Jack grumbled. She continued, "I know it's not easy. Being back. And the therapy, it...sucks, I bet. And when you're stressed it's hard to concentrate which is probably why it's so hard for you to, you know, get there. Maybe."

Jack slowly turned his head to Anne. The light from the TV screen reflected off the moisture in his eyes. "You're right, Anne. It does suck. And it's not getting any better. When I first woke up, at least I could *get* back, but the longer I'm here… Every day it gets harder."

"Because you're angry."

"What else can I be?" he snapped. "You didn't- You have no *idea* what I was when I was there. I was a god…"

Anne reached to touch his hand, but he pulled it away. "What if-"

"Please." Jack gave her a hard glare. "Don't. Don't try to help me. I don't want it. I just want one thing. And no one can give it to me."

Jack's mom helped him into bed. She kissed him on his forehead and wished him pleasant dreams. She turned out the lights and closed the door on her way out. Jack let his head drop to the side. His eyes met with a framed photo taken a few years ago. It was him and his older brother, Bobby. He was smiling with his arm around his little brother, wearing a Jay-Z tshirt. He was Jack's hero. Bobby had been killed in the same car accident that put Jack in a coma. Jack felt a sharp pang of sadness. Yet another awful aspect of this world.

Jack groaned as he reached above his head and under his pillow. His fingers made contact with a small plastic bottle and he did his best to grip it and bring it to his chest. After a struggle to remove the top, three sleeping pills dropped into his palm. "Goodnight," he said as he placed them all into his mouth and began to chew.

18

Annabelle Grimmly sat at her usual table in the spacious cafeteria at Addley High. Hundreds of teenagers and their teacher overseers filled the place with noise. The lunchline was finally dying down. Carl the custodian scanned the area for any potential messes. Construction had begun to fill in a human-sized hole in the far wall.

Anne removed her PB&J from its container and tried to ignore the stares and whispers by searching hidden upgrades for Glug the Troll: Ogre Crusher - a character she played in an online RPG. A month ago she sat at the popular table. And while far from popular herself, a few twists of fate landed her there; a stranger who was generally tolerated by her unlikely companions. A lot had happened in the past few weeks and today, she sat alone. Each and every one of her friends had, in one way or another, become victims to the weirdness of Reverie; a mess she felt she was always cleaning up.

When the final bell rang, Anne grabbed her jacket and backpack and walked down the sidewalk, passing the bus she'd normally take home.

She couldn't get Jack out of her head. The hopelessness in his eyes. Thoughts of Jack moved to Max and Jamal, who'd gone missing after Vic's funeral. And then to Vic, whose ashes had been stolen at some point between the funeral and the repast. To Claire, who was no longer talking to her after deciding to move in with her alternate self's mother.

In desperate need of a win, she walked up to a nice gray and white house with a porch swing and unruly hedges. She knocked on the door and, after a wait, it opened. A little old lady with a wrinkled face stood in the doorway wearing a purple bathrobe. She took a look at Anne and her thin lips curved into a frown.

"Hi, Mrs. Baker," said Anne. "May I speak with Jason?"

Jason's grandmother sighed. "Young lady," she began, her voice coarse and shaky, "Jason's in no condition to speak with anyone, I'm afraid. Just like he wasn't yesterday. Or last week. Or the week before."

"I know," said Anne. "I'm sorry to bother you. I just-"

"Wanted to help," Jason's grandmother said with a sad smile. "I know, dear. You know, that Sparks girl's parents came by today, too. To check on him. They left in tears, poor things. They lost their daughter and now…" Her mind wandered off. "Shame."

Anne started to leave, turning toward the walkway. "Well, if there's anything I can do."

"Take a walk," said Jason's grandmother. "My grandbaby upstairs, he's just shut up in his room. Won't talk. Barely eats. He just sleeps. I gotta be right and ready with a hug and a kiss as soon as my baby comes back to me. So, dear, take a walk. Clear your mind. Do good by you."

Anne nodded and walked off while Jason's grandmother muttered something about dead bodies found in a park on the news.

The sun was setting and Anne was thinking it was time to head home. Jason's grandmother was right. All this walking had helped, though she couldn't fully shake the need to do *something*.

Something caught Anne's eye then. Just some girl crossing the street. Crossing the street to... Wait, she knew that house. Anne had aimlessly wandered to a neighborhood she knew very well. And that house was one she knew almost as well as her own. From a simpler time. In ways, a better time.

And the girl...

At first Anne thought it was the Claire who had recently lived with her and her mom. The one that wore expensive clothes and had destructive dream powers. But, no. Upon closer examination this person was dressed in an old hoodie that covered most of her dirty blonde hair. Teal flipflops smacked against her feet. That Claire would never...

Anne's heart went into overdrive. Her eyes opened wide. "It...it can't be..."

The girl noticed her then. She turned and looked at Anne. First with surprise. Disbelief. Then intense, unbridled joy. "Anne... *Anne?*"

Anne could feel the tears swelling in her eyes as the girl ran for her.

It was Claire. Her Claire.

The two hugged in the middle of the street, crying through "I missed you's," and experiencing a fleeting, but welcome sensation of everything being absolutely perfect.

19

"Sorry I didn't find you earlier," said Claire, not quite truly believing she was sitting on the curb having a conversation with her best friend; someone she hadn't seen in almost a year. "This...thing with paper-white skin led us to a portal and then, poof, we're here. We were in the middle of the woods outside of town and it took us like, more than a day to find the main road. Then we walked for what felt like forever. Fortunately, this old couple picked us up and brought us to Addley. And we've been at my mom's- at my house ever since figuring things out. Well actually, I was coming from Jamal Anderson's house. Did you know he went *missing* a few days ago?"

Anne was listening as best she could, but really just so excited to hear Claire's voice again. See her face. "Jamal." Claire's words finally caught up with her. "Yes. And Max. You know *Dream* Claire and Jamal were- are? -dating, actually."

"Yeah, she really went for it, huh?" Claire giggled. "I had a crush on that guy since before I knew what crushes were."

Anne grinned and leaned close. "Sooo…"

Claire raised an eyebrow. "Sooo…?"

"When do I get to see the baby?!" Anne looked around like Claire was hiding it somewhere close.

"About that," Claire began. "I gave her to the ghost of my brother who said he'd take her somewhere safe because these rock monsters practically destroyed the house trying to get her."

"Wow." Anne only then noticed the damage that had been done to Claire's house and the front yard; like something had just taken giant chunks out of both. "You know, a year ago I wouldn't have believed anything you just said. Or I would have been too shocked to even respond. It's still shocking, but in a different way. It's pretty amazing, how people really can get used to anything."

"I know right?" Claire leaned her head against Anne's shoulder. "So. What have you been up to? Tell me everything."

Anne recounted as best she could all the events since Claire's departure. From her first run-in with that other Claire and her attempted suicide to Guillelmina's funeral and Dion and Jason's relationship to Jack and his current state.

Claire hugged her tight then and said, "I love you so much, Anne, and I'm sorry I wasn't here for you."

"*You're* sorry?!" said Anne through fresh tears. "You had a baby in an alternative universe and *survived* and I couldn't help at all and it drove me crazy. I knew you were strong, but...damn, girl."

They laughed at that.

"Hey," said Claire, "let's go inside and steal a glass of my mom's wine. She's blind now and sees the future so she won't notice."

"Um...what?"

Claire opened the door to the house. Victor was sitting on the couch with his usual worried expression. Satya was next to him, reporter's notebook in hand. Her attention was fixed on the beautiful bald woman in a deep blue dress, with skin as dark as the night sea.

"Uh, hi," said Victor. "This is Olokun, goddess of the unknown...and the deep sea...and dreams."

"Among other things," said the goddess.

Satya pressed her pen to her notepad. "She's going to tell us everything."

20

Satya Shirazi had never felt so alive, so invigorated, as she did by the situation she currently found herself in. The scoop of the century...of the millenium...of all time!

She zipped her hoodie to hide the cute cat and penguin T-shirt beneath (professionalism is everything) and pondered her first question to the literal goddess within arm's reach of her. "Mrs...Ms...Olokun, my first question inv-"

"No, child." Olokun raised a long finger, silencing the other. "This ramshackle estate is no place to conduct an interview." She glanced to the street outside through a hole in the wall. "I require privacy. I merely returned to this home as a courtesy to Victor, who didn't want the others to worry. And I'm nothing if not exceedingly compassionate." She said that last bit with a touch of sarcasm. "Now that we're all accounted for I will be relocating us to a more secure location." Olokun raised an arm. Numerous gold bracelets dangled down her wrist as she did. Dark tendrils emerged from her fingertips.

"Wait!" Claire placed herself beside Olokun, in the middle of everyone. "Where's my mom?"

"Oops," said Satya. "We kind of left her at the diner. I was caught up in the excitement!"

Claire placed her hands on her hips. "Well, we can't just leave her. Someone's gotta go back and-"

"So be it." Olokun snapped her finger and the whole world went black.

Satya waved her arms and legs wildly as she did the first time. She couldn't see, couldn't hear. It was like she was swimming in a sea of utter darkness. She could even feel the coolness of the tumultuous water engulfing her. She couldn't breathe. And then, quickly as it came, Satya was on solid ground again, trying to right her balance before toppling.

She pressed her hands against the cold, marble floor and rose to her feet. The room she found herself in was large with a high domed ceiling. And it was dark; lit only by a large fireplace. All of the furniture was magnificently designed; sculpted, golden, mythical sea monsters adorned it and the cushions were made from the pelts of giraffes and zebras and things she had never seen before. A hundred other trinkets and artifacts on crowded tables and shelves were arranged beautifully and sparsely. Satya also noticed two magnificent golden doors, similarly detailed as the furniture but with humans seemingly at war with the same creatures. One was closed, the other slightly open and emitting a soft green glow.

"Claire! Where's Claire?" asked the girl with the thick glasses in a mild panic.

Olokun, cool as ever, replied, "I left her behind so that she could gather her mother." To Satya, she said, "Sit." And then to Victor, "You too, Mister Soto."

Olokun took a seat in the largest chair, with a high back and the most golden decor. Satya and Victor sat on a giraffe-skin sofa beside her; Satya choosing the seat closest to the goddess.

"Okay. All right. Okay." Satya psyched herself up. "What do you know about the disappearance of Mindy Sparks?"

Olokun cocked her head to the side, obviously confused by the question. "Who…?"

Okay, Satya, she thought to herself, *come on. This is the big leagues!* "Uh…" she began, "What do you know about the portal in the woods?"

Olokun's lips curled into a smile. "A great deal," she said. "Portals act as gateways between the realms. Emergency exits and entrances created by chance or design countless ages ago."

"Did you create them?" Satya asked.

"Some," she replied. "Most precede me. Though few could actually figure out how they work. That's where I come in. You see, the laws of physics demand a certain level of balance. Activating a door between realms requires an even exchange of living beings to pass through each side at the same time."

"There were shapes." Victor sat up. "When Anza and Claire and I were at the door…er…gateway, we saw shapes on the other side. But when we went through…they were gone."

"Shapes?" Satya turned to Victor. "How many shapes?"

"Two, I think."

Satya's mind was racing. She had a crazy idea, but crazy seemed to be all that happened around here. "Max and Jamal." Then to Olokun, she asked, "But there would have to be a third, right? Because of Anza?"

Olokun shrugged. "Perhaps. But Anza is, to put it lightly, a special case." Olokun stared into the fire as if reading something no one else could see. "Any other questions? Questions that are actually worth my time." Satya sunk at that. "Time is of the essence these days and I have much to-"

"The man in white," Victor blurted. "Who is he? He led Claire and I to Anza once when we...lost her. And then he took us to the portal."

Olokun paused. A hint of ice blue flickered in her dark eyes. "So that's how..." She let the sentence drift into quietness. Olokun once again turned her attention to the fire. She then closed her eyes and relaxed herself, sitting comfortably in her seat. "I am an inventor," she said. "For thousands of years I toiled away down here in my lab at the bottom of the sea, ingesting the knowledge of man and immortal and synthesizing it so that I might achieve the goal of most of the great thinkers of history: a brighter tomorrow. The height of my creativity coincided with the height of the war between the pantheons. Gods killing gods, the world was about to end and I made it my great mission to solve this problem. Fortunately, I didn't have to. The gods all but killed each other off. But the damage had been done. By their example, humans became obsessed with power and bloodshed; with a natural distrust of others, other cultures..."

Olokun reached to a copper figurine on a table beside her. It was a tall, thin man with a flowing robe and large wings. "From my time with the ancient Zoroastrians I discovered the spirit plane, Eternia. It was a realm of structure and law. But what intrigued me the most was its physiology. All energy that travels to Cosmos begins and ends in Eternia. And while there, it takes on a crystalline form which I named the Core Substance. It is the origin of atoms and cells and all things. Malleable. Under the hands of a true inventor the possibilities are, well, limitless."

Olokun returned the winged man to its place and grabbed a clay vase with ancient drawings of fire-breathing lions hovering over sleeping children. "Once I had studied this substance I was able to manipulate it. And, more importantly, to detect it. To measure it. In Cosmos, the most powerful occurrences of the core substance happened when humans slept. It practically beams from their untethered minds, taking their thoughts and rising up, up up...then disappearing to another world. A third realm."

"Reverie," said Victor.

"Yes." Olokun winked at him. "It took some doing, but I was able to travel to Reverie, a realm literally created with the power of human imagination made real by Eternia's Core Substance in Cosmos. The scientist in me was elated. I felt like I had finally found the missing piece. That I had finally discovered the complete picture."

She crossed her legs and stared up at the ceiling. "There are two things I find myself sorry for. One, is how this has impacted you, Victor. And Claire. And a number of people in your village, it seems. The second is the grave error I made bringing Nihilo into this world. He played us all for fools. At first I thought, stupidly, that I could not be deceived by my own creation, but his single-minded wish for the destruction of all things outweighed my more multifaceted foci. It is becoming clearer and clearer to me that he manipulated the other manifestations into bringing Anza into this. Among countless other things I know nothing about. He wishes to sow chaos. Chaos, destruction's infant state. For all I know, this plan of his could have been millennia in the making."

Olokun leaned back in her seat. As she raised her hand to her mouth a glass of dark, deep wine appeared in it just in time for her to take a long sip.

"And the man in white...?" Victor asked.

Olokun laughed. "Oh right. Before creating the manifestations I thought I should give them a place to convene, to interact. A neutral place. They think Origin Point is where all three realms began, but I just used a giant knife made of the Core Substance and tore a hole in reality for them to play in; added a little magic to offer some firm footing. But when I created the manifestations, a flaw, more or less some excess Core Substance batter, merged with the Origin Point and resulted in your man in white. Or Speck, as I've named him. I'm not sure what Speck's game is in all of this, but I've learned long ago not to trust anything that's born of my hands."

Anne was pissed. What was supposed to be a lengthy reunion with her best friend in the world had been cut short by some gorgeous goddess teleporter. While Satya and Victor sat down with Olokun talking about...whatever, it didn't matter...Anne opted to sulk in the dark corners of the room and angrily take in the dumb statues piled everywhere.

That is, until she noticed the door.

It was big and gold with scenes of men hurling spears and fireballs at massive sea serpents. It also happened to be slightly ajar, emanating a green glow. Olokun and the others were far too interested in the story the goddess was telling to notice her as she slipped into the next room.

The space was big. It looked like a steampunk laboratory. There was plenty to take in but all that Anne could focus on were the dozens of large cylinders of a thick, green glowing liquid. Most of them were so dusty that she couldn't see what was floating inside of them, but something seemed wrong. Some of the silhouettes looked a little too...human.

A glimmer of light caught her eye from a far corner. It was another cylinder, but this one shone brighter. As she got closer, she realized it did because it wasn't covered in dust. It was considerably newer than the others. The nearer she drew to the cylinder, the clearer its contents became. It was a young man, floating naked, with thick cords connected to his back and snaking down to the base of a copper machine laden with levers, buttons and gauges. Anne placed her hand on the glass. It was warm to the touch. She circled the cylinder in order to get a look at the face of this unfortunate captive.

She gasped. "Dion…"

21

"Dion's in there!" Anne burst into the room, much to the surprise of Victor and Satya, who had likely forgotten she had come along.

"Trespassing, are we?" said Olokun, unphased by the other's arrival.

To Victor and Satya, Anne said, "She has people- lots of people -trapped in vats of green goo in there!"

Victor and Satya's eyes darted to Olokun. Satya started scribbling in her notepad.

"Not people." Olokun rose from her seat. "Gods." She walked over to Anne, towering over the small girl. "More specifically, gods of life and death." To Victor and Satya, she continued, "During the wars between gods, I would pull some of the dead bodies off the battlefield to run my experiments. The gods have such unique DNA.."

Olokun's excitement was met with Anne's disgust. "So Dion's dead?!"

"No." Olokun crossed her arms, in parts amused and irritated by Anne. "He nearly died, but I was able to siphon the power from some of the other gods to rehabilitate him."

"Then why is he still in there?" Anne's cheeks were turning red. "For more experiments? Just in case? I didn't hear all of your story, but from what I gathered you're a pretty crappy scientist."

"HUMAN," said Olokun, her eyes suddenly shining a brilliant cerulean. "You do not come into my domain and speak ill of me or my work."

"I didn't ask to come here. You kidnapped me." Anne was not backing down, though she was shaking from head to toe and finding it generally hard to stand. "Dion is supposed to be your friend. And...and more importantly, Jason needs him. He's home right now. He won't eat or take his meds. He won't- he *can't* speak to anyone. We need Jason. We need him here and we need him in Reverie because he's one of the few people powerful enough to clean up this mess. Your mess." Olokun bared her teeth. "Yeah, I totally heard that part."

Anne took a deep breath and adjusted her glasses. She looked to Victor and Satya who were too taken aback to say anything. Then to Olokun whose nostrils flared, but was otherwise still. "Look," Anne said, almost in a whisper. "You did a great thing saving Dion's life. You've got a chance now to save another."

Olokun's eyes returned to black. She lowered her head. Inhaled. Then looked to Anne. The light of the fire seemed to reflect off a tiny tear in her eye. "I am not a bad person. I merely wanted my life to mean something. Even as a goddess, I will someday be taken from this earth. And in my time I want nothing more than to put an end to the pain and suffering and hatred that has damned so much of this existence."

"You want to help," said Anne. "Then help."

Olokun blinked. Then she started for her laboratory. "So be it."

Interlude IV:
Ben Burnham

Ben tugged on his hood, making sure it covered his face in case the large, dark aviator glasses he wore weren't doing the trick. He looked ridiculous (and quite conspicuous) weaving his way through the cracked alleyways and streets of the mostly abandoned part of town in a three-piece gray suit, lugging a large black leather duffel bag.

Ben compulsively checked his phone every few minutes, swiping through the headlines with sweaty hands. "One hundred dead in apparent mass suicide at John C. Addley Park." The authorities seemed no closer to tying him to the event - the leader could have easily been one of the dead - but Ben had never conducted one of these in a place so public. And it had never been so many at once. In this day and age a hidden camera would have captured sight of him. Not that it would matter much once the one he dedicated his life to achieved his goal.

One of the many abandoned, boarded up townhouses that defined this part of Addley had a strange black symbol painted on its side facing a narrow pathway: a dagger stabbing a lightning bolt. As instructed, there was a door in the back of the house; the only entry point that hadn't been sealed off. Ben trudged through the tall grass and gave the door a knock. There was silence at first then the sounds of assorted items shifting and falling.

"State your business," said a deep voice from the other side of the door.

"My life I give to Nihilo, great liberator of the realms," Ben said this proudly. It was a popular chant amongst his congregation. He heard whispers from inside and then the door clicked and swung open.

Ben nearly gasped. He was greeted by a man who filled most of the doorway. He was easily seven-feet tall, thick with muscles and clad in a fur cloak and heavy armor, all black. His eyes were glacier blue. His skin, pale and smooth as alabaster. And, perhaps most curious of all, his entire body emitted a soft, warm light. "Come inside," the man said.

Ben followed him through the door which led to a staircase down into a gray and musty basement that reeked of mildew and something else.

"Mead?" offered the large man. The basement was a wreck of cobwebs and old, dusty furniture in various states of disrepair, but the one thing that was mostly intact was a fairly well stocked bar and a few stools lit by candlelight.

Ben barely heard the other's offer as he was too fixated on the thing at the farthest barstool.

Though seated, it was clearly taller even than the one who let Ben in. Leaner, too. It wore light golden armor over its ankles and wrists but otherwise was clothed in a white toga. Its skin was like pearl. A pair of massive silvery feathered wings were folded against its back. A large sword rested against the bar beside it.

"Alcohol," said the winged creature as it turned to face Ben. Its face looked quite human except for its eyes which were large, slanted and completely black. A large, toothy smile widened on its face as it raised a stein full of beer. "You humans get a lot of things right. Most of all, your vices."

"This is Arbitryx," said the one with the blue eyes, gesturing to the winged one at the bar. "He orchestrates a number of

Nihilo's endeavors in Eternia."

Arbitryx snickered at that. There was something disarming about him. Something inherently mischievous. "Proud soldier of Nihilo since before either of you were glimmers in the eye of creation."

"And I am Baldr, son of Odin," stated the blue-eyed one with great pride, "Norse god of justice, sole survivor of the Black Companions, a weapon deftly forged in Nihilo's war."

Again, Arbitryx laughed. "What he's saying is that he's a traitorous god-killer with nowhere left to go."

Baldr's cheeks went red with anger. He began to reach for the great axe strapped to his back, but decided against it.

"Have a seat, little human," Arbitryx sang as he pointed to the stool beside him. "Tell us how you got yourself mixed up in Nihilo's games."

Ben had barely begun to process the fact that he was currently sharing a basement with an angel and a god. Still feeling the initial wave of disbelief he took a seat next to Arbitryx. Baldr had already placed himself behind the bar. "Yes," Baldr said, monotone, "who are you?" He planted a mug on the bar in front of Ben and gave him a heavy pour of whiskey.

Ben took a sip, winced at the drink's strength and bad taste, and said, "The great lord Nihilo appeared before me in my time of need and blessed me with eternal truths, opening my eyes to a path most holy so that I might find the strength to connect to something greater than myself and join in his hallowed mission to put an end to all suffering through the return to the sacred void."

There was a moment of silence in which Baldr and Arbitryx shared a knowing look. Then Arbitryx burst into laughter, brought to a swift end by the look of conviction that remained on Ben's face. "Oof," said Arbitryx, "old Nihilo sure did a number on you, didn't he? You humans are gifted with all the freedom in the universe and want nothing more than to throw it all away in someone else's war."

Not quite following, Ben took another sip of whiskey. "What about the two of you?" he asked. "How did you come to receive such a blessing?"

Baldr gestured for Arbitryx to speak.

The winged one obliged. "He first came to me claiming to be the ruler of Eternia, which is funny because I'd been around for some time and never heard of any talking inkblot overlord before that. As a yazata- angels, you people call us - I wasn't happy with the way good and evil is segregated in Eternia. The way families are separated. Or how we yazata are kept in a state of endless servitude, keeping the peace, if that's even what you'd call it. As Cosmos expanded, our jobs weren't getting any easier. Then Nihilo comes along talking his talk and I like what I hear. I gather a small army of like-minded yazata. Then a couple thousand years pass and nothing changes and most of us disband, quite sure the inkblot is a fraud."

"Blasphemy," hissed Ben.

Arbitryx grinned. "Heh. Nihilo can't directly, physically affect anything so he uses us and the others to act on his behalf. I've seen them come and go. He's got agents in Reverie, Eternia, and, obviously, here in Cosmos. Earth isn't the first planet he's pulled this one, lemme tell ya."

Baldr leaned over the bar then. "Arbitryx was supposed to

secure the baby, but couldn't. The all-knowing Nihilo should've sent me in there if he'd known what's good for him."

"What can I say?" The yazata shrugged. "They don't make golems like they used to. And you're one to talk!" Arbitryx pushed a long thin finger into Baldr's armored chest. "You couldn't even kill a single schoolboy. And don't get me started on tact. You were told to do it quietly, quickly...so you decided to burst through the wall of a high school cafeteria?!"

Baldr grunted. "I've a question for you, yazata. As one who has known Nihilo longer than most, what do you think the odds are of him actually achieving his goals?"

Ben placed his focus on Arbitryx, hungry for his response. The yazata took a swig of his drink. "Cosmos, Reverie, Eternia- all three are expanding and have been from the beginning of time. To end it all, to achieve complete and utter nothingness, in my opinion, seems an impossible feat. Honestly, I'm in it for the chaos. In a world rife with existence, nothingness is impossible...but with enough destruction to the status quo, myself and my kind might finally be free to live my life however I choose." He turned to Ben and added, "Like you humans could if you opened your damn eyes for once."

Ben did his best to swallow his emotions, but he was appalled by the lack of reverence, of respect Arbitryx had for Nihilo. Baldr, too, seemed fine with the yazata's blasphemous words.

It was then that Ben understood his new calling. Why he was brought to Addley. He would do what he had for hundreds of men and women over the years: Ben Burnham would instill within these two, within all the people of Addley, a deep and undying love and fear for the great Nihilo, manifestation of the blessed void, so that they would be ready to accept him, willingly, when the Day of Nothingness came.

PART V
THE SUM OF HIS PARTS

22

During the battle at Black Rock- well, the most recent battle at Black Rock -Rumi Inyonara found herself curled on the ground as five hulking cyborgs relentlessly attacked her, kicking and punching, leaving her with excruciating pain and broken ribs. Her leg fractured, Rumi knew there was no fighting her way out of this one. Recalling from her years of training for the rebellion, she unscrewed the hilt of her lightblade. A small glowing spherical battery the size of a pill fell out. As another rib cracked she grabbed the battery with a trembling hand and inserted it into a small pocket in her utility belt.

There was a subtle click and a beep, both sounds swallowed by the clamor of the war raging all around. Then a teal layer of translucent energy surrounded Rumi's body. The sharp kicks from the cyborgs could no longer be felt. The clangs and cries of battle went silent. Rumi couldn't move, but she looked into the eyes of her tormentors and watched as they shone bright red. The cyborgs stopped their torture and, in unison, exploded into an all-encompassing show of fire and light.

Rumi, encased in her translucent cell, was launched into the air. For a split second she saw a vast battlefield covered in smoking craters. The last thing she remembered was the green and brown blur of a forest before she passed out.

When Rumi woke up the sun had long since set. She was high in a tree, lodged between two branches. She grabbed hold of a branch to maintain balance as the forcefield began to fade. Her ribs were sore, but the nanobots released by the mechanism in her belt had healed the worst of her wounds.

She took a moment to thank Pasqual for yet another superb invention.

Rumi climbed down the tree. She checked her watch. She had been out for hours.

She made her way back to the battlefield at the base of Black Rock, the impossibly high, narrow mountain of dark stone. She hid behind the ruined husk of a hulking machine and watched as a group of people- her allies -spoke and cried and dragged corpses from the surrounding woods to be buried in simple, shallow graves. She recognized Aggie and her little brothers. And Mindy with Aemon, who was using his telekinesis to dig more graves. Eliza and Pasqual, her truest friends, were there as well. Rumi wanted nothing more than to join them, hug them, tell them she was okay. But there was something she needed to be sure of.

It was easy enough to repair an old hoverbike she'd found amongst the wreckage of war. She sped off to Futara. Once one of the most remarkable, lively, and technologically advanced cities in all of Reverie, it was now a place of death and ruin. She paused for a moment, remembering her parents, her friends, and all those in the rebellion who lost their lives. The promise she made to finish their work no matter the cost. Jack and the others had been a distraction. Rumi had to finish what she started.

She climbed to the top of the tallest building, where their AI overlord, Nexis was once housed. Nothing. She then scoured the prisons and great arena where Nexis, merged with that psychopath Patrick, created his cyborg abominations. Empty. Perhaps he...it...was finally gone. The overlord Rumi had been trained her entire life to defeat, defeated at last.

Rumi hopped on her hoverbike and headed back for Black

Rock. Her friends were gone by then; the sun was rising on a new day. She produced a device she'd cobbled together from some tech in Futaran arena and pressed a small green button. The device beeped and a screen lit up, a yellow light racing around its perimeter. A few times around and light stopped in the upper right corner and began to blink red.

She blew a stray strand of neon green and pink hair from her face. "There you are," she said.

It wasn't long before she spotted him. A pair of lightweight silver binoculars gave her a closer look. She recognized the face of the man walking with a slight limp, wearing nothing but torn pants, as Zen, a capable fighter and ally during the battle. But it was easy to see he had been altered. Those red eyes. The grayish, almost reflective skin. Nexis had found a new host. She decided to tail him, then put an end to the entire nightmare once and for all.

Rumi watched and listened from a safe distance for days. She watched as he argued with himself over what to do next again and again. Merging with Nexis was hardly a smooth process. For a moment she wondered if Zen was combatting Nexis or Patrick in his mind...perhaps both? It didn't matter much. He had to die either way.

Rumi observed him as he saved the winged child from the cowboys only to then slaughter every single person in that town.

Finally he led her back to the ruins of Futara. She climbed from her hover-bike and climbed down the manhole into the secret lab. This was it, she thought. And she pulled her laser gun from its holster, set it to full power, killed the scientists in the room, then pressed it to the back of Nexis' head. "It's over, Nexis. I'm going to destroy this place and you along with it."

"Rumi Inyonara," he said. "You have no idea how glad I am to see you." Then in a darker tone, "Such sweet pleasure it will be to kill you at last."

"Zen," Rumi said, "I'm sorry, but I have to end this."

"I understand. But you can't. Not yet."

Rumi clenched her teeth at that. "Give me one reason why not."

"I can give you four." Nexis spun around, wrapped his fingers around the barrel of the gun and crushed it in his hand. In his red, mechanical eyes Rumi saw glimmers of terror and rage. "My back-up servers," Nexis said. "Three hidden in the city and two more outside of it. The only way to truly destroy me is to destroy them first. I'll have nowhere left to hide."

Rumi's free hand was already reaching for her second gun. "Where are they?"

She could see Nexis trying to speak, the benevolent side of him grappling with the malicious, but the words would not come out. Then he said, "I will take you to them."

"Zen," she said, her voice lightening. "How much of you is in there?"

Nexis paused then answered, "More than he'd like...they'd like? Sometimes I feel like I'm battling more than one entity in here."

"Patrick," Rumi said. "He's a homicidal maniac who somehow took control of Nexis' entire system. I bet both of them are in there, trying to pull your strings."

"Patrick, yes...yes, that feels familiar." Nexis released Rumi's broken gun and it dropped to the ground, destroyed. "Sorry about that. I'm in control, I think, most of the time. And I think that's because Patrick and Nexis have a hard time agreeing on anything. They're always bickering in here. But when they agree on something."

"Like killing everyone in that saloon."

Nexis nodded ruefully. "Yes. It's a lot harder to keep them at bay. I have stay very focused right now, to keep them- me - from killing you." Nexis raised his arms and unleashed a barrage of laser beams at the lab, destroying servers and screens. He winced as if experiencing a sudden headache. "They didn't like that. He tried to smile but it couldn't quite get there. "Can I ask you a favor, Rumi?"

"Okay."

"Call me 'Zen.' It may seem silly, but it helps to ground me. The memory of who I was...am...should be."

Rumi nodded.

"Thank you. Now let's get out of here so we can slay these monsters and win the war." Zen added, "You should let me stay in front. I wouldn't trust me walking behind you."

23

"DIE, REBEL SCUM!"

Rumi deftly dodged a white beam of hot light. Zen moved in for a punch. She twisted her body out of the way. Zen's fist left a hole in the wall beside her. Rumi launched herself into a backflip, flying over Zen and aiming her gun at the server hidden in a mess of large discs and plastic containers. The server exploded and, as if breaking from a trance, Zen calmed. Frowning, he leaned against a messy shelf full of boxes and said, "My apologies. Again."

Rumi wiped the sweat from her brow. She pulled a stray strand of neon green hair behind her ear. Short of breath, she took her place beside him. "Back in control?"

Zen nodded. "Yes."

"Good." Rumi looked in the messy storage room. It was in the back of a music shop they'd broken into. All over the floor were boxes filled with silver discs labeled things like "Future Pop" or "Deepwave" or "Space Groove." Most of it had been rendered useless by the flood. "I never really listened to music," Rumi said. "When my classmates were sneaking out to raves or smoking Styng while playing bit-discs, I was training. Always training for the rebellion. Training to overthrow, well, you."

Zen let out a breathy laugh. "I understand. One minute I am attempting to save a princess from a dark sorcerer in Grobi Kingdom and the next it is all destroyed and I'm fighting a war against the metal monsters that wiped that entire kingdom from existence...and now I *am* that very monster. Life is funny that way." He turned to Rumi. "How are you faring?"

"I'm fine," she said. "That was the last server in Futara, right?"

"Yes." Zen squinted, as if experiencing a headache. The others in his mind were causing an uproar, no doubt. "After the floods, The Nexis allied himself with a dark creature called Nihilo. He suggested two more places where the servers might be kept safe. Come with me."

"Great." Rumi became uncharacteristically weary all of a sudden. "But before we go, there's something we need to talk about."

———

Zen looked down at the stumps where his hands once were. It was tough and The Nexis fought back, but Rumi was able to lop them off and weld the stumps. Zen noticed Rumi looking at her crude work and, before she could say anything, said, "You had to do it. Every time we reach a server The Nexis will come on stronger."

Futara was behind them now. Rumi and Zen found themselves walking through an old neighborhood at night. The houses that lined the empty road were decrepit, creepy. Rumi swore she could see shapes, sometimes human, watching her from the black windows of the homes out of the corner of her eye. But that might have just been the fatigue setting in. She hadn't slept since waking up in the woods...almost three days ago.

"We should rest," said Zen hungrily, obviously noticing Rumi's wavering spirit.

"No," she said through a yawn. "You'll kill me. Like I said: No sleep. For either of us. Come on, let's go."

They continued through the town, into another; a village of wooden cottages on stilts in an expansive marsh. Zen attempted to bite Rumi twice. On both occasions, Zen was able to regain enough control to let Rumi evade the attacks.

Zen's losses of self increased as they walked across a vast field of grass. Rumi wasn't quick enough to evade one of the attacks, resulting in a fractured ulna from a very powerful kick. She tended to the wound with some stabilizing foam from her belt and they continued.

The field gave way to a jungle so thick it appeared to be a solid wall of twisted leaves, bark and vines. Zen squeezed between two trunks, Rumi followed, and they were in total darkness. Zen's eyes glowed a brighter red and Rumi tapped her temple. A faint blue glow flickered on from behind her irises. Stolen military-grade night vision implants. Problem solved.

Rumi squeezed through a viny tangle. "Well this is a pretty great place for me to die."

"Agreed," said Zen. "Keep some extra distance behind me."

As they continued, the space between the trees widened a little and they caught sight of a clearing up ahead. Quietly they moved toward it.

"Whoa," said Rumi, her heart beating hard as she tried to hold herself together. The clearing contained hundreds of heavily armored soldiers lying dead in the mud and grass; small creatures feeding on their corpses. Deflated, she added, "Is this the world now since the walls came down? Just death and destruction and monsters ruling over all?"

Zen sighed. "Maybe." He pointed to a stone structure near

the middle of the clearing. It had been a tower once, but now the cylindrical building stood little more than twenty feet high, covered in vines and moss, surrounded by its own rubble. "In there. We have to hurry. I cannot hold on much longer."

Rumi nodded and they sprinted for the tower. They climbed over the piles of stones and entered through a still-intact doorway. The space was small and cluttered with even more stones. The beginnings of a spiral staircase went upward, but ended quickly. There was an old wooden door along the far wall.

Zen turned back to Rumi. "The server is through that door." He added, without emotion, "IT'S A SHAME YOU'LL NEVER LIVE TO SEE IT." Rumi watched in horror as the stumps at Zen's wrists began to glow white-hot.

Without flinching, Rumi launched herself forward, ramming into Zen and throwing off his balance. She opened the door, slipped inside and slammed it behind her. A set of descending stairs caused her to lose her balance in the dark, damp space, but she righted herself and ran down them. The closed door behind her burst into splinters as a beam of light tore through it.

Down she went, exhausted and sore, trying her best to retain balance on steps that were slick with moss. She could hear Zen approaching quickly from behind. All that hatred, power and tech driving him toward her.

The room at the bottom of the staircase was pitch black. Rumi's night vision implants allowed her to see the outlines of various shapes around the room, including the one she needed most. A small, oddly-shaped box along the wall. She drew a small glowing bar from her utility belt-

BZZT!

The bar was disintegrated. She turned to see Zen descending the last of the steps, his eyes glowing red.

"Helpless," said Zen, his voice dripping with disdain. "Defenseless. Alone. Poor little Rumi breathes her last breaths in this stank-ass tomb."

Rumi snarled and summoned every last ounce of energy she could muster. She clicked a button on the handle of her gun and out dropped a small pill-sized battery. She caught it in her other hand, squeezed it hard in her palm, and hurled it at Zen. On impact the battery burst into a blinding mix of blue fire and light. In Zen's confusion, Rumi ran behind him, taking his neck in a vice grip and grabbing him firmly by the forearm.

Zen shot a beam from his restrained arm. A moment later his red eyes went dark. Then closed. Then reopened. "Rumi?" he said, his tone sweeter, concerned. "What happened?"

"I aimed your arm beam at the server. Nexis was too enraged to notice." Rumi's breathing was heavy, but she smiled through it. "Are you...?"

"I am me," said Zen. "For now." He took a seat on the stairs. "It is insane, you know. The clarity that follows a broken server is the most myself I feel. And then the closer we get to the next one...the harder it is to hold on."

Rumi rubbed her tired eyes. "One more to go. Maybe when I destroy all the servers-"

"No." Zen stood and walked to Rumi. "I have to die."

"There has to be a way."

"Wow," said a new voice, startling the two.

For the first time Rumi and Zen noticed someone else in the dark room. He was thin, muscular with short black hair. He was also completely naked, tied up with vines on the ground in the fetal position.

The stranger continued. "As riveting as your conversation is, I would love it if you freed me. My name is Vic. And I've got all the answers you're looking for."

24

Simply saying that Vic was angry would have been a gross understatement. In his entire life, the idea of failure of any sort was something foreign to him. He had excelled at any challenge life threw at him and had done so with ease- he had even come back from the brink of death twice -but this current situation was most definitely a failure...and a humiliating one at that.

One minute he was leading a pair of bumbling teenagers through a dense jungle; the next he was swallowed up by syrupy, purple blackness, unable to see or speak or breathe or move.

Vic frowned at the sound of exaggerated laughter. "Escape is futile little man," said Estralus. "For I must further Nihilo's plan. My mission, boy, is one to find the knowledge buried inside your mind."

A sharp, intense pain coursed through Vic's head. He opened his mouth to scream, but only swallowed that thick, heavy purple darkness.

The next thing Vic remembered was waking up on a cold, damp stone floor. Naked. Wrapped in thick vines. All was dark except for a blue light that blinked on and off, illuminating nothing special aside from a staircase leading up.

He wasn't exactly sure how long he had been stuck in the basement before witnessing the arrival of the Asian girl and the red-eyed guy and the curious battle that swiftly began and ended.

"Who are you?" the one called Rumi asked.

"As I just told you, I'm Vic!" he exclaimed. "Now untie me so I can stop whatever havoc Estralus is going to wreak on this world!"

The one with the red eyes stepped forward. A stump where a hand had most likely been cast a light on the small space. "Who is Estralus?"

A wave of refreshing information flowed into Vic's mind. The feeling of new knowledge, triggered by being asked a question, was his favorite sensation. "Estralus," Vic began, "is a powerful, irritating demigod who rules this jungle. He can take on any form and, because that's not enough, can pull the thoughts and abilities of people's minds. So if you would be so kind as to free me, I need to stop a monster from using my greatest gifts to bring Reverie collapsing in on itself."

"Vic…" Rumi leaned in closer. "Victor…?"

"Hey," said the red-eyed one. "I know Victor. This person looks…different…"

Vic sighed, rolled his eyes. "So you've met my lesser half. Joy. Well, let me assure you that I will be of much more use than that evolutionary sinkhole. Now can you please untie me already?"

Rumi's eyes narrowed. "How do we know we can trust you?"

"You don't," said Vic, matter of factly. "That's life. That's especially life in this place. All I know is that you, lady, look like you haven't slept in days, lost your last weapon and have for whatever reason decided to travel with No-Hand Hank over here who occasionally comes down with an unquenchable urge to kill you. I must say this scenario does not inspire confidence. I can most definitely be of service."

"My name is Zen," red-eyes said. "You said you had answers. What do you know?"

Vic smiled. "Whatever you need me to. It's kind of my thing. I know the answer to any question. It just...comes to me."

"Ridiculous," Rumi spat.

Zen cleared his throat, doing his best to banish the excitement that bubbled inside him. "How can I get these monsters out of me?"

Vic's mouth twisted into a toothy grin. "Ah. It's difficult, but definitely doable. How about this? You two untie me, help me stop Estralus, and I will cure Zen here of his affliction." Rumi opened her mouth to speak, but Vic noticed and continued, "Let me guess. You don't believe me. Ask me a question. Something I could not possibly know. Hell, ask me five questions! And prepare to be amazed."

25

"I'm suffocating," groaned Rumi. She was wearing full-body black military armor. She held a massive weapon, part battle axe and part gun, in both of her armored hands.

"Hey," said Vic, "just be grateful you're weaponized...and found a complete set." Vic was in full armor as well, but his was a collection of mismatched parts. He held a black dagger in each hand. "Besides, it'll keep you safe from You-Know-Who."

Zen, who had no new weapons or armor, offered no response.

The three of them walked side by side through a field of tall, golden grass under a dusk sky and Vic shared with them everything he wished them to know.

"So the two you were traveling with. How are they?" asked Rumi.

"Alive," said Vic. "But anything could happen where they've gone."

"Under Reverie," said Zen.

Vic raised a finger. "Under the surface of Reverie. It's a place of raw energy and chaos; a sort of high-speed cosmic furnace where new dream realms are born and die and occasionally make it to the surface. It is not a kind place."

Rumi shook her head. "What sort of damage can Estralus do down there?"

"A lot." Vic turned to Rumi. "Normally one would get

swallowed up by the insanity of the Underrealm, but Estralus has my thoughts. And with those he can potentially shape parts of Reverie to his will...or destroy them completely."

Rumi and Zen were more or less returning the way they had come. They walked through Futara and dropped down a sheer cliff face into a wet, sandy plain with the help of Vic's armor's jetpack feature. In the center of the plain was a tall, brown, rocky mountain rising from the sand. A hole had been blasted into the base. The three stepped over the corpses of strangely feline beasts and entered the mountain, hit with a wave of intense heat as they did so. A path led downward, deeper into the earth. It was lined with more corpses. At the bottom of the path they were on-level with a magma lake. They crossed the lake and entered a large domed room. On one end of the room was a beast that resembled the others, but enormous in size. Dead. In the center of the room, another hole had been blasted through the floor.

"Down there," said Vic, pointing to the hole.

The three stood at the edge and beheld at a sight unlike any they had seen before. Islands, big and small, floated in a backdrop of whiteness. Some housed cities, others, forests...some were just a simple garden or shop or stretch of road.

"What am I looking at?" Zen asked.

"This is the Underrealm," said Vic. "We're witnessing the birth of potential worlds. Not every place that a person dreams ends up on Reverie's surface. Only the ones that are reinforced and given time and attention to solidify make it to the top. On Earth they call them recurring dreams. If a person goes to the same place over and over, sometimes over the course of years, that place might rise up and become a new realm in Reverie."

A sudden cloud passed by in the hole beneath them, rife with bolts of pulsing lightning. Visibility into the hole was nil for a few seconds before returning. Vic shrugged with a smirk. "If you thought Reverie's surface was chaotic, you haven't seen anything yet."

Just then, a huge island of purple grass passed beneath the opening.

"It's now or never!" said Vic before jumping into the hole and landing softly on the island. Rumi and Zen followed him. From the grassy surface they looked up and, surprisingly, only saw a vast empty whiteness...except for the hole through which they jumped which offered a view of the interior of the cave.

"Now observe." Vic gestured toward crystalline veins stretching out of the whiteness above and disappearing into the whiteness below. They were thick as redwoods and reflected iridescence. "These feed all realms, finished or otherwise, with dreamstuff, the core substance of all life in Reverie. They reach all the way to the core of this world and are tethered to their respective realms." Just then a small island rose into view, this one not much more than six feet in diameter. It was a chunk of desert with a heart-shaped cactus and nothing more. A thin crystal vein was attached to the bottom of it. "These tethers are strong, of course," Vic continued, "but not indestructible." He reached one of his daggers out to the vein. With the press of a button the dagger's blade was alive with blue bolts of electricity. In a swift slash, he tore through the vein. Seconds later, the island and all its contents, exploded into a hundred chunks of iridescent crystals. "See?"

Zen quickly dodged one of the larger crystal shards that

nearly removed his head from his shoulders.

"Where's Estralus?" asked Rumi, finally seeing the direness of this mission.

Vic pointed down. "Let's drop." He leapt off the edge of the grass-covered island to whatever awaited them below.

26

Reverie's Underrealm offered a tumultuous environment. Floating islands of half-formed ideas, abominations of scenes and settings being born of the dreamstuff, moved through clouds of fog pierced by blue or pink or green streaks of lightning. The larger islands rose up at blinding speeds, connected to thick iridescent veins. Other islands sped wildly in any direction, crashing into one another or simply appearing or disappearing from existence when their tethers tangled. The rumbling of near and distant thunder filled the air.

"STAY BACK!" shouted Jamal as he stood over Max's unconscious body. His massive weapon was pointing at the monster that shared the floating rock island with them.

The monster, Estralus, resembled a sentient glob of dark purple slime, stretching fifteen feet from the ground. Its large, almost cartoonish blue eyes were fixed on Jamal while one of its tendrils, shaped like a giant sword, was hacking away at an incredibly thick iridescent vein, with a diameter wide as a bus, that reached so high and so low neither end could be seen.

Everything flickered in and out of view as clouds of fog whipped by.

"Shut your mouth and help me destroy," said Estralus in its radio host voice, "or risk winding up like this redhead boy." It burst into laughter, stopped dodge a purple rock hurtling through the sky, then returned to laughter once more.

"I am not your slave," said Jamal. "Neither is Max. And, honestly, I am sick and tired of being someone's minion in this ridiculous, ridiculous world."

A white, toothy smile emerged from Estralus' dark, slimy form. "Fine." Its eyes narrowed and turned fire red. "Then die." Estralus raised his sword-shaped tendril and then brought it down over Jamal. Jamal pulled the trigger on his gun and launched a glowing blue orb. The orb made contact with the tendril, exploding and dispelling it into shards of black. One of the shards left a scratch in Jamal's helmet.

"You're going to have to try harder than that!" Jamal taunted.

Estralus' smile widened and widened. Its teeth became sharp. Eight long black tendrils rose from its glob form, each taking the shape of a smaller sword. Jamal could see that its body shrunk as it displaced most of his mass to his weapons, throwing off its balance a bit.

"If you won't help me cut this cumbersome tether," Estralus began, "I'll eviscerate you both now altogeth- ARGH!"

One of Estralus' eight swords was disintegrated by a beam of white light. Jamal watched in awe as three individuals fell from the sky, landing on the island between him and the enemy. Two were in full armor like he was and the third was a gray-skinned creature without hands.

"It's Vic," said the one in the mismatched armor. "To the rescue." Vic turned to Estralus and said, "I'm growing quite tired of living a life riddled by people claiming to be me."

Estralus tried to mask the surprise in his eyes. It twisted its gooey form once, twice, three times, then landed a cyclone of slashes to the vein. The gash was a brutal one. The vein was one or two blows from breaking.

"You're too late," Estralus hissed.

"Enough talk," said the one in the black armor. She held a massive firearm with an axe blade at the end of its barrel. "How do we kill it, Vic?"

"Thanks, Rumi," Vic said. "All we have to do is-"

BZZT!

A beam of light hit back of Vic's helmet and he was down. The attack had come from the stumps of the one without hands.

"Zen!" shouted Rumi.

Estralus twisted his body again, preparing for a second attack at the damaged vein. He burst into maniacal laughter then said, "Hail, Nihilo."

"Hail, Nihilo," echoed Zen.

Interlude V:
Vita

The manifestation could hardly comprehend what she was seeing. Her Eternia, her perfect crystalline paradise of order and beauty unsurpassed, falling into ruin before her eyes. "What…" said Vita in a whisper. She began to feel faint. Screams rose up from a city descending into an enormous sinkhole as chunks of core substance the size of skyscrapers collided with her realm from above. "H-how…? Nihilo, he's- he's done the impossible. That foul beast, he's laying my domain to waste…"

"We have to get out of here!" shouted Patrick, but Vita barely heard him. She was mesmerized by the destruction as they watched from her balcony high above.

More screams. The winged yazata swooped in for the rescue, but it was too much too fast. And, what was that-? Yes. Yazata wearing black robes attacking the others. Nihilo had gotten to them, as well. How long had he been planning this? How could Vita not see it coming? "Your arrogance blinds you to the truths of this life." Initia had said once. How annoying she had found her when she said it.

"Vita. Vita!" She felt a tug at her elegant white dress. It was Guillelmina. "Patrick's right. I know this is against the rules, but…" Vita didn't hear the rest. She was too busy experiencing the odd sensation of tears forming in her eyes. Of pain in her heart.

More explosions and constant screams from below. The black-clad yazata ramming their weapons through the bodies of their brethren. And then a light, bright even in this world of brilliance, caught her attention.

Vita turned to Guillelmina who was using her gifts to open a portal at the other end of the balcony. Patrick, with the child in his arms, stood close.

Vita's brow furrowed. She wiped a tear from her eye. Finally, something she could control. The tall, silver-haired being stepped toward the others. "What," she hissed, "do you think you're doing?"

"We're getting out of here," said Guillelmina. "I'm taking Anza to Origin Point."

"You will do no such thing." Vita was standing before Guillelmina now, towering over the old woman. "There are still rules, Guilly. Rules have kept peace in Eternia for millennia and rules will return us to peace soon enough. Using your abilities to leave this fated realm are strictly prohibi-"

"Screw your rules!" Patrick shouted. "Your realm is falling apart!"

Vita turned to Patrick. Anza began to whimper. "You *dare* raise your voice at me, human," Vita said. "I am the embodiment of existence itself. I am old as time." She pointed her finger at Patrick's chest. "I am the ruler of-" Vita stopped and gasped. Her finger pressed against Patrick. Since the very beginning, no manifestation had ever been able to make physical contact with a single creature of Reverie, Cosmos, or Eternia. "What...what is happening?"

"Whatever it is," Guillelmina began, "Anza can't stay here. In any of the realms. She's our only hope. We have to take her to Origin Point."

Vita's eye twitched. "But- but what if that's a part of Nihilo's plan as well? What if this child is nothing more than yet another weapon forged against us? Against me!"

"No," said Patrick. "She's just a baby. My niece. She's no one's weapon."

"Look," Guillelmina spoke calmly and placed her hand gently on Vita's, a strange sensation for them both. "Whatever rules you set into motion, five of the six beings who set them did so with the best intentions. You, Somni, Timor, Mortem, Initia- you all sought to create a savior, a peacemaker...one twisted being's twisted thoughts can't compete against the goodwill of the majority."

Vita closed her eyes. She had never felt such a lack of control. "You'll be lost, darlings, if you step into that portal. The Origin Point is nothing but endless white. Enter like this, without preparation, and you all will starve or worse; have nothing to occupy yourselves." Her eyes opened and she extended her arms to the iridescent castle to which the balcony was attached. Suddenly, chunks of the crystal wall began to liquefy, coalescing into a floating stream that pulled more and more from the castle and flowed into the bright white portal Guillelmina had opened. "The uses of the core substance are limitless, darlings. The manifestations found we could transfer it into Origin Point and create whatever we might need ad infinitum."

The liquid crystal continued to flow. The castle was half gone. "If you insist on going, I hope I have supplied enough arrangements for you, darlings," she said, gravely.

"Thank you," said Patrick. He looked to Anza. "You made the right choice."

"Get out of here," said Vita. And to Guillelmina she said, "Pray that you remain hidden from our enemy."

Guillelmina nodded and gestured for Patrick to follow her. She stepped into the portal, disappearing into the whiteness. Patrick followed with Anza in his arms.

Vita watched as the portal began to close. And then a third surprise, something she had never experienced before: Pain, as a spear cut through her belly. She turned and looked into the eyes of a yazata wearing black, smiling sadistically. Vita winced. "So it's come to this, darling." Barely able to stand, she screamed into the closing portal, "ORIGIN EXISTS OUTSIDE OF TIME AND SPACE, GUILLY! USE THAT TO YOUR ADVANT-"

Another yazata in black arrived and swung its broadsword at Vita's neck just as the portal closed completely.

"Hail Nihilo," it said as Vita's severed head hit the ground with a thud.

PART VI
COLLISION COURSE

27

When doctors, teachers, and friends asked Jason Baker what it was like when his mind was like this, he would say it felt like disappearing. Like the parts of him that made Jason Jason went away and in its place was just a husk that felt separate from the rest of the world. Helpless. Meaningless. And sad. When friends would stop by or his grandmother dropped off a meal he would hardly eat, none of them could understand that the Jason they were trying to reach simply was not there.

Days had passed since the incident in the cafeteria and the images of Dion, his first boyfriend, the first boy he ever loved, getting carved to death by a mad god's axe played over and over in his mind. Dion took Baldr's attack. The attack meant for Jason.

Each night Jason would eventually go to sleep. And when he did he would wake up in a similar space: an expansive land of rolling hills stretched out in every direction. All the hills were emerald green, except for one in the center which was covered in dead, black grass. This is where Jason sat and stared blankly forward. A small thunderstorm raged only above the blackened hill. The rest of the sky was blue and sunny.

Jason heard the sounds of footsteps crunching against the dead grass well before the one who made them stepped into view. Jason found himself staring at a pair of brown pants stained in oil and dirt. He tilted his head up, taking in the leather belt with a rusted tiger buckle; the old red flannel shirt.

The man crouched down to see Jason eye to eye. By the look of him, he was in his forties. The first thing Jason noticed was his thick, wild, red hair and sunken green eyes. The crook in his nose. His face was covered in scars. Thick stubble covered his chin. He grinned with crooked, yellow teeth.

"Well, what have we here?" said the man. "*The* Jason Baker. I traveled quite a ways to see you."

Jason said nothing.

"Name's Ezekiel," the man continued. "Friends n' foes call me 'Zeke.' Man of few words. I like that. Respect it. A man's actions are what makes him anyway, am I right?" Ezekiel's laugh sounded more like coughing. "Word's gotten around these parts of Reverie. A Lucid, one of the most powerful anyone had ever seen. Piqued my interest because, well…" A thick cigar materialized in Ezekiel's hand then lit itself. He took a puff. "…I, too, am quite the capable Lucid."

Jason sighed and looked to the ground.

"Woo-ee!" Ezekiel stood up and placed his hands on his hips. He looked up to the storm clouds above then to the dead grass below. "You've got a gift, I'll give you that. Why don't we, I dunno, swap tricks of the trade?" Jason offered no response. "Oof, okay. Gotta do this the hard way."

Jason felt his body lifting from the ground, but did very little to resist it. He dangled in the air by an unseen force. Once again, he was looking into Ezekiel's eyes. "I get it," said Ezekiel. "You're down in the dumps. Failed your exam. Your girlfriend broke up with ya. Happens to the best of us. But your ol' friend Zeke's got a surefire solution to your situation."

A gentle popping sound and Jason found himself in an altogether different place, Ezekiel beside him. Both were floating high above a scene like something out of a fairy tale. Cute wooden cottages were built into the sides of a rocky valley with a crystal stream running through it. Birds chirped joyfully and lush trees with colorful flowers grew all over. Populating the village were a hundred or so chubby-cheeked gnomes with pointy hats singing or whistling with glee as they went about their day gardening or reading or frolicking.

"Thing you gotta remember," Ezekiel said, "is that dreams aren't real. They're the stuff of our imagination. Psychologically speaking, a way for us to sort through and untangle some of the thoughts that are racking our brains throughout the day, you see. They're meant to give us perspective. To heal us. To serve us." Ezekiel took a puff of his cigar. "My daddy was the worst man I'll ever know. People call me a monster, but woo-ee, that guy. When I discovered Reverie, I was just a kid. But I found my confidence here. My power. My freedom. From that cruel man. From this cruel world."

Jason's eyes landed on two gnomes snuggled close under a tree. They were holding hands, kissing and giggling. A chill went through Jason's spine.

Ezekiel put his arm around Jason. "Makes you sick, don't it? All that glee. Tears you up, huh? All that love. Pisses you off that they have it and you're back on Earth- back in *reality* - with nothin'!" Jason turned his head, looking at Ezekiel with glazed eyes. "Ah, there he is. My boy. It's okay. Get angry. Life's out to get you and sometimes you just need to find the strength to strike back. Let that rage build up and show them all who's in charge."

Ezekiel gestured to the gnomes. "Go on now, Mister Baker. They're just figments of your imagination. Little fantasies here to help you heal. Taunting you with their joy, those bastards. So, go on. Show them your power."

A single tear trickled down Jason's face. He was fixated on those two gnomes, so alive, so in love. And it made him furious. Hands shaking, he slowly lifted his arms above his head. He closed his eyes. His teeth were clenched. He could feel his heart thumping in his chest. Then he brought his arms down fast. Beyond the darkness of his eyelids he heard the sound of rocks crumbling and a hundred agonizing cries.

28

Claire stepped out of her shiny red Porsche onto the muddy forest floor. Brown leaves crunched under her designer shoes. She inhaled, exhaled, trying to keep her cool and keep the memories of her last visit to this place at bay. Her feelings sufficiently suppressed, Claire marched deeper into the woods.

The place looked quite different in broad daylight, but she remembered. How could she forget? The anguish on Jamal's face. Max's terror. Anne's impassioned speech; one that probably saved her life. But the rules were different now. With that *other* Claire back on Earth, she no longer had to worry about falling apart or turning to dust like Vic (Though she felt an odd pull to be near that Claire. This made her all the more certain she had to go.)

This was exactly the spot, she was sure of it. One Claire was enough for this world so she decided to give her original plan a second try: returning to Reverie where she was worshipped; where she belonged.

Claire stood in the exact spot the doorway was supposed to be. She tugged on nearby branches, hoping one of them would unlock a secret entrance. No luck. "This is ridiculous," she said, "If that lesser Claire could find a way to stumble through this portal, why can't I?"

She waited there, attempting everything from strange gestures to secret words. Nothing happened. The sun was setting and she shivered in the cold, autumn air.

It was dark when she finally left, exhausted, defeated. Screw Reverie. Screw her lesser other self. Claire was a fighter, a winner, and a cut above the hand life had recently dealt her.

She raised her head high, shrugged off a mountain of disappointments. Claire climbed into her car and drove away; as far from Addley as she could get.

29

Mindy sighed, her breath leaving her like a ghost as a heavy snowstorm raged all around her and those she had promised to protect. Many of them had never seen snow before. So many of these dreamworlds were stuck in a single season, a single time of day even, that something so commonplace as rain was shocking to them. They were ill-prepared for this blizzard. They shivered as they trudged through the snow, nearly two feet deep, ascending to a ridge that would hopefully lead to a warmer place.

She felt Aemon's arm around her. Trying to comfort her, still weak from the poison as he was. But it was no use. She heard the crying babies. The whispers of those who were losing faith in her ability to lead. She could already feel them turning on her well before the fight with Aggie. Though nothing they said could contend with the disdain she harbored for herself. It's not like she asked to be their leader. It just sort of happened. The people of Black Rock had never experienced freedom or power, and then Mindy showed up; the bride-to-be of their overlord, doing what she always did, survive. She connected to their loss, being lost herself, and showed compassion. That's all it was. It should have never gone this far.

She should be at home preparing for a recital.

"Your staff," said Aemon, sweetly. He could barely stand on his own. Mindy shook her head, gritted her teeth against the cold. The orb at the top of the staff would emit a warm light when she held it. But she refused to hold it since the light couldn't warm everyone. Whatever the fate of her people was, so, too, would hers be.

"M-Mindy!" A voice from up ahead, faint. Whoever said it

was shrouded by the storm of snow.

"Mindy!" Louder this time. A faint, gray silhouette came into view. Small, having trouble moving through snow that was piled nearly half its height. Moments later the creature made itself clear. A small velociraptor, his green scales tinted blue, a scarf around his neck. His entire body trembled with cold.

"Miles," said Mindy, so relieved to see her scout returned. "What is it?"

"Warmth!" he exclaimed. "Freedom from this storm! I think we're here, Lady Mindy. I think we've reached-"

Mindy's eyes widened. She smiled. "My dreamworld."

———

There it was. At the edge of the ridge of ice and snow was a smooth downward slope, a green grassy hill under a sunny cloudless sky that led to her dreamworld; her Addley. Spirits lightened as, one by one, her people stepped out of the blizzard and into a perfect spring day.

Even if it wasn't the real thing, Mindy was thrilled to see her hometown as she had imagined it. She recognized Addley Park, the high school, the mall, her own cul-de-sac and the many landmarks of her life, made compact in this miniature version of Addley. She stopped to take it all in as the group moved down ahead of her. Her old elementary school, the dance studio, town square. She then noticed a dark spot in the northwest corner of her tiny town, no more than a small city block in size. Even from this distance she could tell the houses there were in disrepair, overrun by trees and vines. One house in particular was larger than the rest, darker than the rest, and wrapped in something large and gray that glimmered in the light of the midday sun.

Mindy clutched her chest, her heart pounding, head spinning. How could she be so dumb? How could she not have thought-

A commotion at the bottom of the hill snapped her back to the present moment. Her people crowded along the edge of the road, surrounding something she couldn't see. But the red and blue blinking lights were enough. Wiping the tear from her eye, she ran down, weaving through the masses until she reached the police car and the thin man in uniform. The officer was sweaty, nervous, clearly overwhelmed by the assortment of strange creatures at the edge of his beat. That is, until he laid eyes on, "Mindy..."

The officer raised a hand over his eyes and squinted to make sure what he was seeing was real. "Mindy, is that you?"

"Officer Chang," said Mindy. The officer, or the officer that he was based on, had been a friend of Mindy's family ever since she was a kid when he rushed her to the hospital after a particularly nasty spider bite. "It's me." Mindy tapped her finger to the left side of her belly where the spider had bit her, as proof.

Chang was so overjoyed, he was nearly crying. "It's been a year, Mindy. We all thought you were- Then these other worlds started appearing. It's just so good to see you." Once again taking notice of the myriad of creatures surrounding him, Chang asked, "What happened to you?"

Mindy thought it best to leave out the part about Cosmos and being transported to a dreamworld. She started with getting kidnapped by goblins at the edge of town. Everything after that was truth. "These are my people," she continued. "My responsibility. I promised them a safe haven and there's no place I can think of that's safer than here."

Aemon hobbled beside Mindy and took her hand in his.

Officer Chang thought for a moment. His expression was unreadable. Then, a big smile appeared on his face and he raised his arms into the air and said, "Any friend of Mindy's is a friend of Addley! Let's get you all out of those wet clothes and get you fed and lodged."

Mindy breathed a sigh of relief. Ever since she was a child, the Addley of her dreams was a place where she saw the best in people; where the sun always shone brightly and people truly cared for one another. This would be paradise, she thought. Everything they had been through, all of the pain she'd caused them, would have been worth this.

And then she remembered that dark house and the thing that lived inside it. Would she ever truly escape the trauma from her childhood? "This is paradise," she said softly, only to herself, fully knowing that there was no such thing.

30

"Well color me impressed," said Ezekiel between drags of his cigarette. "How do you feel?"

Jason floated in the sky next to Ezekiel. He could not find it in himself to respond. His eyes were wide open. His breathing, heavy. An energy coursed through him that he had not experienced before. The power caused him to tremble all over.

Minutes ago, he hovered above a world of gleeful rosy-cheeked gnomes, cheerfully going about their simple goals lives in a picturesque forest village. But now he hovered over nothing, just a giant hole of bright white light where once trees and cottages, men, women and children, a babbling brook, chattering squirrels and chirping birds had been. Even the sky above, once blue and filled with the scent of wildflowers, lost its form, fading to that empty, formless white.

"Speechless, eh?" Ezekiel's thin lips stretched into a sinister smile.

Jason turned to Ezekiel, his mouth agape. His throat was dry. Tears were beginning to swell under his eyes. He looked at his shaking hands as the feelings rushed into his head. The guilt. "What did I do...?"

"He speaks!" Ezekiel flicked his cigarette into the vast emptiness below. There were shapes in the whiteness, distant formless islands floating far beneath them in a world that existed below Reverie's surface.

"I killed them," Jason said, tears streaming down his eyes.

Ezekiel laughed in response, running his rough hands through his graying red hair. "Killed? Ha, you kill me, kid. You can't kill what isn't real. Soon as whoever dreamed up those happy little elves goes back to sleep- Poof! -they'll come right back." A lit cigar materialized in Ezekiel's hand. He smelled it. "Mmm, Cuban." He placed his arm around Jason, the smoke from Ezekiel's cigar filling Jason's nostrils, causing him to cough. "You felt it, though, didn't you? The power. Gotta say I didn't think you had it in you. Didn't believe all the hype. And here I am. Impressed. Plucked a whole dream clean outta existence. Brought the color back into your cheeks. Come on, man. Tell me. How do you feel?"

Jason inhaled. "Alive," he said.

Ezekiel floated higher into the blank sky, spun around, and clapped his hands together. "Woo-ee! Now that's what I'm talkin' about! So, look around, kid." Ezekiel gestured all around them. Beyond the crater of white and the pale sky above it there was an endless expanse of jungles and beaches and towns and cities and snow-capped mountains. "Where to next?"

31

Claire tried her best to ignore the smell as she examined herself in the mirror. To her relief, despite the stress, she remained beautiful. She took a pair of scissors and a comb from a plastic bag on the sink and cut her long platinum blonde hair short. No more than a few inches long. Taking more supplies from the bag, she dyed her hair honey brown then styled it into a fashionable pixie cut. People knocked on the door a couple of times, but she only uttered the phrase, "I need everyone to use the other restroom," and the problem was solved.

Perhaps Vic had the right idea, she thought. While she refused to change her name (she was the ultimate Claire), she had no trouble donning a new appearance; something stunning that would separate her even more from her lesser copy.

Claire exited that disgusting restroom into the harsh lights of a roadside mini-market. The old man behind the counter ogled her as she approached him. "Give me forty-five dollars on number three," she said.

He leaned forward, licked his lips, and said, "I'll give it to you for free, cutie, if you come with me to the back for fifteen minutes."

"I need you to stop," she said. And like that, the old man froze. He was terrified, unable to move a single part of his body, a prisoner in his own skin. "I'll also need a protein shake while we're at it." Just then, a pickup truck crashed into the glass storefront, ramming through aisles of sugary snacks and into the beverage refrigerators. Glass shards and food items exploded all around. Claire casually raised her hand and a protein shake landed in it. Not her favorite brand, but it would do in a pinch.

She took a sip of her drink as the dumbfounded driver of the pick-up truck cursed from within his vehicle. Then something on the flat screen TV that hung awkwardly over the hot dog oven caught her attention. A news anchor with salt and pepper hair spoke and two familiar faces were displayed just above him: "Max Grayson and Jamal Anderson, both star players on Addley High's varsity team, are still missing. This is the third disappearance in a once sleepy town now rife with-"

Claire left before she could hear the rest. It didn't matter anyway. At least that's what she told herself. Addley wasn't her world. It was bland and unspecial. The people were bland and unspecial. Claire was so much more and so very tired of playing normal. She had the looks, the confidence, the power, and it was high time she stopped feeling guilty because of it.

.

32

Mindy couldn't sleep. Even though she was lying in her own bed for the first time in over a year. Well, not her bed technically, but what she imagined her bed to be. Aemon slept beside her, moaning in his sleep. The poison hurt him more than he let on, she thought. Damn Aggie for what she did to him.

The people of Mindy's Addley had been more than accommodating to the hundreds of refugees she brought to the town. The Addley of her dreams was eager to please her. They offered their spare bedrooms, couches, and hotel rooms to them, as well as food and drink. Many had never experienced such hospitality and comfort in their homeworlds; certainly not in the past year. Mindy had instructed everyone to meet at noon the next day at Town Square to plan next steps. She would work with the mayor and town council to find ways to give them all permanent homes.

Mindy pulled her fluffy pink blanket over her head and closed her eyes, hoping they would stay closed this time. She controlled her breathing. Slow. Measured. Inhale. Exhale. Inhale.

"There you are."

Mindy's eyes snapped open and she sat up, clutching the bed as if something was going to yank her out of it. The voice seemed to seep out of the surrounding darkness.

"I've been waiting for you." It was a man's voice, soft and with a drunken slur.

Mindy turned to Aemon. He was squirming in pain, but fast

asleep. That voice. It had been so long and she had come so far, but it was unmistakable. Unforgettable. The most terrible sound she had ever heard.

"I'm coming for you."

"No," said Mindy. She let go of the bed and climbed out, slipping into a T-shirt and jeans and some running shoes from her dream closet. She reached under the bed and produced her staff. The orb at the top of the staff was already glowing bright red. Mindy gazed out through her window into the night sky. "This time I'm coming for you."

Mindy marched out of her house and into the darkness. Her dream father had poked his head out of his bedroom to ask if she was all right. Mindy ignored it and kept walking. If she stopped now she may never find the strength to keep moving again.

She swiftly made her way down the empty suburban street, lined in houses with curtains drawn, lights out. She passed through the eerie park at night, wind howling through the black trees. Town square was empty as well, save for a few locals and some of her people too excited to sleep. They called her name, but she kept moving.

Mindy was close now and the terror inside her was becoming harder to contain. Every step she took toward that dark, foreboding block on the edge of town was more difficult than the last. The orb began to flicker. She'd come so far, she told herself over and over again. Through impossible odds. Imprisonment, threats on her life, surviving a cyborg war and leading her people to paradise...

There it was.

Mindy paused at the edge of the curb. On either side of her

was a beautifully maintained sidewalk lined in leafy, flowery trees and bright streetlights. Behind her, lovely suburban homes and shops and restaurants. Across the street from where she stood the street lights flickered, if they worked at all. The trees were bare and long dead. The homes resembled ruins with their broken windows and overgrown yards. One house in particular, the one she stood directly across from now, arrested her.

It was darker than the rest, a little more narrow, taller. Three stories of pure horror. Unlike the other houses, this one had all of its windows, but inside was only blackness. The front door was a slab of rotting wood that seemed even more rotten in the time Mindy had been standing there. A red "X" was painted over it. Massive heavy chains wrapped around the entire house as if keeping something inside. This house had been the stuff of Mindy's nightmares for years.

"You brought friends for me to play with," the voice from the house said, fading off into a low cackle. "Sweet, young things…"

Mindy raised her staff and pointed it at the house. The orb glowed a brilliant orange. "You will not. I've come too far. We've come too far." Tears were collecting under Mindy's eyes.

Again, the voice laughed. "Look at you, Min. All grown up. A far cry from the little niece I used to have so much fun with."

The staff shook in Mindy's hands. Through clenched teeth, she said, "I will destroy you. Once and for all."

"I don't think you will, Min. I truly don't think you can." Something banged hard on the door from inside the house. "I've been caged up in here for years, just waiting, waiting,

waiting, until the day you'd turn all weak again. Confused. Terrified. Helpless and in over your head. Just like you were when I'd come into your bedroom and-"

FWOOSH

A torrent of flame burst from Mindy's orb, tearing through the old wooden door and into the dark house. Flames took hold onto the door frame and began to spread outward, widening the hole into the abyss within.

Mindy's heart was pounding in her chest. Her hands were slick with sweat. She wanted nothing more than to run away, but would not allow herself to move.

The gruff, masculine voice spoke again. "I knew I could count on you."

And then the dark house exploded.

"I can't do it." Jason floated above a small fair, complete with a Ferris wheel, rollercoaster, merry-go-round and a ton of those cheap carnival games.

"Come on, killer," said Ezekiel. He gave Jason a playful punch to the shoulder. Jason gave him a hard look in response. "Come on, kid. I just saw you annihilate an entire beach."

"No." Jason folded his arms. "Look at them." Jason pointed at a young couple taking turns tossing darts at a wall of colorful balloons.

Ezekiel grabbed Jason by his T-shirt, something sinister in his eyes. "They ain't real."

"They're real enough!" Jason shouted. He could feel himself-his real self -returning in small, clumsy steps. With a thought, he sent Ezekiel flying backwards. Ezekiel stopped himself before he would have crashed into the top of an old haunted house. A few people looked up, noticing the two men hovering above them for the first time.

Ezekiel's bushy orange eyebrows lowered and a frown appeared on his face. He floated back to Jason's side. "Now that's no way to treat the guy who plucked you outta your rut. You're lucky I ain't my daddy. I'd string you up and-"

"You manipulated me," replied Jason.

"I gave you life!" Ezekiel's face was barely an inch away from Jason's. "You were nothing but a sad little crybaby when I found you on that hilltop. Now look at you! Alive, alert, damn near a god!"

"You're right." Jason shrugged. "I was lost. I lost something...someone very special to me and I went away for a while. You brought me back. But I was always gonna come back, Ezekiel. You took advantage of me when I wasn't fully myself. You made me-" Jason stopped himself. "But now I'm enough of myself to see that you're the bad guy here."

Ezekiel took Jason by the arm. "All of this is crumbling with or without you. The walls came down. Chaos ensued. This world is expanding too fast and we gotta stop it. So you got a choice. Work with me or crumble with the rest of it."

"You're crazy," said Jason.

"So be it." Ezekiel rolled up the sleeves of his flannel shirt, revealing tattoos of skeletons and fire and blades and bullets. "I'll handle you just like I handled my daddy. Hail Nihilo."

An explosion boomed in the distance. The people at the carnival fell silent.

Ezekiel and Jason, along with the onlookers, turned to the direction of the sound. Beyond the fairgrounds, nestled in a valley surrounded by snowy mountains, golden corn fields and a volcanic wasteland, was a small town. And in a dark corner of that town something bulbous, hideous, was growing like rising dough.

"Damn it," said Ezekiel before disappearing into thin air.

Jason knew exactly what he was looking at. That town wasn't some random place in some random corner of Reverie. It was Addley. Mindy's Addley.

33

Rumi stood perfectly still on the floating island in this hellhole of white, planning her next move. Two men were down. She and another faced Estralus and a corrupted Zen.

"Nexis," Estralus exclaimed, "is it really, truly you? I must say I'm quite a fan of your work." Estralus swung his sword-shaped tendrils in unison, lowering the iridescent vein's strength a substantial amount. One more similar attack and it would shatter; whatever world was attached would be destroyed.

Zen stepped over Vic's unconscious body and addressed Estralus' gloopy, purple bug-eyed form. "T"is I indeed! Had a bit of internal struggle, but it's been taken care of. It's complicated. I'll explain the details later." He paused. "Twist my arm, why don't you? My robotic half is suppressing a corruption in my programming, while yours truly, the artist formerly known as Patrick Ashford, takes the reins! Boo yah!"

Rumi took the villain's conversation as an opportunity to sidle next to a young man in full armor, holding a blue-lit gun. "I'm Rumi," she said.

"Jamal," the young man replied. "Guess this is it?"

"Unless we're zagging exceptional." Rumi pulled her trigger, sending a rapid fire river of red beams of light at Estralus. One, two sword tendrils were destroyed but two took their place. Estralus' mass decreased just a bit.

"We just have to keep hitting him!" said Jamal. "Every time he takes a hit, he gets smaller and-!" Jamal found himself on the receiving end of an abnormally strong headlock.

"Enough," said Zen...no, Nexis. He was all Nexis now. "Now stand still while I pop that little head off your little shoulders, heehee!"

Rumi tried to aid Jamal, but was quickly grabbed by one of Estralus' tendrils. She dangled upside down and rose up, up until she was in line with Estralus' massive, cartoonish eyes. "Before your death, here's a fun fact Ms. Inyonara," said Estralus as one of his sword-arms moved toward her. "Once I break this tether, say goodbye to your precious Futara." It burst into laughter.

"What? No..."

Jamal felt heat intensifying around his neck as Nexis' entire arm glowed bright white. "ARGH!"

Rumi clenched her teeth. "Zagging no." She pressed a button on her weapon and the axe tip shot from the barrel and hit Nexis hard in the chest. Zen lost his balance, stumbling backwards, close to the floating island's edge. Taking advantage of the situation, Jamal rammed his weapon backwards into Nexis' face. The surprise of both attacks was enough for his grip to loosen and Jamal to break free. Wasting no time he launched a blue orb at the tendril holding Rumi. It exploded, freeing her. She dropped ten feet but her armor broke most of the fall.

"This is getting fun!" Nexis chimed. "This ends now."

Rumi rolled to her feet. "You're right. It does." With all the strength, she could muster, Rumi charged at Nexis, using her momentum and plowing into his surprisingly hard body, throwing off his balance just enough to send him teetering over the edge,

"Impressive," said Estralus as the swords disappeared into his body, growing his form substantially.

A hint of fear shown on Nexis' face. Rumi placed her armored hand around his neck; the only thing keeping him from falling into the abyss, the horror of lightning below. "B-but-," he pleaded, "the last server."

Rumi looked to Vic then and said a short and silent prayer of hope before returning her gaze to Nexis. "This is for everything I lost."

"You're done," said Jamal. He launched eight orbs that lodged themselves into Estralus' body as Rumi released her grip on Nexis, watching him fall and disappear below.

Only a purple puddle remained where once Estralus stood.

"Care to do the honors?" said Rumi as she joined Jamal. Jamal nodded and stepped forward, aiming his weapon at the puddle.

Then a thick fog blew in. They couldn't see anything. "Shit!"

From the cool, misty, white Estralus' voice emerged, a whisper, from everywhere at once. "The battle, I'm afraid, I no longer can endure, but rest assured I've won the war."

Visibility returned just enough for Rumi and Jamal to watch as the puddle morphed into a single blade leaping from the earth and making contact with the weakened vein, destroying what was left of it. They watched as it exploded into crystal shards both upwards and downwards.

"NO!" cried Rumi, feeling a level of helplessness she had never before known. "No, no, no, no, no…" She tore the helmet from her head, dropped to her knees as Max groaned and Jamal rushed to his side.

"What happened?" asked Max weakly, to the backdrop of Rumi's primal cries. "Did we die?"

"No, dude," Jamal said. "We're alive. But I think we're lost."

Lightning struck, taking a chunk out of the island. Deafening thunder followed.

Jamal helped Max to his feet. To Rumi, he said, "We have to get out of here."

She turned to him, her eyes red and full of tears. "Futara...he- he destroyed my home..."

"Look," Jamal crouched down beside her. "We don't know that, okay? Bad guys lie. It's what they do. And regardless-" A small crystalline rock crashed into the island, knocking everyone to the ground. "Shit. Okay. Regardless, getting to the surface is the only way we'll know for sure, either way."

"Jamal is right," said Vic, who was already climbing to his feet. He dusted himself off a little. "We have to go. Now."

Jamal rose, bringing Rumi up with him. Rumi pressed a button on her weapon and the axe head returned to the end of the barrel. Another rock crashed into the island.

"How?" asked Jamal.

Vic, instantly enlightened, said, "Jamal, turn on your anti-gravity field. Rumi, in roughly forty seconds a fairly stable new dreamworld will rise up over that ridge. Be ready to hit it with that projectile axe of yours."

A blue, translucent light formed around Jamal. "Done."

163

"Great," said Vic. "Now everyone make contact with Jamal. Combined with my jetpack it will make us light enough to allow the magnetic pull of Rumi's weapon to lift us out of this mess."

Everyone did as they were told and they rose up, up toward Reverie's surface world. Rumi could not help but feel terrified of what they would find once they got there.

34

Vita's head lay severed in a bed of her sparkling hair. Where blood and bone would show at the cross-section of her neck, instead was solid iridescence. Her insides were nothing more than the Core Substance breathed into a living being. Vita blinked as she looked at her body, crumpled and limp at the other end of the balcony. "Such a beautiful figure," she thought.

Vita winced as something or someone scooped her head off the floor. It was Nihilo. She sneered at his eyes - or where his eyes would have been were he not a hulking humanoid-shaped shadow of opaque blackness. Vita tried to shake her head in disgust, but that was no longer an option.

"I've won," said Nihilo.

"Darling," Vita said, with an airy laugh, "you've done no such thing."

"Look around you, woman." Nihilo reoriented Vita's head to see the gargantuan sinkhole in the otherwise gorgeous Eternia.

"Perhaps if you were the manifestation of chaos and temper tantrums." Vita sighed. "But you are the manifestation of nothingness. Destruction isn't nothing. Disarray isn't nothing. As long as there is something, you do not win. I do."

"Where is the human child?" asked Nihilo.

Vita smiled at that. "I haven't the faintest, darling. You must do a better job keeping track of your things."

"So be it." Nihilo tightened his grip on Vita's head before tossing her off the balcony and into the darkness of the sinkhole far below.

35

The staff's forcefield flickered out of existence as the explosion of dust and debris settled around Mindy. As her visibility returned she saw something massive and grotesque growing, growing, growing from where the dark house had been. It was like a bulbous tumor, ballooning as it pulsated. It was made of pale human flesh, covered in long thick hairs. Fleshy roots began to take hold, destroying the yard and sidewalk and streetlights; the run-down houses on the block. Fingers, toenails, eyebrows grew out of the mass. A pair of puffy pink lips opened like a wound across it, yellowed teeth and a tongue forming in the dark, wet mouth.

"I will destroy everything you love," said the familiar voice from those pink lips.

The ground began to shake. Mindy was barely able to maintain her balance in the tremor.

The fleshy thing had grown a nose and part of an eye. Bushy brown hair emerged in thick tufts at the top of it. A new limb that ended in partially-fused fingers moved to touch the skin charred by Mindy's staff. "You burned me!"

"I'm just getting started," said Mindy as she scorched the monster's new eye.

The ground was growing more unstable. A deep crack broke through the asphalt of the street. It spread quickly like a bolt of lightning, branching off in every direction.

Jason Baker appeared directly in front of Mindy.

"Jason?" She could barely stand, barely believe that her best friend, who had disappeared days ago, was here. Now.

"Mindy," said Jason, taking her by the shoulders. "We have to go!"

Mindy was excited to see him but the feeling was quickly dwarfed by her rising anger toward the monster. She pushed Jason to the side with her staff, her eyes locked onto it. "I'm sorry, Jason, but I'm not leaving here until he's gone."

"Forget this thing," Jason hovered back to her side. "Some psychopath named Ezekiel is-" His words were cut short. A man in a flannel shirt with messy red hair materialized beside Jason and grabbed him by the neck, then threw him high into the sky with great strength.

Chunks of yard and street and sidewalk were crumbling into the depths of the earth.

The monster's face was burned but complete, a spitting image of her Uncle Kenny. Its head was now as big as a house with more fleshy, hairy parts growing beneath it. Mindy was finding it hard to breathe. Memories she'd hidden deep within her were making it hard to concentrate.

Mindy lost her balance and fell to the ground. Nevertheless she aimed her staff and screamed as an endless river of flame burst forth from it, burning the monster's skin.

A snake-like arm, thick as a pick-up truck, reached from the monster's newly formed neck to Mindy with hungry fingers, growing as they grasped. Mindy's attack turned the monster's skin red and pink and black but it continued toward her. Before the charred hand would have crushed her in its grip, the monster, now growing a chest, sank into the crumbling ground, throwing off its aim. Mindy watched as the earth swallowed him.

Mindy tried to get up then, but the ground was too unstable, more a chaotic pattern of deep fissures and uneven platforms than solid surface. She caught sight of two men quarreling in the sky, silhouettes against the full moon. That was the last thing she saw before she felt the earth drop beneath her and a great light blinded her.

Aggie woke up to a gentle rumbling sound. She looked to her brothers, both were fast asleep in the woods they had slept in days before with Mindy and the rest. Now it was only she, the twins, and Eliza, who didn't require sleep as she was mostly machine. She was on high alert as well, scanning the surrounding forest for a source of the sound.

"What is it?" asked Aggie.

"Not sure," Eliza responded. Her robotic eye glowed green. "I'm scanning for any disturbances. There seems to be some seismic activity, barely detectable, but definitely there."

As if in response, the ground began to shake. Softly at first, then increasingly more powerful. By the time Aggie reached for her brothers everything was blanketed in total, impenetrable light.

36

Claire Ashford rested under a blanket on the couch in her living room. She had hardly been able to sleep the previous night. Partially because of her sleep schedule being thrown off after a year of living in alternate realities. And partially because she was worried about the people she cared about the most. Anza and Patrick. Victor and Anne. Complicated could not begin to describe what Claire's life had become.

When Olokun and the rest had gone, Claire walked to Eddie-O's Diner to pick up her mother and bring her home. The local police had been called to the house, of course, by prying neighbors after the commotion. Claire and Karen cited an earthquake and promised to begin reconstruction of the lawn and damages to the house as soon as possible. In the meantime, a handyman had put up some wooden boards to cover the holes in the walls. Both he and a gardener were scheduled to stop by the following day to finish the jobs. Living in the house while it was being repaired wouldn't be ideal, but with everything else going on, finding another abode just seemed too daunting.

Enough light shone through the curtains that it was clear the sun would soon rise. Claire sighed, trying to think of her mother fast asleep upstairs or Jack or Futara or anything that would get her mind off of her lost friends. Even the other Claire.

Whenever Claire's thoughts quieted, she could feel it. The connection she had to her other self. It was strongest when they were in the living room together, something pulling at her, drawing her to the other. But she wanted nothing to do with that Claire, a feeling she sensed was mutual. Even now though, she could feel that other Claire getting farther and farther away. Mostly she was grateful the other Claire was distancing herself, but another smaller part felt weirdly incomplete without her.

Claire's wandering thoughts were jolted to the present as the earth began to shake. Her first thought was that the monsters had returned so she jumped up, off of the couch. Before she could take her first step, light shone so brightly that it was impossible to see anything in its blinding brilliance.

And then the light faded. The tremors stopped.

"What was that?" shouted Karen from upstairs. "Don't tell me those things are back."

When Claire's vision returned, everything seemed normal. "Everything's fine, I think," she said in response.

Then came a commotion from outside. Low muffled conversations. Then screams. An explosion. Silence followed by more muffled talking, more screams.

If Claire had not lived the recent life she had, this would have terrified her. She made her way to the front door.

"Doesn't sound like everything's fine to me," said Karen. Her voice was closer now.

Claire grabbed the door knob and paused for a single moment of serenity before opening the door. In all she had seen, what awaited her outside left her speechless.

The quiet town of Addley, a town like thousands of others across America, had been invaded. Broken towers, tall and beautiful and carved from iridescent crystals, appeared on front yards and roads, some rising up through the insides of the sea of suburban houses. Stranger things littered the scene as well. A rusted swing set, a fallen over palm tree with purple leaves, the skeleton of some monster sliding down a shingled rooftop.

Among this chaos the locals of Addley ran or hid from the creatures that had suddenly come to share the space with them. Winged creatures, like angels, flew above. Animals, some normal and others downright fantastical, scurried or stalked on two or four or seven legs. Other things, more humanlike, wandered around, transparent like ghosts. All were united in their utter bewilderment of what had happened. How they had gotten here.

Before Claire closed the door she noticed one more thing at the other end of town, blocking half of the rising sun. It was a craggy mountain, narrow, dark, and impossibly tall, rising up to meet the clouds.

"Black Rock," Claire whispered, not fully believing what she was looking at.

"It's happened, hasn't it?" said Karen, her black eyes wide open. She was now in the living room, clutching the arm of the couch. "Just as I envisioned. The end of all realms."

Interlude VI:
Initia & Mortem

In another place, outside of conventional reality, two lovers gazed upon the chaos of Addley.

"I do not have the words," said Initia, manifestation of growth. She allowed the tears to flow freely down her dark cheeks, a proper ode to the ruin she watched through a window in Origin Point. One hand rested on her pregnant belly, the other rested on the shoulder of her beloved, Mortem, manifestation of decline.

Veins of lava glowed brightly under Mortem's chalky, gray skin. His heavy brow quivered and he rested his head against Initia's, lost in the viny tangles of her thick, green hair. "Neither do I, my completion," he said.

"Glorious, isn't it?"

The familiar voice startled the pair. They had for the past hour been alone in the endless expanse of Origin. They turned to see Nihilo, the opaque shadow of a hulking being, standing directly behind them. He seemed larger somehow. His once sharp silhouette, pulsing with life.

"What do you want?" asked Initia, venom in her tone. Mortem instinctively wrapped his arm around her waist.

Nihilo guffawed. "Initia and Mortem, growth and decline personified. Rulers of Cosmos. Distant even now from your precious realm, when it needs you the most."

Initia bared her teeth. "Nihilo." She slipped from Mortem's grasp and marched to the manifestation of nothingness.

"What did you do?"

"I won," was his reply. "While you fools watched lazily and without vision, I took action. And now witness the fruits of my life's work."

Initia turned away and grabbed Mortem by his great bicep. "Let's go find Vita and the others and-"

Initia and Mortem found themselves unable to move. As much as they tried they were held in place by a crippling fear. It took some doing, but Initia was able to mouth one word: "How…?"

Nihilo stood perfectly still. "Timor," he said, almost playful. "You've heard of him? Manifestation of fear? Co-ruler of Reverie? He gave it to me. Well, that's not entirely true. I took it." Initia's terror-twisted face trembled. "Confusing, I know. But with the collapse of the realms as we know them, the old rules are fading. The laws that governed our incorporeal state are dissipating like the walls of Reverie." Two bright red orbs appeared where Nihilo's eyes should be. Then, in a fraction of a blink, his right arm lengthened and he took Mortem by the neck. "Fear. Decline. These are necessary concepts for the coming nothing."

Initia watched in horror as Mortem, her truest love, was pulled into Nihilo's void-like body without a trace. Nihilo's creepy red eyes vanished and Initia found herself free enough of fear to unleash a devastated scream, to land her fists on Nihilo's rock-hard chest, demanding, "Give him back! Give him back!" over and over again until she had sunk to the ground, wailing, having never grieved so powerfully. "Kill me, as well," she said. "I cannot live without him."

"No," said Nihilo. "I have no need for you. If you wish to

be of use, perhaps you can find Somni. She isn't handling the loss of her brother Timor well. Spend your final moments as you spent those leading up to it: wasting away on frivolous emotions. The age of hope, of growth, of existence itself, has ended. Now, and forever more, there will be nothing."

With that, Nihilo disappeared.

PART VII
HOMECOMING

37

"Don't panic, Claire. Don't panic." Claire was most definitely panicking. She peered through the curtains from the living room, only to gasp and hide away once a ghost of an old man in a sweater materialized in the middle of the street.

"This is it," said Karen, sobered up. She sat on the couch, her black eyes wide and wet with tears. "Where's Anza? We need-"

"She's gone," snapped Claire, surprised by the anger she still harbored about it. "It was your idea, remember? And even if she wasn't gone, she's just a baby!"

"You're right." Karen moaned, at once looking tired and confused, as she massaged her temples. "You're right, sweetheart. There's time. More work we must do."

A black portal opened in the middle of the living room and Victor and Anne stumbled out of it. With them was someone new: a young man, sopping wet, with tan skin and thick locks of dark brown hair. He wore a colorful robe of West African design that reached down to just below his knees. He lost his balance, but Victor caught him before he fell. The portal closed behind them.

"You're back!" Claire caught Anne in a big hug.

"Claire. What's wrong?" Anne could see the fear on her friend's face.

"Anne's back?" Karen searched the room with eyes that could not see.

"Yes," said Claire. "With Victor and..."

"This is Dion," Victor said. "He's a god that Olokun had trapped in her lab."

Claire sighed. "Of course he is. And where's Satya?"

Anne shrugged. "She stayed behind. By choice. Said she wanted to learn more about Olokun's whole thing."

"Enough of this talk," said Dion in an accent Claire did not recognize. "I must find my Jason Baker." Dion took a step forward and collapsed to the floor. "Damn these mortal legs." Claire joined Victor and Anne in helping him to his feet. "I am fine. I will be healed in mere minutes. Seconds!"

Claire backed away from the others, exhaled, then said, "Something's happened while you were gone. Addley, maybe more than Addley, has transformed. It's like-"

"The realms are crumbling," Karen continued.

Anne and Victor ran to the window and peeked out. Victor shuddered. "Oh my God."

"No matter." Dion took more measured steps toward the door. "A crumbling realm will not keep me from my love."

"You can't go out there alone," said Anne.

"You can't stop me," Dion spat. "Neither can anything on the other side of that door."

Victor placed his hand on Dion's shoulder. "Then we'll go with you."

"NO!" The word came from Karen's mouth like a howl. Red-faced, she charged in the direction of Victor's voice, taking him by the arm. "You cannot leave this house!"

"Mom-"

Karen spun in the direction of her daughter's voice. "You either, Claire! I've- I've seen it. You must stay here. You and Victor. Right here." Karen was trembling. Tears streamed from her eyes. "I know I haven't been the best mother. That I made your childhood a hell. But if you listen to nothing else, understand this, my beloved daughter. If you- or the boy -step out into that war zone, you will die."

"Hey," said Anne, pointing to an open front door. "Dion's gone."

38

Ben Burnham stood on a corner in the center of Addley's modest downtown, wearing a three-piece white suit he'd purchased specially for the occasion. He surveyed the chaos all around him. Large, crystal structures protruding from the earth. People and other, stranger creatures running in every direction. Angelic beings soaring overhead. Ben felt a sense of calm. This is what it was all leading up to.

He straightened his red bowtie. He checked that his strawberry blond hair was properly positioned over his bald spot. He sucked in his belly a bit and puffed out his chest. Ben lifted a megaphone to his pink lips then loudly proclaimed, "Dearest people of Addley, the apocalypse is nigh! From nothing we came and to nothing we shall all return. But, do not fear. Do not panic. For there is another way. If you wish to be a part of the liberating wave of the abyss and not merely a victim of it, join me. Pledge your allegiance to Nihilo and you will become part of something far greater than yourself!" With that, Ben grinned, taking in the handful of people who stopped to listen to his words, and then strolled confidently to another corner.

———

Arbitryx soared above Addley on majestic wings of silver feathers. He was unfazed by the bustle that had taken everyone else's attention. Instead, he was only happy to be free. To feel the fresh Cosmos air on his face, no longer in hiding. To take in the sounds and smells and near-limitless spectrum of colors that were not available to him in his mundane crystalline realm of Eternia.

"Sir!"

Abritryx stopped and turned, mid-flight. Another yazata hovered beside him. She had long hair, the color of copper. Like him, she was wearing a black toga. It signified allegiance to Nihilo's plan.

"What is it?" asked Arbitryx, annoyed at having been pulled out of his bliss. He now flapped his wings, flying in place.

"Orders, sir," she said. "Some of the more recent recruits and I are not sure what to do next."

"Next." The word left Arbitryx's lips like a whisper. His dark eyes darted around where yazatas in both black and white togas filled the sky. He shrugged. "Whatever you want, my dear. You've been liberated. Take in the splendor of this untamed planet. Eat, drink, love." The copper-haired yazata stayed there, awkwardly. She seemed concerned. Arbitryx smiled a sad smile and placed a finger to her chin, tilting her head slightly upward so their eyes met. "I know, darling sister. We have been kept as slaves for so long, the very concept of freedom seems too foreign to grasp. How about we start small then? With a simple choice instead of unabashed possibility. You have two options. Rid this town of any threat to Nihilo's master plan---anyone who looks as if they are anything less than terrified...including our white toga-wearing brethren. Or don't."

Arbitryx grimaced and said, "Spread the word," and flew off to once again enjoy the splendor of the world around him.

...

The last thing Rumi remembered was rocketing upward. Then everything went blank. At first she thought she had been blinded. That would, after all, have been the perfect ending to a series of days that had included her barely avoiding death multiple times and witnessing the alleged destruction of Futara. It was then a small pleasure when her eyesight returned to her and her feet landed on firm ground.

"Am I alive? Are we alive? What just happened?!"

Rumi heard Max's voice before he came into view. Jamal was there as well. And Vic. They had all survived Estralus' attack and were now somewhere strange and new, even by Reverie's standards. Rumi had her weapon ready as she surveyed the area. They were all standing on a round plane of concrete at the end of a long road. Vehicles with wheels and no discernible hover-capability lined the road and pastel two-story living units were scattered throughout the grass. Other people and creatures, as disoriented as she, moved around at a distance. Crystal rocks littered the ground and other things flew high above.

Jamal stepped forward, scratching his head. "Dude, am I crazy or is this the cul-de-sac on North Street?"

Max took it all in. "Oh my God, dude. Yeah. Remember you and me and Asher used to play street hockey like right over-?"

"Enough," said Rumi. Then to Vic, "Where are we?"

"Shit." A wave of surprise washed over Vic's face. "We-we're here. I mean, we're home. I mean...it's Addley. Cosmos Addley."

Jamal's muscles tensed. "How is that even possible?"

"Nihilo," said Vic. "This was all part of his plan to destroy all of existence. And, ARGHH!" Vic dropped to his knees and clutched his head with both hands. "So. Much. Information. The realms are broken here. I can know it all. See it all. Nihilo used the chaos of Victor and Claire, the baby, to weaken the borders between the realms. He pinpointed Addley...gathered allies from...Aemon to Nexis to...Estralus- AGH God, it hurts!" Vic took to the fetal position. "It's too much...Nihilo's plan stretches back centuries…"

Max tapped Jamal's shoulder. "Ask another question, man! Maybe it'll, like, reset him!"

Before Jamal could come up with something, Rumi asked, "How do we stop it?"

Vic's convulsing stopped. More than that, he seemed calm. No, something else. Numb. As he climbed to his feet, it was clear he was trembling. Sweat poured from him. An expression of horror plagued his face. He made many attempts to speak before the words finally found their way. "No," he muttered, almost a gasp. He turned to Rumi, shaking his head in disbelief. "I...I don't know."

Vic turned around and ran from the others as fast as he could.

39

Jason Baker was hurtling through the sky, attempting to save Mindy from Ezekiel, when a bright light washed over everything. The next thing he knew he was in some completely wrecked version of Addley. "Mindy!" he shouted. "MINDY!" Jason was certain this was one of Ezekiel's tricks, that the evil Lucid had transported him to another dreamworld version of his hometown.

Nihilo materialized under a large willow tree. He paused for a moment, disgusted as he watched Ezekiel peer up at Jason as he flew by.

"You failed," said Nihilo. Ezekiel showed only the slightest bit of surprise at Nihilo's presence.

"Well, if it ain't my old friend," Ezekiel said. "To what do I owe the pleasure?"

"You were tasked with turning the Baker boy to our side," Nihilo continued. "He was weakened. Susceptible."

A cigar appeared in Ezekiel's hand. The way it shook betrayed his bravado. "Looks like your intel was wrong, bud. I gave him a master class in manipulation and he was more than strong enough to go racing after his precious Mindy. Who, from the looks of it, didn't make the jump. Heh." He took a puff.

Nihilo pressed his large, black hand against Ezekiel's face and watched with satisfaction as the other winced at the pain. Nihilo pulled back revealing rotting skin and bone where his hand has been.

Ezekiel dropped his cigar and touched his hand to the wound. "What in the-? How are you doing this?"

"The rules have changed, Ezekiel," said Nihilo. "With the realms collapsing, my abilities, once spread thin between them, have condensed. Your affliction is courtesy of a former colleague of mine that I have absorbed into my insatiable void. Now quit your whining, Lucid. Heal yourself. Reap chaos."

Ezekiel's scars were already being replaced with healthy, living skin. He grinned a little and looked out of the window to Jason above.

Nihilo sighed. "Not him. If you must salve your shattered ego, do not go after this one. You must kill the primary Jason Baker."

40

Dion moved toward Jason's house as fast as he could, weaving past manic crowds and scrambling over the ruined buildings and fallen trees. A winged creature, absolutely beautiful, descended from the sky and blocked his path. It had flowing cerulean hair and wore a black toga. It raised a spear to Dion's neck and said, "Hello, little human. You seem like you're up to no good. Not filled with righteous terror like all the rest. Nihilo's plans will not be challenged."

Dion looked the winged creature in its violet eyes. "Allow me to gift you with a fraction of the desperation I've felt; the longing and loneliness for the one I love." The winged creature immediately lowered its weapon and dropped to its knees, overcome with tears, wailing to the heavens.

"H-how did you do that?" It was Anne, who it appeared had been following him all this time. "Oh, right. You're Dionysus."

"More or less, yes." Dion flashed his playful smile. "Since I have no time to express why you should not have left the house, and I can already feel my spell fading from this winged creature, I will merely ask that you stay close."

Dion, with Anne in tow, reached Jason's front door. He knocked.

"Can't you just tear the door off the hinges?" Anne asked.

Dion shook his head. "Lady Anne, I am a god of class, of nuance, of substance."

"Who's there?" rang a muffled old voice from the other side of the door.

"Mrs. Baker," Dion said, "it is I, your Jason's beloved, here to return him to his sense-"

KA-CHOOM!

Splintered wood and glass rained down from the second floor, sliding off the porch roof to the lawn.

"What was that?" Mrs. Baker's voice was panicked. "Get off my property!"

Dion moved off the porch and to the walkway, crouched down, and grabbed a large chuck of wooden plank from the ground. "My patience is fleeting." He rushed to the back of the house. Dion ascended the few stairs onto the back patio and, grasping the plank like a battering ram, rammed it into a glass backdoor. It barely left a crack. "Damn it!" He tried again. The crack spread a little more. "Damn it!" Before he could strike the door a third time, Anne appeared with a smile on the other side of the door, opening it from the inside.

"They keep a key under the doormat," she explained as Mrs. Baker threatened to call the cops from somewhere deeper in the house.

"You are a delight." Dion pushed past her, darted down the hall, up the stairs, and burst into Jason's room. There he found Jason, in bed wearing a T-shirt and boxer shorts, struggling as a muscular red-headed man attempted to choke him to death. The red-headed man turned to Dion and said with a gruff, dark voice, "I like to be close. So I can feel the last bits of life fade right outta my victims."

Dion looked the man in his eyes and the man, suddenly and uncontrollably, began to laugh. He laughed so hard he could barely contain himself. So hard that he released Jason's neck and fell off the bed and onto the floor, his face beet red. Barely able to breathe. Anne appeared in the doorway just as the red-headed man disappeared.

Dion went to Jason's side as Jason coughed and gulped for air. Their eyes met and both grinned, tears in their eyes.

"D-Dion," said Jason, "I knew it. I knew you'd be back."

Dion kissed him on the forehead. "Death is a mere inconvenience to creatures such as ourselves. Our story is written in the-"

"Mindy!" Jason sat straight up. "Oh my God, I have to go back to sleep! I have to find her! Ezekiel sent me to some messed up version of Addley. I have to go back to sleep and get there and find her before he destroys her like he's made me destroy things and- and…"

Dion raised a finger. "Uh…my darling? Might I suggest you regard your altitude."

Jason stopped talking and noticed he was somehow floating a few feet above his bed. "What's happening?" he asked. "Am I dreaming? I'm dreaming, aren't I?"

"You're not," said Anne. "You don't have to go to Reverie. Reverie's come to Addley. This monster named Nihilo…"

"Nihilo." Jason floated toward the giant hole in his wall. "Ezekiel mentioned that name. So, if Reverie is here then Mindy's gotta be here, too." He looked to Dion. "I'm so happy you're back. But I have to find her."

Dion smiled. "You have mentioned this Mindy enough for me to know I cannot stop you. Good luck, my Lucid love."

Jason blushed. "I love you, Dion. I'll be back soon." He flew off into the distance.

Anne placed her hand on Dion's shoulder. "You okay?"

Dion nodded. "I got to see my Jason fly. How could I not be?" Dion took Anne by the hand. "What shall we do now, my dear?"

Anne blushed. "First, we should get Jason's grandmom out of the closet I may have locked her in. Second, there's someone else who we should visit. I think we'll need the extra firepower."

41

Satya sat on a thick rug near the fireplace in the dim, domed room. She looked with morbid curiosity into a gold-framed mirror, about the size of a dinner plate, floating in front of her. Within the mirror was a window into Addley. "This is madness," she said.

"Quite the opposite, dear," said Olokun, unseen from within her lab. "It's actually quite brilliant. Nihilo craves the end of all things, but that was impossible as long as the three realms exist. Destroy Reverie, Cosmos creates a new one. Destroy Cosmos, Eternia creates a new one. Destroy Eternia, well- hm -I'd have to do more research, but since human imagination has been known to produce Core Substance I imagine it was a risk Nihilo wasn't interested in taking. By bringing all the realms together in one place, destabilizing them all at once in a cascading, collapsing expanse…this is his best chance."

Satya watched a building explode within the mirror. "You almost sound impressed."

"Oh, I most certainly am," said Olokun. "Proud, even." Satya could hear her tinkering in the other room. The subtle sound of glass and metal clinking and clanging from within a lab that, less than an hour ago, Dion had been kept. "And, to be honest, a little jealous. That depthless brute made a grander impact on the world than I ever have."

Satya had seen enough destruction. She set the mirror on the rug and stood up, letting the warmth from the fire calm her. "So, what are you going to do about it, Olokun?"

The noises from the lab ceased. The patter of bare feet on a hard floor grew louder until Olokun emerged. No matter how many times Satya looked upon the goddess she could not help but be in awe of her beauty. She had changed into a flowing white robe that fit perfectly against her lean, muscular frame. The jewelry around her neck, her wrists, her ankles, reflected the eerie green light from the lab. In her hand was a small vial containing a blue liquid. The liquid shined so bright it lit the room. Olokun raised it to her lips, twisted those lips into a smirk, and said, "That is the question of the day, is it not? Whatever it is, my dear, it will be spectacular."

42

As the light faded, the first thing Mindy noticed was the smell. It was unlike anything she had ever experienced. Rancid. Overwhelming. She fought the urge to vomit as the unique sensation of cold water, ankle-deep, pulled her fully into her new reality. She took in her dark surroundings, the old concrete tunnel she found herself inside. In front of her, the path snaked ahead, dimly lit from grated holes above. Behind her, it was blocked by something too lost in shadow to identify.

She noticed something in a filthy flowing stream of water and gasped in spite of herself. It was her staff, broken in two. The orb was shattered into chunks of cloudy, gray glass.

"Poor baby." The familiar voice echoed down the tunnel. Mindy winced at the sound of it. "Not so powerful without your little stick, huh? A helpless little girl, just like I remember you."

It was then that Mindy got a closer look of what was blocking the tunnel. It was bulbous, squirming, alive. For a moment she lost the ability to think, to breathe. He had followed her here...the sewer of her nightmares.

From the writhing mass a fleshy appendage stretched out from the shadow and into the light, reaching and reaching for Mindy as it formed stubby, hungry fingers.

Mindy made a run for it.

She ran as fast as she could, splashing her way through the foul-smelling labyrinth, taking turn after turn, unsure of where to go. "Help!" she shouted. "I need help!" The only reply was an unsettling chuckle from something far too close behind.

A strong, calloused hand caught hold of her ankle and she went down, crashing onto the hard, wet ground. Mindy couldn't scramble to her feet before another hand took her by the forearm. And another by her hair. Her neck. Her mouth. Her thigh.

And another.

And another.

And another.

A heaviness, a mound of soft, warm, hairy flesh enveloped her, blocking out all light. All hope. A hundred fingers terrorized her body as she gasped for air. She inhaled the taste of old beer and cigarettes.

"The Unspeakable," the voice said coolly. "That's what you called me before you could bring yourself to ruin my name. We had fun together, you and I, before you betrayed me." Mindy squirmed, thrusted, to no avail. Her lungs burned. She could barely move. "You were such a frail, little thing," he continued. The lack of oxygen was making her feel faint. "Always crying for mommy and daddy. You hate me so much, but if it wasn't for me you'd still be that weak. Little. Girl."

Something awakened in Mindy. His words tapped into some deep, primal part of her; a final burst of strength. She bit one of the fingers nearest to her mouth and one of the dozens of hands recoiled. "If I die...before I die...Let me tell you who I am," she spat. "I am the girl who won dance competitions when I was four. I am the girl who made head varsity cheerleader my sophomore year. And maintained a 3.92 GPA." The grips began to loosen around her. "I literally fell into another reality and became queen." She felt her suffocating coffin opening up around her. "I created a refuge. I fought in a war. Where good people died." The last fingers left her skin. A glimmer of light emerged from above. "And, yes, I failed, I hated myself, because no one should have to live through the stuff I did. But that's life." The mass of flesh opened up and she could see the sewer ceiling. "It hurts. It sucks. You rise. You fail. You rise. You fail." Mindy felt the ground, again; the flowing water against her body. She began to rise. "I am the girl who will always rise."

Mindy stood up. At her feet was a shrinking glob of pulsating, hairy pink flesh about the size of a melon. She snatched it up before it would have been washed away. She brought it to her face. It was the size of an orange now. "You are a weak, pathetic memory of a man who attacked little girls. You didn't make me strong. You were just another example in my life of something I had to overcome." Mindy looked at the thing on her palm, no larger than a walnut. She crushed it in her fist and wiped the remains against the side of her pants. "Goodbye, Uncle Kenny."

Mindy took a few steps, then lurched forward, vomited. She composed herself, took a deep breath, and continued down the tunnel.

43

Rumi ran off after Vic between two of the houses that lined the cul-de-sac. "Wait!" she shouted, "Come back! You have to tell us where the last server is!"

"No, I do not!" Vic said from ahead. The distance between them was widening already. "Just because I know everything doesn't mean I have to share it, okay!"

Rumi had so little energy left that she could feel herself starting to slow. Still, she pressed on. "At least tell me, is really Futara gone?!"

"Yes!" Vic shouted as he leapt, deftly flipping over a fence, and disappeared to the other side. "Now stop following me! Leave me alone!"

His answer hit her like a Mach Two Mech-Fist to the face, but she'd have to process that later. Max and Jamal helped Rumi over the fence. "Come back here, Vic" she yelled, "or I swear you'll regret it!" By the time she reached the other side, he was gone.

"Zag!" Rumi cursed as she fought the tears in her eyes.

"Over here!" shouted Max. He and Jamal had run to the street. "We see him! He's running to the park!"

Rumi met the others in the front lawn and the three ran past a few lawns full of crystal formations and weird sculptures and ghosts, before reaching the corner. Directly across the street was an expanse of green and a sign that read "John C. Addley Park."

"This place makes no sense, even by Reverie standards,"

Max commented.

"Oh!" Rumi smacked her hand to her forehead. All those sleepless nights watching Zen had gotten to her. She was off her game. She tapped her finger to her temple twice and a green light flickered behind her eyes. Suddenly a hundred lifeforms came into view as vibrant blobs of red, yellow, and orange. Heat sensors. She scanned the park for anyone running away, but something else caught her eye.

Her sensors were picking up a human-shaped blob in the center of the park, but it was showing up as blue. She only knew one person who gave off a signature like that. Beside the blob was one colored more like a normal human and two smaller blobs beside it. A rush of joy went through Rumi's tired body. Forgetting almost completely about Vic, she darted off in the direction of the blobs. She could hear Max and Jamal mumbling something as they tried to keep up.

44

Jack woke up on his living room couch, not completely certain how he got there. He was groggy, hardly able to move his body or fully digest the strange muffled sounds coming from outside. The last thing he remembered was falling asleep in his room and then going to Reverie in search of Aggie. He was worried about her and wanted to be her hero like he had been for almost three years before. The years before he was taken out of his coma. Before he was cursed to his scrawny, powerless, broken, real world body. It was a better time. A much better time.

Jack gathered the strength to lift his skinny arm over his head and feel around a smooth wood surface until he made contact with his glasses. He put them on and turned his head slightly so that he could see the time on a clock above the TV. Almost three in the afternoon. How long had he been asleep? It didn't matter. His mom was working extra shifts to cover his physical therapy, which was great because she'd force him to practice his stretches or do his homework or eat. No. Jack had to get back to Reverie. Had to find Aggie.

Jack reached into the pocket of the shorts he was wearing. His concentration shot, he fumbled around for a bit before he found what he'd been looking for. He produced the small white pill and offered it a lazy smile. Goodbye stupid Cosmos, he thought, as he raised it to his mouth. Closer. Closer to power. To love. To feeling like he mattered at all.

Just before it reached his lips the pill was smacked out of Jack's hand. The surprise of the moment put Jack in a level of alertness he had not experienced in days. He searched for the source and, to his complete astonishment, saw a face that he had not seen in almost three years. "B-bobby?"

Jack's older brother had been driving the car that dark afternoon when Claire's brother Patrick, drunk, crashed his own car into Bobby's, instantly killing the both of them and putting Jack in a coma. Bobby now stood over Jack, dressed in the denim jacket, Kendrick Lamar T-shirt and black jeans he remembered him wearing on that final ride. Despite being translucent, Jack could make out the color of his brown skin and short-cropped black hair and his unmistakable eyes: a gray that was almost purple. Bobby didn't look pleased.

"What the hell do you think you're doing, bro?" Bobby asked, brow furrowed and hands firmly on his hips. "You trying to kill yourself or something?"

This was all happening too fast. "Bobby?" he said again, lethargic. "Where...where am I? Did I make it to Reverie?" Another option dawned on Jack. "Did I die?"

"No, you idiot." Bobby smacked Jack lightly on the back of the head. "But keep drugging yourself and you will. Look, the truth is, I don't know how I'm here, bro, but I'm glad I am. Addley is a war zone- like there are literally military planes flying over this mess -and we need to get you and Mom to safety." Bobby looked at Jack, who only returned the gaze with his mouth hanging open in disbelief. "Come on, man, say something."

Jack burst into tears in response. "I missed you, Bobby. I missed you so much." He nearly fell off the couch reaching for him. Bobby knelt down and gave his brother the biggest hug.

"I missed you, too, bro. More than you know." Bobby stopped, then looked around. "Where's Ma?"

A knock at the door. Bobby hopped to his feet, standing between Jack and the door. "We need to get you in the basement," said Bobby. "Now."

"I..." Jack hesitated. "I can't walk that well."

"Jack! Are you in there?" The voice came from the other side of the door. "It's Anne! Please, let us in!"

Bobby turned to Jack, suspicious.

"Let her in," said Jack.

Bobby walked to the door and opened it cautiously. Jack couldn't see her yet, but heard her gasp and say, "Oh my God. You're Bobby, aren't you?"

"And you're Anne." Bobby grinned. "When I was able to get a glimpse of Earth I saw you once, reading to Jack in the hospital. Nice to meet you."

"Uh...you, too."

A curly-haired young man dressed in African garb barged past Bobby and into the house. "It is best we continue this wholesome moment indoors, I think." He spotted Jack on the couch. "And who might this be?"

Anne stepped inside as well. She lit up at the sight of him. "This is Jack!"

"Um..." Dion cocked an eyebrow and crossed his arms. "This is your great hero of Reverie? Apologies, but I do not see it."

Despite the series of events leading to this point, Jack was finding it hard to stay awake. He'd taken three pills earlier that day already. He was starting to disconnect with the people around him as sleep pulled him farther and farther away.

"Jack?" said Anne, concerned. Her voice was like a distant echo in his head. "Are you okay?" She turned to Bobby. "Is he okay?"

"No." Jack could hear the anger in his brother's voice. "He's not. He's been drugging himself. Sleeping pills."

Anne's eyes widened. "Sleeping…? Oh. Oh no. He must have been trying to return to Reverie. Poor thing."

"Well, he is certainly of no use to us like this," said the curly-haired young man. His voice, all the voices, were getting softer. "Fortunately, you are all in the midst of a professional."

The last thing Jack remembered before his eyes closed were two warm hands touching the sides of his head.

———

Jack sat up, awake, alert and drenched in sweat.

"He's awake!" said Anne. "How do you feel, Jack?"

"Good," he said. Honestly, he felt better than he had in a long time. The sadness, the depression, had been relentless and now he felt truly alive for the first time since waking up. But he looked down at his frail figure, his little legs, and the feeling began to creep back.

Bobby stood beside the curly-haired young man. "Dion," Bobby said to the other, "what did you do?"

"It was quite simple," said Dion. "I am a god of life and death. Of all of your complex human emotional states.

Chemicals of the body and chemicals of external substances are all mine to command. I simply gave his biology a purge...chemically. Now he can be the Lucid powerhouse I have heard so much about."

"No. I can't." Jack turned his head away from the others. "Look at me. I'm...nothing."

Anne knelt down beside Jack and took his hand in hers. "Jack, you're not nothing. You are an amazing person-"

"Enough of this." Dion pushed Anne aside and took her place on the floor beside Jack. "The realms have merged. Reverie and Eternia are here." He gestured to Bobby. "Obviously. So if there's something you want to be, be it. We do not have time for more motivational speeches. Only action."

Jack looked to Anne who nodded warily. A big smile formed on Jack's face. He could feel it now. That familiar crackle in the air. The unlimited possibility.

He stood tall and looked to the front door. As he walked toward it, he willed his skinny limbs and thin chest to grow tight with muscles. He grew a few inches taller and a uniform, black and skintight, replaced his old clothing. He clutched the doorknob, transformed into a version of himself he dearly missed. He turned to the others, his eyes bright purple, like amethyst struck by a ray of light, and dashed off into the world.

45

Claire Ashford sat, legs crossed, on the deck of a fancy restaurant overlooking an Autumn-hued mountain range. She'd gotten hungry on the road and a quick search on her phone led her to this establishment, one of the most exclusive and expensive in the area. They were only taking reservations, but she worked her way around that. She gazed upon the beauty of nature as she sipped from the priciest glass of chianti available (it's not like she would have to pay for it). As long as she kept her requests small and specific, she surmised, the chaotic effects of her abilities wouldn't be too much trouble.

Claire thought about where she'd go next. New York City, maybe. Or Los Angeles. Maybe Paris. She figured she'd fit in quite well in Paris. All she'd have to say was, "I need to speak French" and- poof -she'd be as good as a native.

Unless it backfired and her consciousness was transported into an ugly old woman who spoke French.

Or she suddenly found herself only able to say the word, "French."

Best to not use her powers on herself, she concluded.

Claire brushed that out of her mind and waved for the server, a freckled young man with rosy cheeks and a round face. He blushed and came to her. "How can I help you, ma'am?"

"I'll have the truffle deviled eggs. And-" She was startled by the vibrating of her cell phone. Ignoring the server, she looked at her phone. "Local news update - Addley" read the alert. She'd have to change her location settings, she thought.

Then she read the news headline:

Witnesses Say Military Closing in on Small Town in America's Heartland.

"Anything else, ma'am?" The server grinned stupidly, simply happy to be near her.

Claire shook her head and swatted him away, eyes never leaving her phone. She clicked on the alert and was taken to a blank webpage that read, "Sorry! We can't find the page you're looking for."

Odd, thought Claire. She searched "Addley military strike" and a few relevant results came up. She clicked on a few and they each led to error pages. Next she clicked on a video link. After a toilet paper ad ended, there was shaky footage of a gruesome scene. Soldiers were racing into action. Shots were fired. There were screams, then the camera angle went sideways, dropping to the ground and pointing skyward. A military helicopter flew by, something smaller chasing it. An explosion sounded. Someone, a little girl, moved into view, staring curiously at the camera. She was translucent and dressed in clothing that had not been in fashion for a hundred years. She reached to the camera and static followed.

Claire shoved her phone into her purse, not quite sure what to think about what she just saw. She reached for deviled eggs realizing they had not yet come. Hand trembling, she reached for the chianti and took a sip. Then a gulp. Then it was gone.

What had she just seen? Was it real? No. No, that would be crazy. This isn't Reverie. Crazy things like ghosts and flying monsters don't happen here. Frazzled, she stood up. She left the deck, entering the main dining area, then headed for the exit.

"Ma'am?" Her server caught sight of her and tried to cut her off. "Ma'am, where are you going?"

Claire pushed past him, "I need you to move." She gasped, realizing what she'd said. Claire caught the look of pure panic as the waiter was plucked into the air by an unseen force then hurled through the glass window, past the deck, disappearing with a scream over the railing into the valley far, far below. The patrons of the restaurant were in a frenzy.

"I- I didn't mean to-" Claire made a run for it and drove away as fast as she could in her lovely red Porsche.

She wiped the wind-swept tears from her eyes as she sped down the long, lonely road. She hoped the waiter was okay. Hoped she hadn't- No, no time to think about that. It was an accident. That's all. She had to move forward, move on, just like before. To New York. Or Los Angeles. Or Paris.

And then she saw it again - that poor, stupid waiter falling, so confused how something so extraordinary could happen in his menial life.

She felt terrible. But there was something else, as well. Magnified by her guilt, the empty feeling that had been inside her since she ran away took hold of her mind. There was no doubt that it was somehow related to her other self. Her original self. That mediocre, lesser Claire.

And Addley. Again she mulled over what she had seen. Impossible things. Dangerous things. Things that another, lesser Claire could not possibly face. And if that Claire were killed by bombs or bullets or flying beasts or ghosts...what would happen to this one?

Claire Ashford slammed on the brakes. She did a U-turn on the empty road.

There were a number of reasons she decided to go back to Addley, but she dared not acknowledge a single one.

46

Rumi hadn't slept in days. Her joints and muscles were sore. Even standing was becoming more and more of an issue, especially in her armored battle-suit. But none of that mattered right now. The closer she moved towards the heat signatures, the blobs taking a clearer shape, the more sure she became. The four figures were crouched within a dense tangle of shrubs.

She opened her mouth to speak, but an arrow shot out of the bush and bounced harmlessly off her armor. Then another. Aggie then leapt out from her leafy cover, daggers in hand, ready to attack...until she saw Rumi's face. Aggie's rage turned to suspicion then.

"Stay back," Aggie warned.

Rumi tapped her temple twice and her view of the world returned to normal. "Aggie. It's me. It's Rumi."

"Rumi!" Osip and Oleg's little blonde heads perked up.

"Behind me," Aggie said to her brothers. Aggie took two steps toward Rumi, out of the shrubs and into the grass. "Who are you?"

Rumi stepped forward as well. She raised her arms in the air. "It's me, Aggz. It's Rumi." She then turned to Max and Jamal, who had just caught up with her. "Put down your weapons, boys."

Jamal shook his head, his gun firmly aimed. "There's a half-robot, a crazy lady with a knife, and murder twins fifteen feet away from me. I am not putting down my weapon."

Rumi was too tired to argue.

Fortunately, Eliza emerged then, seeming far less skeptical. Her human eye showed genuine hope as she approached Rumi, passing Aggie. "Rumi, how are you...?"

"Pasqual's skin-shield," Rumi replied. "I popped the battery out of my sword, transferred it to the generator in my belt and shielded myself in the explosion. Was knocked out for a bit then woke up and figured I'd hunt down any zagging cyborg scum that might have survived that battle."

The human half of Eliza's face smiled wide. "The skin-shield worked?"

"Like a charm, girl." Rumi could feel the tears swelling in her eyes. "It's good to see you." She looked to Aggie. "You too, wild woman."

"We- " Eliza's intense, green machine eye flickered. "-we thought you were dead." Eliza took Rumi into a hug so strong that only an advanced AI could achieve it.

"I know. I'm sorry. I had to make sure the mission was complete. That Nexis was gone for good."

"And is he?" asked Eliza.

Rumi pulled out of the hug. She made eye contact with Aggie before continuing. "Short story, yes. Slightly longer one: It's complicated."

"What have you gotten yourself into, girl?" asked Eliza. "And when was the last time you slept? No offense, but you look like death."

"Hi." Max wedged himself into the conversation. "Hello,

ladies, I am Max. Three-time MVP of the Addley High Varsity League- Go Ospreys! -and recent hero of Reverie. My bro Jamal and I are more than happy to join you in any quests against the powers of evil or whatever. Just point me in the direction of evil and I will..." Max raised his weapon and unleashed a torrent of fire into the air. "...scorch it dead."

Eliza narrowed her eyes and grinned. "And where'd you pick up these energetic young men?"

Rumi shrugged. "Another long story, but they're harmless."

"Harmless?!" Max patted his large, smoking gun. "Um, massive fire blaster. Hello?"

Rumi ignored him. She placed her heavy hand on Aggie's shoulder. "It's good to see you again. Thanks for keeping my best gal safe."

Aggie nodded solemnly in response. "There is a lot we must catch up on."

"Wait. Where's Pasqual?" Rumi looked to the trees as if he were hiding there.

"He's fine," said Eliza. "Like Aggz said. A lot to catch up-"

A sudden WHOOSH and the distinct sound of crumpling metal cut the conversation short.

"No." The utter shock on Jamal's face was the first thing Rumi noticed. Then Aggie ran to her brothers and hovered over them like a shield. A thud drew Rumi's attention to the ground where Max dropped to his knees, then to the grass with a large, iridescent spear, drenched in blood, through his chest.

"No! No, no, no, no..." Jamal was on his hands and knees beside Max, who had barely begun to process what had happened to him.

Rumi followed Eliza's gaze and saw five winged creatures wearing black togas flying above them, weapons at the ready.

47

Roughly ten seconds into swiftly flying down the street, past a smattering of suburban ruin, three thoughts raced through Jason Baker's mind. The first being how insane it was that he was flying in Cosmos, in the small, boring town he grew up in. The second, that he had no idea where Mindy was. And third: Dion was freaking alive! He was alive and he saved him and how did Jason respond? By rushing off to save Mindy. *Okay, Jason*, he thought. *Let's think about this for a sec.*

Jason floated to a porch swing in a relatively tranquil piece of town, trying his best to ignore the shouting and explosions in the distance all around. He sat, gently rocking as he tried to focus on his training. The first time he'd ever used his Lucid powers was to find Mindy. So instead of flying around like an idiot, that's what he'd do. Jason closed his eyes and pictured her: her auburn hair and wise-beyond-her-age eyes. Her knowing smile and unexpectedly boisterous laugh. Suddenly the darkness beneath his eyelids gave way to another scene. A dark corridor. Running water. And Mindy, searching, searching for something. Possibly a way out. Jason clenched his fists and prepared to teleport to her.

Then the house across the street imploded.

Jason's eyes opened just in time to see the robin's egg blue house with a slate gray roof collapse into a pile of splinters and pipes and then be swallowed by the earth in sinkhole. An all-too familiar evil hovered above the wreckage.

"Hey, kid," said Ezekiel between puffs of his cigar. "You're dead."

An old, gothic church haunted the corner of a block at the edge of Addley. The local preachers had moved their congregation to a more modern building closer to the town's center decades ago, making this building an abandoned relic in a part of town that had been derelict long before Reverie and Eternia came crashing down.

The church, empty for so long, had found new residents. Its boarded-up doors had been knocked down and a new flock huddled nervously amongst its old, dusty pews. Ben Burnham, proud as ever to be fulfilling his most holy duties, stood behind the pulpit, preparing to speak to the five hundred frightened humans and assorted other things he led from the streets.

The church was massive and unevenly lit by the sparse rays of sunlight shining splotches of color through the few remaining stained glass windows. The space behind Ben was thick with shadow save for a large, muscular man in black armor who wielded a great sword and seemed to give off a pale golden light: Baldr, the once-great god of truth and justice.

Ben cleared his throat.

"My brothers and sisters," he began. A rogue sun beam shined upon his bald spot. "You are safe here." Soft murmurs rose and fell from the congregation, hundreds of living and ghostly humans. "You are safe because you have chosen the righteous path. The only path that can bring a true end to your suffering, your doubt, your loneliness. A return to a simpler time. The great Nothing." Ben waited for a reaction, but received none. He scrunched his red nose and straightened his bowtie and said, "It is my greatest honor to introduce you to the one true beginning and ultimate end, the great Nihilo."

From the shadows behind Ben emerged a hulking beast carved of impenetrable black. He stood nearly fifteen feet tall. Muffled gasps rose from the audience, but all went quiet when Nihilo's round eyes glowed red.

"Fear." His voice was low and piercing, a powerful sound that reached every corner of the church. "It is what brought you to me. It is what shall guide you to your higher purpose, stripping you of hope and wonder for these are the frivolous playthings of the living."

Ben looked at the people. They stood perfectly still, bug-eyed, teeth clenched. Frozen with purest dread.

Nihilo continued, "And when you are cleansed of such trifles as I am cleansing you now, all that will remain is precious fear. And it shall overtake you. It shall become you. And you shall become instruments of eternal nothingness. You shall keep at bay those who wish to thwart my dark cleansing. You shall be mine."

Agonizing howls erupted from the audience as they began to transform, every one of them, man, woman, and child, into monstrous versions of the things they feared the most. Gray and sharp-toothed clowns, mythical monsters, and murderers took shape, their eyes glowing red like their creator's.

Nihilo lifted his hands to the heavens and the church began to crumble. The wood and stone began to decay. "Now, go forth, my loyal slaves," he said. "Go forth and pave the way for the end of all things!"

The horrid things erupted into unearthly fervor and charged into the light.

Addley's town square was mostly abandoned. The action had since spread outward into the more suburban corners of the small town. That's why few were there to witness the bright white tear open in space just in front of the fountain statue of John C. Addley.

From the white, shapes began to emerge. Four, to be exact. The first was Patrick, followed by Guillelmina. The young man and old woman were translucent, ghosts. Each wore hardened expressions. Concerned. The third shape had no expression at all, for he was a man with no face, hardly any discernible characteristics at all; his entire body as white as the tear they had emerged from. Speck, he was sometimes called.

And finally, from the tear walked a young woman with shoulder length, black hair with skin, tan like her father's. She wore a sleeveless shirt and pants and boots that, like the large sword she wielded, looked as if it were crafted of iridescent crystal. Her eyes were sharp, intense and green like her mother's. She surveyed the area, overwhelmed by a world so different than the one she had known the past seventeen years.

"Did we get it right?" she asked.

Guillelmina gazed upon the broken buildings, heard the cries and sounds of battle. "I'm not sure, child. But it's not too late."

Patrick smiled his mischievous smile and placed his hand on the young woman's shoulder. "Well, Anza, ready to do this?"

Interlude VII:
Esperanza Ashford-Soto

Year 0, Day 1

Patrick held on to his young niece tightly, not quite knowing what to expect when the two of them, along with Guillelmina, stepped into the strange tear in reality. Origin Point. He had never experienced anything quite like it, standing in the midst of ultimate emptiness, a vastness of white in all directions. He had assumed death would be a lonely void, free of all the burdens and boons of life. There was only a large pile of what looked like shattered iridescent crystals, as high as a three-story building, not too far from them.

"Don't think about it too much," said Guillelmina, "or you'll get lost in it." She tapped her foot on the ground beneath her. Patrick could make out a subtle hint of texture, hardness, that signified the existence of a floor. "I'm glad Vita spoke true," said old Guilly, as she eyed the small mountain of Core Substance. "Or else we would have been dead in a week." She laughed a little. Patrick found none of this funny.

"What's the plan, Old Lady?" Patrick asked, Anza cooing in his arms. "Because from where I'm standing we have no food, no water, and no way out."

"The plan is to keep your niece safe," Guillelmina said. "There's no easy way out which means there's no easy way in. As for food and drink." Guillelmina walked to the pile of broken crystals. "This is Core Substance. You know this as the stuff from which Eternia is built, but in reality it is the first substance, the proto-element, the building block of life

214

and all things. And, due to its nature, it can become anything we need. And we humans, as the first beings of Cosmos gifted with imagination and creativity, have the unique gift of manipulating it with a certain application of practice or sheer will."

Guillelmina took a small piece of the solid substance in her hand. She walked it over to Anza and placed it to her lips. The Core Substance instantly came alive, liquifying and spilling into Anza's mouth, down her throat. The baby giggled as she, for a moment, sparkled white and pink and green like the substance itself.

"Ah," Guillelmina nodded. "Unsurprisingly, this special child takes to it quicker than most."

"What just happened?" Patrick asked.

Guillelmina explained, "The Core Substance exists to expand, to grow all of existence. You and I are dead, made eternal by the Substance that flows through us. A soul, some might call it. But for those creatures that still live and have much more life potential within them, it can merge with them...sustain them."

Patrick scratched his head. "So she won't need to eat?"

Guillelmina grinned. "Not much. The Substance will sate her far longer than any nutrients on Cosmos."

Patrick sighed. "Okay. Good. Weird, but good. So, what else? What's the rest of the plan?"

"I'm not entirely sure." Guillelmina had already grabbed another piece of Core Substance and was molding it into something as if it were made out of clay. "But I think he can help."

Patrick noticed Guillelmina was looking past him. A chill went through him as he held Anza tight and slowly turned around. To his great surprise, standing behind him was a strange man with no distinguishable features, barely visible against the backdrop of white.

Year 0, Day 15

Guillelmina lounged on a soft, iridescent couch with Anza tucked in her arm. She held an oddly shaped rattle in her hand, shaking it much to the baby's amusement. The rattle, too, was iridescent but also adorned with a crudely-drawn blue elephant. She had been training Patrick in the art of manipulating the Core Substance and this was one of his first attempts.

"If I get good enough do you think I'll be able to conjure a TV with some half-decent reception?" asked Patrick as he toyed with a shard of the substance as he paced back and forth. "I'm going to go crazy in this-"

A light "pop" preceded the unexpected arrival of the manifestations of growth and desire. Initia, beautiful with her thick green hair and pregnant stomach, and Somni, slight and cute with robin's egg blue hair and wide cerulean eyes.

"Whoa!" Patrick stumbled and almost fell.

Guillelmina rose from the couch and smiled. "Mighty manifestations, what a pleasant surprise." As she walked to them, the depths of sadness in their shared expressions became clear. Guillelmina had never seen either of them appear as anything less than all-powerful. Much like Vita, their confidence had taken a hit in these dark times. "What's wrong? What's happened?" she asked.

"Nihilo," Initia snarled. "Mortem is gone." A single tear rolled down her dark cheek. She then gestured to Somni who was whimpering now. "Timor is gone. Nihilo absorbed them both and uses their abilities to wreak absolute havoc on the realms."

Guillelmina shook her head. "I'm so sorry. For you both."

"It's fine," said Somni, sounding less like the child. She forced a wavering smile and brushed the back of her small hand against Anza's face. "Hope is still alive."

Patrick stepped forward. "What's it like out there? In the world?"

Initia said, "The collapsing of the realms continues to spread and pick up velocity as it does. On Cosmos, it has far surpassed Addley and crept across most of North America. He has twisted hundreds of thousands into dark creatures, soldiers in his destructive cause. He makes great spectacles of some of his conquests, televised and streamed for the world to see. Presidents, Prime Ministers transformed into ravenous beasts." Initia turned to Guillelmina. "Nihilo murdered Olokun. She had arrived to face him, to do...something...but he was prepared. Before she could act, he immobilized her with Timor's fear and stripped her to bones and ash with Mortem's gift. It was a grim sight."

"No." Guillelmina began to feel faint. She handed Anza over to Patrick. To the manifestations she said, "You must stay here. You'll be safe. The man in white-"

"No," said Somni. Her resolve was evident and seemed to outsize her youthful appearance. "These are our realms. Nihilo might be stronger, but so are we. We have to fight. We have to. Right, Initia?"

Initia, brow furrowed, lowered her head and looked away. "I do not know who I am without him…" With those words, Initia disappeared.

Somni sighed. "I'll find her. I'll make sure she's okay." She took Guillelmina's hands in hers. "The man in white, as you call him, has been around as long as we manifestations have. Origin Point is his realm. Just as he led us to you, he will keep Nihilo from finding you here. And he is most definitely looking for you." Somni slightly bowed her head. "Until next ti-"

"Somni, wait. Before you go." Guillelmina stroked her wrinkled chin. "I have a favor to ask. Something I need you to find for later."

Year 0, Day 45

"Earth is gone." Initia's words startled Guillelmina and Patrick, who had not heard her arrive. Anza sucked away at a red polka-dotted pacifier. "It is a crude business," she continued, "the collapse. As the structural cohesion of the planet became undone, molten rock beneath earth's crust merged with the chaotic storms of Reverie's Underrealm giving birth to great unnatural disasters, tearing the planet apart. The atmosphere destabilized and soon all living things died and their souls now float in the endless abyss of space." Initia let out a cry so terrible that cracks formed in the hardly visible floor beneath her. She dropped to her hands and knees. "I can't do this anymore. I can't be witness to an existence so bereft of life. And without my beloved."

Anza began to cry.

"No, no, no," said Initia, calmly. She climbed to her feet,

standing taller than anyone else. "You must not be sad. As Somni said, you are our hope. We have lost so many to a vile cause. Now we must even the score."

"Initia?" Guillelmina scratched the hairs on her chin, perplexed. The old woman didn't understand what had to happen.

Initia's grass-green eyes reflected the certainty in what she must do next. "Timor and I understood, inherently, that for life to truly flourish, something must come to an end." Initia reached out and caught Anza by the wrist. The baby fell silent and both began to glow. "We manifestations were never truly worthy of the gifts we had." Initia glowed brighter and brighter until she was a silhouette of brilliant green. "I want to feel what it's like to be one with something again."

And, with that, Initia was absorbed into baby Anza. For a moment Anza's brown eyes mimicked the green of Initia's light. And then Anza, as Patrick and Guillelmina stood silent and still, giggled joyously.

Year 1, Month 4

Patrick Ashford watched with pride as Guillelmina rocked on the swinging bench. The bench looked and felt almost exactly like wood and the chains that held it aloft, almost exactly like metal. Guillelmina waved at him as she sipped her cup of almost-tea from the porch of the small single-floor house he'd spent the better part of a month building from the Core Substance. Guillelmina could've done it faster, but he needed to keep busy or else the boredom would be too much to bear. Fortunately, his niece was anything but boring.

"Uncle Patrick!" screamed the little girl with that high-pitched voice. She was walking now. Running, even on wobbly baby legs. "Throw the ball!" she sang. "Throw the ball!"

"Alright, kiddo." Patrick tossed the soft ball he'd made, underhand. Anza reached for it, missed, then lost her balance and fell down. The practically-grass Patrick made softened her landing. "Get up Anza, you're fine! You're fine!" Anza giggled and climbed to her feet. "That's my niece!"

Anza picked up the ball and gave it her best throw. It landed about two feet in front of her.

"All right," said Patrick as he reached forward to pick up the ball. "Let's try again."

Anza clapped and smiled, her big brown eyes full of glee.

Patrick tossed the ball. It slipped out of his hand a little too late, sending it flying a little too far to the right. Incredibly, the ball changed trajectory, mid-flight, and found its way to Anza's hands.

Patrick's mouth hung in disbelief. An expression mirrored by Guillelmina.

"Her abilities are waking up," Guillelmina said, quite pleased. "Now we will see what a chosen one can do."

Year 8, Month 7

"I wanna fight!" Anza grumbled from the dining room table. Her arms were folded and her nostrils flared. She had already turned the bowl in front of her into a very impressive dagger.

"This is boring, Uncle Patrick."

Patrick drew from a pile of flashcards on the table. "Two more and you can go outside."

Anza flung her hands up. "You're killing me, man!"

Patrick laughed. "Just spell the words, Boogerhead." He showed her a picture of a street with an arrow pointing to the sidewalk.

"S-I-D-E-W-A-L-K," she said through pouty lips.

Patrick tapped his fingers on the table. "And..."

She groaned. "A-C-E-R-A."

"Honestly," said Patrick, "I have no idea if that's how you say sidewalk in Spanish, but I've had about enough of this so go forth and be violent!"

"Yay!" Anza grabbed her dagger and ran out of the house to the small backyard under the vast white sky. Guillelmina and the man in white were waiting for her. Guillelmina held a long pearl-colored staff and the man in white was dressed in bulky cushioned armor, similarly iridescent. "Prepare to die!" she shouted before charging right at them.

Guillelmina nonchalantly stretched her staff forward, tripping Anza and sending the girl to the ground. "Think before you strike," Guillelmina said. "Assess the situation. Or perish."

"Ouch, Guilly!" said Anza. "How'd you learn to fight so good?"

Guillelmina said, "When most of your old friends are gods

and warrior mystics, you have to prepare for a lot of sudden dangerous-"

Anza noticed something large moving toward her. The armored man in white charged at her but, instead of making contact, moved right through her as if she wasn't there.

"Nice try!" she said, hands on her hips in what Patrick had called a 'bad-ass Super Anza pose!'

"Not bad," said Guillelmina.

"I'm gonna squash Nihilo like a little baby bug!" Anza cried.

Suddenly a piece of hard, craggy Core Substance hit Anza in her forehead. "Ow." Anza touched her head and felt the blood against her fingers. Tears filled the girl's eyes.

"What gives?!" said Patrick who had been watching from the porch. Anza had never heard him so angry.

"What gives?" Guilly's teeth were clenched. She held another piece in between her thin wrinkled fingers. "What gives is that this is not a game, Patrick. We can't forget that. Outside of this place everything we know is gone. Everyone we love is dead. All of existence is in ruin. And the only people who can stop it are here. Now. We cannot take this time for granted. We must train seriously and leave the frivolousness for the appropriate time. Our chance of pulling this off- of reversing the damage that has been done -is minimal. But when we make light of the battle ahead, we are making light of trillions of lives lost. When we shirk our responsibilities, Nihilo wins."

Anza sat on a mound of grass she had molded into a crude chair. She was dripping with sweat, her muscles sore. There were bruises up and down her arms and long legs. She would heal them eventually.

Guillelmina and Patrick were inside doing who knows what. Guillelmina was probably coming up with some new way to torture her and Patrick was doing his best to maintain the peace.

Anza tossed her large, Core Substance sword to the ground and buried her head in her hands. She began to cry. She cried because of what was expected of her. She cried because of Origin Point, which was more like a prison. She cried because of her loneliness which, despite her uncle's best efforts, ran deep.

Anza jumped when a hand softly touched her back. It was Somni. The manifestation had not been a frequent visitor, but she was always pleasant. Anza remembered her sweeter, happier once. What was the world like outside of Origin Point? When would she know?

"You're crying," said Somni. "What's wrong?"

Normally, Anza would keep her thoughts to herself. After all, what would sharing how miserable she was do to make her feel any better? But Somni had caught her in the right moment. "It's all wrong." Anza wiped the tears from her eyes and faced the weary manifestation. "I'm supposed to be some chosen one. To save the world- no, more than that. Everything! Can you even-? How can I even wrap my head around that when this house, this yard, are all I know. Guillelmina and Uncle Patrick show me pictures, but what are pictures?! It's not real, NONE of this is real! But Nihilo is… Nihilo is…"

Somni sat beside Anza, taking her hand in his. "I can't imagine what you're going through. To have experienced so little, but to have so much expected of you." The two sat quietly for a while before Somni continued. "When you absorbed Initia you received the gift of growth. Hard to put something like that to the test when there's so little alive around you."

"I can make stuff bigger, though," said Anza, under her breath. "Heal."

"That you can," Somni agreed. She exhaled. "Initia's abilities were based on biology, on space, mass. But me… My brother and I, we ruled the world of dreams. Hopes and fears. Imagination. Matters of the mind." Anza began to lose interest, moving her attention to an especially painful bruise on her left thigh when Somni took her sharply by the shoulder, looked into her green eyes. Anza had never noticed the specks of purple that danced in Somni's irises. "I have all the desires of the people of Cosmos inside of me. And I've done very little with them. The rules that controlled the manifestations were flawed. Heh. We were flawed." Somni tightened her grip, never breaking her gaze. "Right now, more than anything, Esperanza, you need hope. Let that be my final gift to you."

Somni was absorbed into Anza in a beautiful display of soft blue and purple light.

Year 17, Month 9

Guillelmina poked her head out from the back door. "Do you have everything you need?"

"You tell me!" Anza's heart was pounding. It felt as if she was feeling every feeling she'd ever felt at once...and then some! After so long. After spending every moment in her memory in one place - today was the day. She had grown into a strong young woman. She looked almost identical to her uncle in age now.

"I can't believe we're going back," said Patrick as he shoved Core Substance into a giant duffel bag made from the same stuff. "Back home. Words cannot describe how excited I am to leave this place." He looked to Anza. "You're going to see your parents! How weird is that?"

Claire Ashford and Victor Soto. Anza had no memory of them. Only the stories Guillelmina and Patrick told, with some bits of Somni's memories of them (she was still getting the hang of that part of Somni's abilities). From Patrick, she learned so much about the girl that was her mother. Her knowledge of Claire greatly outweighed what she had learned from Guillelmina of the nerdy, skinny, adventurer with the heart of gold that was Victor. Patrick often told her how she had her mother's strong will and fierce eyes.

"Bring it out!" shouted Guillelmina into the empty white sky.

A moment later the man in white appeared. And with him was a curious, furry creature with large floppy ears and big turquoise eyes. Its fur was cream colored except for the tip of its ears and tail and its front and back paws, which were light purple.

"A Waypoint Grobi!" Anza exclaimed. She had heard the stories of Claire and Victor using one to travel in Reverie. As well as how the manifestations used it to transport them from Origin Point. "This is our way out!"

"That's right, my dear," said Guilleilmina with a chuckle. "I had Somni gather one from Reverie before it was too late and our friend in white kept him secure in another pocket of Origin so we wouldn't accidentally trigger it ahead of schedule. But today is the day. You have grown into a formidable woman and I have taught you all I could hope to."

"You really thought of everything," said Patrick.

"I did the best I could." Guillelmina scratched her head. "As you know, the world as we knew it was destroyed many years ago. But Origin Point exists outside of time and space. The Waypoint Grobi gives us the means to go back. But we'll need to amplify its ability to send us to a specific place and time. Ideally, before the realms collapsed. From there we can consult the manifestations, search for Mindy and her army, Olokun, too, and take the fight directly to Nihilo, neutralizing him before it all gets out of hand." The man in white stepped forward. He and Guillelmina shared a nod. "The manifestation of Origin will focus on the past. Anza, take his hand and let the power of Somni's desire strengthen his resolve." Anza did as she was told and an indigo aura emanated from her. "Now, Patrick take my hand." Patrick did so and Guillelmina touched the grobi's tail. "Whenever your mind is clear and your vision true, you must-"

And they disappeared.

PART VIII
NOTHING HAPPENS

48

Anza stood ready, a sparkling sight of strength and beauty in a world in ruin. At least that's the image she struggled to maintain as her senses were overtaken by surroundings more stark, more complex, than anything she had experienced before. Creatures flying above. Percussive sounds and unintelligible voices howling in the distance. It was all so much; too much at once. All of the flash cards and fabrications in the world couldn't have prepared her for reality.

Something small whizzed above and crashed into a building, producing a fiery explosion on impact. A bomb? No, what was the word...missile. Yes, a missile.

"Looks like we may have overshot a little with the time traveling. I thought we'd get here earlier," said Patrick as the Waypoint Grobi leapt from the portal and onto his shoulder. He was more translucent, more ghostly, in this realm. He reached into his backpack and produced a ball of Core Substance. Its shape began to change.

"Better now than after the planet was destroyed," Guillelmina responded. Then, to Anza, "I think the best course of action is to find cover and then devise a plan to find Nihilo."

"No need." The voice was big, deep, and cut through the rest of the world's noise like it were silence. Anza couldn't believe it. Not ten feet in front of her stood Nihilo, the towering void, the manifestation of nothingness who she had been trained her whole life to defeat. Though, at this current moment, she felt especially unfit for the task. A gentle touch against her leg caused her to jump. It was the grobi, as frightened as Anza, trembling against her.

Nihilo laughed. The most horrible sound she had ever heard.

"So this is what you've been up to," he said, most likely to Guillelmina. "Using Origin to travel through time. Quaint. Unfortunately for you all, it's too late. And you've gifted me the final piece."

From the ruins and wreckage of crystal and stone surrounding them, creatures began to appear. Warped and monstrous things, ogre-like or skeletal, slimy or covered in spines. A long blue monster like a centipede with a woman's head skittered into view.

"It's over," Nihilo said.

"No. It's not." In front of Anza two figures appeared. One she did not remember, but her description fit perfectly the growth manifestation, Initia. The other, Somni, manifestation of desire, she had not seen in years. She was surprised, as they had both given themselves to her, but she quickly recalled that was from another place in another time that had not yet occurred.

"We will not let you hurt her," Initia continued as around her the grass and weeds began to grow.

"You won't break us," Somni added and Anza felt a rush of pure hope rush through her.

Nihilo tilted his head to the side. "She is not who I was waiting for." His arm extended forward, zigging and zagging like a solid black lightning bolt until, a fraction of a second later, it found its home in the chest of the man in white. Anza gasped as Nihilo's darkness overtook him like a virus or a curse. The man in white convulsed, unable to stave off the attack. "Weak."

By the time Anza raised her sword it was done. Nihilo yanked the man in white into his abyss. He was gone.

"It is right that you were all here to witness this," Nihilo said. "It brings me great pleasure that the final moment I have in my cursed existence is to witness the sting of failure as you realize what I've done." He took a grand step forward. The others stood their ground, not quite sure what, aside from the loss of the man in white, had just occurred.

Three jagged black projectiles extended from Nihilo's torso, one each piercing the chests of Initia, Somni, and Anza. Initia and Somni shrieked in agony as the dark arms writhed back and forth, back and forth, hacking their bodies into uneven horizontal pieces which dropped to the ground on either side of Anza, who watched in horror. She would have suffered the same fate had she not turned intangible at just the right moment. The attack moved through her body as if she were air.

"Intriguing," Nihilo mused as Initia and Somni watched from the ground, from heads no longer attached to bodies. Anza could have sworn she saw the vile manifestation shrug.

"Where was I?" Nihilo said. "Ah, yes. The endgame." Moving like a shadow, like liquid night, he stretched forward, diving into the hole they'd left and entering Origin Point. The tear in reality, once filled with blinding white, was now overtaken by impenetrable black.

"What's he doing?" Patrick asked no one in particular.

"Allow me." Nihilo's voice was booming, pouring from the tear. "Since the beginning of time, my very existence was dedicated to the singular pursuit of the end of all things. Through millennia of machinations to destabilize the realms,

I have sown destruction, certainly. Collapse, indeed. But still, existence prevailed. In secretly watching over the many moving pieces of my great scheme, I became aware that the aberrant manifestation of Origin, Speck, had allied himself with that treacherous goddess, Olokun. And, in spying on them both, I learned more. That our existence is a lie, my sisters. We manifestations are parts of the same twisted whole. A single identity. A single experiment, by Olokun, our creator, to save the world. Bah! A simple exertion of will on my part and I was able to absorb my brothers, undoing Olokun's cruel thinning of our true power. And I also learned Origin Point is no realm at all. Void of life or law, it was, I realized for the first time, what I had been craving all along: true nothingness. By capturing its manifestation, I have become what I was always meant to be. And with the gift of decline given to me by my brother, Mortem, I can expand the tear, transforming Origin Point into an REALM-CONSUMING, ALL-DEVOURING VOID!"

The tear opened wide and gained the form and dimension of an uneven rippling sphere, growing before Anza's eyes. She jumped back as it swallowed the sliced remains of Initia and Somni, their faces twisted in horror as they had sacrificed themselves for the second time in her life.

"My servants," said Nihilo, his voice distant as an echo, "kill them all."

The hundreds of living nightmares surrounding them now, charged at them from all sides. Jagged black arms extended wildly, like lightning bolts from the ever-expanding void that was Nihilo, removing anything it touched from existence.

"Aiieee!" Guillelmina was caught by an arm of the jagged, black void. She offered Anza a sure smile and a knowing glance as she was pulled into the nothingness.

"GUILLY, NO!" Anza cried. She started for the void, but Patrick grabbed her arm and pushed the grobi to her chest. The monsters were practically on top of them.

"Take her away!" shouted Patrick. "To anywhere! Now!"

Anza protested, "I'm not going any-!"

Anza vanished as zombies and killer clowns and men with Uncle Sam masks and automatic weapons piled on to Patrick Ashford.

49

As the forest thinned and the sky opened up, Addley emerged hazy in the distance. At first, it appeared to be the drab, infinitely uneventful town Claire had dreamed of leaving. But, as she and her bright red Corvette drew closer, that quickly changed. Pillars of smoke rose from Addley. Explosions happened here and there. The terrain had generally been mutilated by giant crystals and other, weirder structures (like a massive treehouse or an old roller coaster). There was also a narrow black mountain that reached to the clouds.

Perhaps, strangest of all, was the outer edge of town. The sight was hard to digest, let alone describe. In a circular perimeter that surrounded all of Addley were two layers of land, like a pair of thin dimensions, fading in from the sky and merging with the earth, expanding outward in all directions. One was iridescent and the other, a random patchwork of colors and structures. Eternia and Reverie, Claire assumed. The circling helicopters maintained a wide berth between the half-formed realms in the sky, which slowly fell and integrated with the earth like pages of a book.

"This is about a million times worse than I thought." she said to herself.

Claire's wasn't the only car on the road. Old rusty sedans and dirty white vans with stickers and decals with things like "We are not alone" and "It's the end of the world - Let's Party!" written on them clogged the road. Idiots. Claire groaned as all traffic came to a stop. The military had set up barricades. Unfortunately for them, the forests and farmlands that surrounded Addley were too much to monitor completely. Nerds and conspiracy theorists began to abandon their vehicles, grab their nonsense equipment, and head for the town on foot. In this alone, Claire thought they had the right idea.

Instead of scurrying into the woods like some animal, she walked directly to the gate and told the six soldiers guarding it, "I need to get through." The soldiers froze in place. Good enough. She kept walking. A few more incidents like that occurred before she finally made it to the town's edge.

"STOP RIGHT THERE!"

The sharp beat of helicopter blades pounded above. A woman with a megaphone hung out of the door on the side. Claire found herself surrounded by about a dozen soldiers with weapons pointed at her. Claire had been so set on reaching town that she didn't notice them sneaking up on her.

"MAKE ONE MORE MOVE AND WE WILL FIRE," said Megaphone Lady. You could hear the nervousness in her voice. No one could have been trained for this. "YOU HAVE...INCAPACITATED THIRTY MEN. YOU WILL SURRENDER OR BE SHOT ON SIGHT."

Claire rolled her eyes. Under her breath, she muttered, "I need you to stop talking."

Megaphone Lady fell silent. Claire couldn't see her well, but the lady dropped her megaphone. It crashed a couple of feet from Claire. One quick glimpse and it was clear the woman had lost her mouth. *That was a new one*, thought Claire.

"What did you do, you freak?!" spat one of the soldiers with a weapon pointed at her.

Claire didn't have time for this. Her lesser half was in there and could be in trouble which meant that she could be in trouble. "I need you soldiers to disappear," she said. And they did. They all did. Their clothes and guns, no longer held by soldier bodies, dropped to the ground. Megaphone Lady was gone. The multiple tanks creeping nearby came to a stop.

Claire felt a tinge of guilt, but shrugged it off and continued into Addley; a trail of destruction, of lost daughters and sons, behind her.

50

Aggie was quick to place herself between her brothers and the five winged beasts preparing to attack. "Stay behind me," she said. Rumi and Eliza were on either side of her, their weapons ready.

Aggie let loose a pair of throwing knives. Rumi shot the axe-head from the muzzle of her gun and Eliza a beam of green light from hers. The knives practically bounced off of the neck of one of the winged monsters. Rumi's projectile axe hit another right in the stomach, only mildly irritating it before falling to the ground. Eliza's laser beam left a small burn mark in a third monster's forehead. It flinched and nothing more. Two arrows launched from Osip and Oleg's bow had a similarly pathetic effect.

There was a crunching sound from behind as Aggie watched a golden spear zoom past her and return to one of the monster's heads, drenched in Max's blood. It had been pulled from his corpse as if by telekinesis.

"We are the Shadow Yazata," one of them pronounced, "proud servants of Nihilo, the Great Liberator."

Aggie considered her next move. Both fighting or fleeing seemed like equally futile options. Perhaps she could distract them long enough for her brothers to escape. That seemed the best option.

Fortunately, it was a choice she did not have to make for something fell from the sky, a great glistening blur, taking one of the winged things down to the grassy ground. It was another winged creature, this one with long fuschia hair and teal eyes beaming from its silver-skin face. Unlike the others, it wore a white toga and iridescent armor. It pulled a crystalline sword from the corpse of its prey.

FWOOM! FWOOM! FWOOM!

Three more of them came down. Two of the four remaining attackers were killed on impact. The two left were able to avoid the assault. They drew their weapons and squared off against the ones in armor.

"Go now," commanded the one with the teal eyes to Aggie and the rest. "Seek shelter. We are the true yazata, Guardians of Eternia. We will finish these traitors."

Aggie nodded and took Osip and Oleg by their wrists, dragging them off as the black-clad yazata battled with their foes.

"Come on, kid," she heard Rumi say. She was pleading with the young man, Jamal, to leave his dead friend.

Aggie, under almost any other circumstance, would have kept going. Her brothers' safety meant more than anything. But this was Rumi. If not for her, her brothers would probably be dead. Aggie would have probably been dead.

The yazata continued to fight as Aggie knelt down beside Jamal. "If we do not move now, we all will die, do you understand?" One close look into Jamal's eyes and she at once saw his innocence. He was not of Reverie. He had never known true grief. Or war. This death was his first glimpse into the darkness of the world. The sadness in his eyes affected her more than she thought it could.

"We can't just leave him here!" Jamal said through sobs. "We can't!"

Eliza grabbed Jamal by the forearm and effortlessly lifted

him to his feet. "We'll come back for him," she said. "I promise. But for now we need to get somewhere safe."

Aggie caught a glimpse of Rumi, who was barely standing, barely keeping her eyes open. It took her a second too long to react to Jamal being on his feet.

"We're going," said Aggie. She took Rumi by the hand and guided her away. Eliza followed, practically pulling Jamal along as he reached for his dead friend. Osip and Oleg stepped from behind a hedge of bushes. They all walked away from the yazata and out of the park; Aggie all the while keeping watch for the next threat.

"Where are we going?" Eliza asked as Aggie led them along a white fence and into the backyard of one of the many houses that lined the park. Behind the house was a smaller house. It was simple, wooden, and closer in size to the ones Aggie had been used to in her village. The inside was dark and lined with all sorts of tools. Some she had even seen before. It was a tight squeeze, but she climbed inside and the others joined her.

"We are headed to Black Rock," Aggie said.

"What?" remarked Rumi, her voice slurring a bit.

"There is a small entrance in the side," Aggie explained. "It is doubtful anyone has found it in the chaos. We will enter and ascend a narrow flight of stairs to the Great Hall. There is no safer place."

"No safer place," Rumi repeated, ever so slightly losing her balance before righting herself with help of the wall.

Aggie swiftly, firmly pressed her fingers against certain spots on Rumi's neck. Rumi protested for a fraction of a second before falling unconscious. Aggie caught her before she fell. "She was too exhausted to be of any use to any of us," Aggie explained. "Eliza, please?"

Eliza took Rumi from Aggie and gently hoisted Rumi over her shoulder, carrying her weight with ease.

Jamal stared out into the yard, mouthing "Max" over and over, shaking his head.

Aggie placed her hands on either side of his head and looked into his dark brown eyes. "When I was a child and my brothers could barely crawl, my parents were murdered before my eyes. I know death. It is ugly and unfortunate and it never leaves you. But we are not dead. And so we must carry on for the ones we lost. Continue the wars they fought. Live a life they would be proud of. Only then have we earned the right to mourn." She took her brothers by the hand and headed out into the chaos. Jamal wiped his eyes and followed; Eliza after him, Rumi hunched over her shoulder getting much earned rest.

In the distance, looming above all else, was Black Rock. Or, as Aggie saw it, for better or worse, home.

51

Jason Baker watched in horror as four adjacent houses sunk into the ground, one by one. Ezekiel laughed his sinister laugh, cigar smoke pouring out of his dry lips.

"STOP THIS!" Jason shouted. The two of them faced one another in the middle of an empty street.

"Oh, I'll stop when I'm good n' ready, kid," Ezekiel said. "Besides, I like to torture my victims before I kill 'em."

Suddenly, the ground beneath Jason's feet opened up. Jason simply floated in place and rolled his eyes. "Seriously?"

Ezekiel snarled and then grunted as he stabbed at Jason with a butcher knife that had materialized in his hand. Jason disappeared well before the knife would have reached his chest and reappeared a few feet to the left.

This was getting old, Jason thought. Ezekiel was a powerful Lucid, sure, but what he had in power, he lacked in creativity. Just a bunch of sinkholes of various sizes and the occasional conjured knife, firearm or cigar. But the longer Jason could keep him distracted, the longer his hometown wasn't swallowed by the Earth. He could use some time to think, though.

Jason concentrated on a car parked on the sidewalk and it rose from the ground and hurdled towards Ezekiel. Ezekiel crouched and the car slammed into another car across the street. Ezekiel grinned. "You're going to have to do-"

Jason quickly conjured a white cube where Ezekiel stood. It surrounded him completely. Jason watched with some joy as Ezekiel said things like, "What?! Where am I?!" or "What dimension'd you send me too, boy?!" Then he stopped. Jason removed the cube and Ezekiel was gone. As Jason hoped, the unexpectedness of his second attack jostled Ezekiel awake wherever his real self was.

That's it! Jason thought.

If Jason wanted to get rid of Ezekiel, he'd have to find the real Ezekiel. Possibly the only good thing about the realms collapsing in on themselves is that he could use his own Lucid powers to seek him out and make it so he can't go to sleep...at least until this whole mess was done.

Jason sat in the middle of the street and concentrated, picturing Ezekiel in his mind, trying to find where he was hiding. Nothing came to him. "Dammit," said Jason. Jason shrugged. He had a first name and general description. Maybe a targeted Internet search would succeed where his powers failed.

Jason Baker rose from the ground and flew in the direction of his house, over the post office and the park- even flinging a couple of those angel-things into a lake- to embark on what could be the most important Google search of his life. That is, until he spotted someone familiar, though he could hardly believe it. Someone more useful than a million Google searches.

"Vic?!" Jason landed in front of the young man who looked very similar to his former displaced classmate and guy who coaxed him to becoming a Lucid in the first place. "Is that you?!"

Vic pushed Jason aside and kept running. "Out of my way!"

"Yep," Jason said. "That's you." With a thought, Vic was lifted into the air and, despite his protests, plopped on the sidewalk in front of Jason. "Didn't you die?"

Vic groaned. He was wearing a ultramodern military suit like something you'd see in a video game. "I did," he said. "But I found a loophole," He frowned. "Now please get out of my way."

It was then that Jason saw Vic; really looked at him. He seemed tired, and scarier than that, unsure. "Hey, man," said Jason. "Are you okay? You look like you've been crying." At that, Jason noticed the tears welling in Vic's eyes. "Do- do you want to talk? I've never seen you like-"

"I don't want to talk!" snapped Vic, his tan skin turning red with shame. "I don't want any of this!"

"Fine. Okay." Jason put his hands in the air. "Just tell me how to beat Ezekiel. How do I beat Ezekiel?"

"You can't," said Vic, seeming suddenly more deflated than he had at the beginning of their conversation.

"Come on, man." Jason pushed against Vic's chest plate. "Just tell me where he is. What's his name? I know you know!"

"His name is Ezekiel Christopher Clarke!" Vic shouted. He wiped his eyes. "He's in the max prison in Millsborn. Unreachable! You can't stop him! You have to stay here and keep him at-"

"We'll see about that!" Jason launched himself into the sky. He knew the prison well enough. Some of his oldest memories were of his parents driving him by on the way to an old roadside amusement park. He tried to teleport there, but again, nothing. So he flew as fast as he could out of Addley. If he was going to do this, he had to do it quickly, before Ezekiel found his way back.

Jason passed over the "Welcome to Addley" sign and zoomed toward the town limit where he was taken aback by what appeared to be two worlds blending into this one. No matter. He just had to imagine himself intangible and keep going. Keep going. Keep-

Jason passed through the merging realms and over the vast farmland when he realized he was no longer flying. His powers, all of them, no longer worked outside of Addley. His body flew forward on his own momentum before angling downward and crashing hard into a cornfield. It all happened so fast. Bones broke on impact then he rolled, his face pelted with dirt and rocks, his body bent by the stalks, until he stopped, broken, bloodied, bruised.

Unable to move.

Unable to call for help.

He uttered the words, "I'm sorry, Mindy," and then he closed his eyes.

52

Mindy marched through the dark sewers, doing her best to ignore the stench that had gotten less repulsive with time. She also did her best to ignore her hands, still trembling from the run-in with a monster she'd kept imprisoned for so long. *Destroyed is better than contained*, she thought over and over again.

Destroyed is better than contained.

She rounded a corner and was met with a strange sight. The tunnel had been partially blocked by what could only be described as a giant white crystal with hints of pink and green, purple and blue. Mindy approached cautiously, examined it and placed her shaking hands on it. It felt...alive somehow. Unlike anything she had ever touched. She looked up. She could see the sky through a crack left between the crystal and the concrete.

"I have to get out of here," Mindy said aloud. "I have to find Aemon. I have to be there for my people."

The crystal, once hard, began to soften to her touch. Startled, Mindy pulled her hands away. The crystal had changed shape. Faint ridges formed and some of the sharp, craggy details faded. The crack above, she swore, had widened.

She placed her hands on the crystal as before. And, as before, said, "I have to get out of here. I have to find Aemon. I have to be there for my people." Again, the crystal shifted like clay. This time her hands remained and the faint ridges became more pronounced, enough to take hold of. The crack above opened up into a hole large enough to fit through. Mindy climbed out of the sewer and into a garden at the center of a roundabout. She was in Addley. And Addley was in ruins.

Reverie, she thought, *where nowhere is safe*.

Mindy, covered in filth, crossed the roundabout and headed toward her house. She passed another crystal and pressed her hand against it while asking for a weapon. When she pulled her hand back, she was holding a small dagger.

Mindy tried her best to remain unseen as she moved from tree to tree, from house to house. There were what appeared to be angels fighting above and regular people and ghost-like people roaming at street level. Most didn't notice her and those who did seemed more wary of her than she was of them. On one street a military helicopter had crashed.

"Hello, meat." The voice came from a lanky young man with messy brown hair and hungry red eyes. He sat perched atop a roof. His skin was gray and he wore a suit of a similar color. He smiled, revealing a set of long, sharp teeth. By the time he'd jumped from the roof, Mindy was already running.

The young man moved on all fours like a wolf. Mindy ran through a front yard and was hit with a sprinkler's shower. She moved back onto the street, crossed it, and jumped the black iron fence on the side.

She was surrounded by trees now, thick enough to block out most of the sunlight, and kept running. "Yes, fear, delicious," said the thing that chased her. It drew closer. Closer still. She could hear its footfalls directly behind her.

Mindy spun around and stabbed the thing right in its neck, then pulled out her knife and slit its throat. The thing didn't die, but instead sized Mindy up with its eyes, decided she wasn't worth the effort and ran away as if it were late for something.

Mindy caught her breath. Her hands were shaking again. Worse than before. But it was fine. It would all be fine. She could see the gravestones in the clearing ahead. All she had to do was walk through the cemetery and her house was on the other side. Aemon and the others will be there. Safe. Sound.

She saw a light about fifty feet away, illuminating the dark forest. She tried to ignore it at first, stepping into the clearing where so many ghost-like figures quietly observed the gravestones. It called to her. Its glow was not unlike the dagger she held.

Mindy crept toward the light, her hands no longer trembling, but instead her heart pounding with strange exhilaration. A fulfillment, a connectedness that she had never known before. She stepped over a fallen branch, rounded a thick oak tree, the dead leaves crunching beneath her feet. And then she saw it, the source of her sudden obsession.

It was a severed head, a woman's with flawless diamond skin and hair to match. The head blinked and looked at Mindy with eyes that sparkled like a star's. "Come now, *darling*," she said, playful but not without urgency. "You have the honor of escorting Vita, the all-powerful manifestation of existence itself, to her next destination."

53

Aggie kicked aside a broken, slate-blue board. One of many littering the dark rocks. There had been houses here before the Black Rock invaded this land. Aggie sneered. Destruction and Black Rock went hand in hand. Though, part of her felt comfort in its presence. Despite the pain she associated with it, the mountain reminded her of home.

"Under here." Aggie pointed to a pile of wood and other materials that had once been the wall of a child's room. It was propped up by the sheer face of the mountain. Her brothers, the people she cared the most for in this or any world, took to it, picking up small pieces of wall and tossing them to the side.

Eliza, with Rumi still unconscious on her shoulder, stepped toward the pile and smiled; still an unnerving sight since half of her face was mechanical. "Once I find somewhere to set down my carry-on luggage, I'll go ahead and take care of this."

Eliza lay Rumi on the ground as carefully as possible. Aggie caught sight of Jamal out of the corner of her eye. He hadn't spoken since they left Max's body behind. He simply stared blankly forward, his eyes red from crying.

"Out of the way, muscle men," said Eliza to the twins as she prepared to lift the debris.

"Need a hand?"

The voice sent a rush of joy and rage through Aggie. Though both quickly cooled to irritation. She turned her head just enough to see Jack marching toward her. He resembled the Jack she had first met. Strong. Confident. Clad in a black uniform that accentuated his best features. With him were twenty or so people, none of whom she recognized. One of them was translucent.

"Allow me." Jack, with a face Aggie once saw as heroic- now smug, false -placed his hands against his hips and the debris floated a few feet to the side, revealing a small wooden door embedded in the side of the mountain. Then he turned to Eliza and winked. "Hey there. It's been a while." He noticed Rumi for the first time, lying on the ground, lifeless. "And...wait, is that...?! I thought she died! Is she okay?!"

"Never better," was Eliza's response. "What now, Aggz?"

"Grab Rumi," Aggie said. "Osip. Oleg. Jamal. Come." Without so much as a look to Jack and his crowd, Aggie opened the door and entered Black Rock.

It seemed like a lifetime since Aggie had last ascended the dark, narrow, stone staircase carved from the guts of the mountain. She had been part of a procession of horrified women forced to parade themselves in front of an evil overlord so that he might name one his bride. Now she led a group of friends and strangers to the same great hall, this time, ironically, as a safe haven. A place to recover. Her brothers, young but old enough to understand the horrors of the recent past, clung to her as they ascended.

"Excuse me. Pardon me. Excuse me," said Jack as he made his way up the stairs toward Aggie.

She could feel Osip and Oleg's tension fade as Jack caught up to them. He had been their hero. The thought deepened her distaste.

"Aggie," Jack began, all smiles. "Are you okay? I missed you so much."

"Never better," she replied dryly. She picked up her pace but, with the twins weighing her down, he easily kept up.

"Come on, Aggie!" he pushed. "What's wrong? I have some people I want to introduce you to!"

At that, Aggie stopped, forcing Eliza, Jamal and the others to come to an abrupt halt as well.

"Do you even remember?" she asked through clenched teeth and lips curled into a frown. "Do you recall your visits in these past weeks? Popping in at all hours of the day or night, mumbling nonsense, disrupting our peace, embarrassing yourself like some sort of drunken animal?"

"I..." It was clear from Jack's expression he did not. "I'm sorry, Aggie. I- I was depressed. Being in Addley, away from Reverie. Away from you! So I- I took some pills to be with you. To make me sleep, but..." Jack shook off the sadness creeping across his face, replacing it with a veneer of hopefulness. "But I'm better now!"

"You are welcome for that!" echoed a voice from farther down the stairs.

Jack continued, "I'm me again! And I rescued some people-"

"Ha!" Aggie shook her head. "You?" Aggie took Jack by the chin. "This is not you, Jack. I have seen you. You are a skinny boy in a man's body. This thing I see before me is a costume. A mask. Something you hide behind because you hate your truth. You hate yourself." Aggie released him. "I have no place in my heart for liars, Jack. And, even if I did, there are things much bigger than us to tend to now."

Aggie took her brothers by their hands and sped up the

stairs. This time Jack didn't try to keep up.

54

"Damn it! Damn it! Damn it!" Anza slammed her fist against the damp, green earth. She was on her hands and knees after losing her balance from being unexpectedly teleported.

And Guilly...

Anza found herself in a jungle, thick with thin-trunked trees that twisted upward and disappeared into a canopy of green and purple leaves. Colorful flowers of all shapes and sizes flaunted their lush petals. It was overwhelming. All of it. Everything was new. Every sight. Every smell. Not to mention she had just failed at the thing she had been trained her whole life to do. Nihilo made a fool of her in minutes, Guillelmina was gone and her uncle Patrick sent her away to this jungle.

The grobi rubbed its furry head against her thigh. Anza patted its head and rose to her feet, her legs and arms covered in mud. She examined herself. Her clothing sparkled like Core Substance. There was nothing inconspicuous about it and, honestly, all she wanted to do was disappear. With a thought her shirt turned forest green and her pants, tree trunk brown. She picked up her sword from the ground and wiped it off.

"Now what?" she said aloud. Through the dense jungle she could see houses and streets. To the grobi, she said, "Where are we? Is this where you're from, little guy?" The grobi purred as it cleaned its large ears. "You could take me right back to Nihilo, if I wanted, huh? But what good would that do? You could teleport us right into the middle of that black death ball he turned into. What was he even talking about?" Anza leaned against one of the twisted trees and sighed. "I let everyone down."

A sound, many sounds, rose from the general din of the madness happening all over. They were soft, but firm. A dozen puckering sounds in the mud. Anza turned to notice eight creatures she had definitely never learned about on her flashcards. They stood easily ten feet tall. Their bodies were like that of a horse, but where normally one would find the head, there was a human torso, arms, and head. There was a mix of male and female.

"Trespasser," said the one in the front. His horse half had pale gray fur. His human hair was black and his eyes, a cool blue. A beautiful beast were it not for the bow and arrow he had pointed at her. "I am Nikkylos, King of the Centaur of Pholos. In the Great Undoing, we have claimed this land as our own."

Centaur. The word did sound familiar. Like something from Guilly's stories before such things ended and the training began. *Oh my God, Guilly*, she thought. *Did Nihilo- No. I can't think about this right now.*

"I'm sorry," said Anza with a slight bow. "I didn't know. I'll just be on my way." She reached for the grobi.

"Stop," Nikkylos commanded. "You are going nowhere. You could be a scout, a spy. And my centaurs have suffered far too much for me to risk leniency. You must die."

Anza pulled her hand away from the grobi. Then clenched it to a fist. Despite her current feelings of doubt, of shame, of failure, she bled and she sweat for years to take down the ultimate threat to all of existence. And despite feeling utterly useless at the moment, she remembered her uncle's words of advice, when Guilly had pushed her to the limit and she thought she couldn't go on: Fake it 'til you make it.

Anza glared at the centaur king with her piercing green eyes. "Do you know who I am?" she asked. "I am growth." The trees around them began to quake. "I am desire." Despite their discomfort, all the centaurs but Nikkylos lowered their weapons, enamoured with her. "I AM THE CHOSEN ONE!"

Nikkylos let loose his arrow, but it passed through Anza as if she were air.

The trees came alive and snaked downward, wrapping themselves around the centaurs who, aside from Nikkylos, did not fight it. In fact, they relished the embrace.

"What are you?" said the centaur king as he struggled to break free. "What have you done to my people?!" Then, in an instant, his expression betrayed him. His youth showed. "Please," he said, his voice weighed by melancholy, "don't hurt them. They've been through so much. We've lost everything. Everyone. Please, show mercy..."

Anza waved her hand and the trees released them. Her enchantment lifted from the minds of Nikkylos' seven remaining subjects.

"Thank you," said Nikkylos. He added, "Chosen One."

"Call me Anza," she said. "I was sent here to save us all. To stop this Great Undoing, as you call it. But I failed. He was too strong. Too strong."

"An-za," Nikkylos pronounced, confidence returning to his voice with each word, "point us in the direction of this foe. We have little, but if your words are true, allow us to lend hoof and hand in taking down the one who is to blame for this."

55

Olokun, goddess of the unknown, the dark depths of the sea and dreams, had, over the millennia, abducted thirty gods of life and death for her experiments. Gods were hearty creatures, immortal and durable, each with their own unique genetic properties. It took a couple thousand years of intense scientific study to crack them all. Now she stood with the distilled essence of forty-five gods inside of her, experiencing power unlike anything she had ever felt. She looked at the empty vial in her hand, lined in glowing blue residue, satisfied. She placed it on a wooden table in her dark, fire-lit living room and reveled in her power.

"Now what?" The shrill, intrusive voice pulled Olokun from her bliss. Satya, the girl she had invited to her home, was staring into a scrying mirror, gasping and shouting and ceaselessly yapping about the events in Addley.

Events Olokun no longer cared about.

As Satya watched, she jotted notes upon notes. She would move from one moment to the next, bidding the mirror to keep track of every being she thought important to this tale.

"Nihilo's big, dark sphere is growing and destroying everything!" she said. "Anza is in a jungle with centaur! Ezekiel disappeared, but-!"

"Enough," said Olokun in a low, measured tone. "I am beyond such things. And, so you understand, it's not Nihilo's orb, the orb is Nihilo. Using Speck as a conduit, he merged with the dimensional tear I created, expanding the void into a bubble spreading outward to devour all of existence. It's basic science, dear."

"You have to do something!" Satya pleaded.

"Clearly," Olokun replied. She let the conversation drop there.

Satya placed the mirror on the carpet near the fireplace and marched to Olokun, looking up at her with her serious, human eyes that were in stark contrast to the stupid cartoon cat and penguin on her T-shirt. "You have to go down there and save them."

Olokun feigned a yawn. "Do I? In four thousand years of enduring humanity, I must say I'm not so sure."

Olokun silently observed as Satya went through a plethora of very intense emotions before her. Her brown skin reddened and she stood on her toes to close the height divide between them before saying, "Then I'll go. Send me back."

Olokun raised an eyebrow then flicked her wrist and a spiralling portal of black appeared before Satya. "Then go. Simply imagine a place you wish to go, a person you wish to go to. That's that."

Satya nodded and stepped toward the portal, but stopped short of entering. She turned to Olokun and said, "I can see the truth behind your eyes when you talk about humans. It's not hatred, it's hurt. And I can't begin to know your experiences, but I'm a brown woman raised by lesbian, immigrant parents. I get how cruel the world can be. But there's good, too. Much more good. Like the people who are down there fighting for their lives to clean up the mess you-"

A dark blue tentacle wrapped around Satya and pulled her into the portal. Olokun had heard enough.

The goddess ran her hand along her wooden table as she

moved toward her favorite chair near the fireplace. It was then that she realized the vial, empty except for that glowing blue residue, was no longer there.

56

Claire paced back and forth in her living room. "It's not fair, Mom. There's a world at war on the other side of this door and we're not doing anything about it. Our friends are out there. Anne is out there!"

"And my parents," Victor realized as he said it aloud. "My parents are at the hospital. What if they're in trouble?"

Karen stood in front of the front door, her arms stretched wide and her black, sightless eyes searching for Claire and Victor. She was not pleased. "And tell me, children, what do you plan on doing when you're out there, huh? What could you possibly do to stop a war?"

"I, uh…" Victor looked around and noticed his sword on the floor near the dining room. "I have a sword."

Karen laughed. "Yes, your master swordsmanship did wonders when those things ruined my house. The hospital is on the other side of town. You'd never make it."

Victor raised his voice. "With all respect, Mrs. Ashford, your daughter and I survived for months in Reverie, with Anza, and-"

The door swung open sending Karen stumbling forward, catching herself on an old coat rack only to tumble over with it. Claire, of Reverie, entered in a huff, beautiful as ever. She closed the door behind her and calmed at the sight of her other. "You're safe. Thank God."

The other Claire was too busy helping her mother to her feet to pay the other much mind.

"Look who came crawling back," sneered Karen.

"Shut up, Karen." Claire ran her hand through her lush blonde hair. "And you're welcome, by the way, for stopping a nuclear apocalypse from falling on this waste-of-literally-everyone's-time town."

A hard knock on the door.

A louder one followed.

"Let me in, you idiots, before I change my mind!" It was Vic.

Karen closed her dark eyes. Softly, she said, "And so we have arrived."

It was Victor who opened the door and let his Reverie counterpart inside. A strange sensation accompanied a long pause as they saw each other for the first time with the same curious eyes, Victor's gleaming with wonder, Vic's darkened with hurt. Victor's hair, shoulder length and messy. Vic's, short and maintained. Victor's large T-shirt draped over his skinny frame. Vic was in full armor, accentuating his already impressive physique.

Vic looked tired, his eyes red as if he'd been crying. "I'm going to get to it," he said. "All of existence is coming to an end."

"Nihilo's plan," said Victor. "We know."

Vic sneered. "Congratulations. Now let me finish. While my abilities do not allow me to see into the future, per se, I can, using unsurpassed knowledge of the present, make educated guesses regarding the appropriate paths to a desired result."

Claire of Reverie threw her arms up. "Get to the point,

nerd."

To which the other Claire added, "What she said."

Vic grunted. "Ezekiel Christopher Clark."

"The Crosstown Killer?" Karen stepped closer to the children's voices.

"Yes." Vic massaged his temples. "A true monster of a man. Used to ride the rails to small towns in the tri-state area, brutally murdering people in a five-week slaughter spree that managed to take sixteen lives. Well, it turns out he's also a powerful Lucid and one of Nihilo's henchmen. Jason Baker is doing his best, but Ezekiel can't be stopped. Not like this."

"We need to take care of him," said Claire of Reverie. "The real him. Like Jason and I did with Karl, er...Aemon."

"Yes." Vic sighed. "The small obstacle being that, for the past sixteen years, Ezekiel's physical form is contained one hundred and thirty-seven miles north at the Monroe Valley Supermaximum Penitentiary."

"Then we'll go," said Victor, already reaching for his sword. "The four of us will storm the prison and...um...deal with it...somehow."

"Do you know how crazy you sound right now?" said Claire of Cosmos. "We're not in Reverie anymore. We can't just fumble our way through zany situations and hope Jack or someone will swoop in and save us."

"But they can!" Victor exclaimed, gesturing toward their Reverie counterparts. "They're everything we wish we were! Everything we're not! I mean, look at them."

Claire of Reverie laughed, dark and short.

"About that." Vic paused. He closed his eyes and frowned. He shook his head and said, "We're not going. This mission is too precise and our abilities, our personalities, are too unpredictable, too volatile to ensure success." A tear streamed down Vic's eye. "It has to be you two." He turned to Claire of Reverie, who immediately understood what it was he wasn't saying. "We do this, victory isn't guaranteed. Nothing is guaranteed. But the knowledge-"

"I'll do it," said Claire. "I'm doing it. I'm so tired of this- this constant feeling of being incomplete. Of being a reflection; a shadow. Of doing everything I can in my misguided mind to fill this void in my soul when the only thing in the universe that can complete me is…" Claire turned to her counterpart. She could feel the tears swelling in her eyes, but for once she didn't care who saw them. She looked to Vic. "You feel it, too. I know you do. I know it." She smiled a tired smile. A teardrop slipped into the crevice where her lips met. "Remember that time you stormed into my house and tried to convince me that something was wrong? That we don't belong here? I didn't want to believe you then, but you were right. That Vic, the one who was as scared as me, he was right." Claire grabbed her counterpart by the forearm and said, "I would tell you to be better than me, but you're already there. Tell Jamal he was too good for me. Also, a facemask wouldn't kill you, babe. Reverie did no favors for your pores." Claire of Reverie winked and, in a blink, was pulled into the original Claire's body. Claire, the only Claire, gasped as if she'd had all the air knocked out of her.

"What…?" Claire hunched over, her hands grabbing her knees, breathing heavily.

Victor was at her side immediately. "Claire! Claire, are you okay?"

"I'm fine," she said. She stood up.

"What's happening?" Karen asked. "What happened to my baby girl?"

"Claire- the other Claire -is gone," said Victor.

"Not gone," said Vic, his voice soft and uneven. "They're one now. Like it was in the beginning. Like...it's supposed to be." Vic let out an angry scream and kicked over a small table with an expensive-looking lamp.

"What's happening now?!" Karen shrieked.

"Nothing," Victor said calmly. "It's okay."

"Is it?" Vic snapped back. "All I wanted was freedom. Freedom from a mediocre, uninspired life. Freedom from you, Victor. You'd think for the person who holds the knowledge of the entire universe, that, of all things, would be a goal easily obtained. But it would seem that knowledge is worthless when at odds with fate. Somehow you are the one the universe favors, Victor Soto."

"Y-you don't have to do this." Victor was practically pleading. "When I reunited with my parents, I knew they were happy I wasn't dead, but I could tell, I could *tell* -they were disappointed that you weren't their real son. I'm a loser, Vic, but you- I could ask you something like, 'How do you cure cancer?' and you know it, right? You know it!" Vic offered a somber nod. "See? Why would the universe want me?" Victor wiped his eyes. "Why would anyone?"

"You are making excellent points," Vic said. "Surprisingly so, I must say. But here's the truth: I couldn't care less about cancer cures or starving children in Appalachia or whatever.

My singular aim is to be powerful, perfect, and, most importantly, not you. That's why you created me in the first place."

"You dumb idiot." Claire slipped her fingers between Victor's. "You built this guy to be everything you're not, but forgot all the parts of you that make you the best." She placed her palm against his chest. "Your heart. You are the kindest, sweetest guy I have ever met. And I want you, Victor Soto. You gave me hope in a hopeless place. You saved my life."

"I love you, Claire Ashford." Victor blurted it out.

Claire blushed. She looked to her mother who, for once, remained silent. She squeezed Victor's hand and said, "Me too."

Vic cleared his throat. He had removed one of the gloves from his battle suit and now stretched his bare hand to Victor. "There is nothing I am that you are not capable of manifesting, you sensitive nerd. Now, please, spare me all this YA romance and just promise not to disappoint me."

Victor took Vic's hand in his and, just like that, there were only Claire Ashford and Victor Soto. Complete, perhaps, for the first time in their lives.

"All right," Karen announced. "You may go now."

57

It was another hour before Aggie reached the top of the staircase. There was a flat surface with nothing of note besides the crumbled ruins of a statue. To the left was the entrance to the great hall: two marble doors, each one two-feet thick. The entrance was tall and wide enough for one of those houses outside to easily fit through. Aggie remembered how utterly small she had felt the first time she'd seen these doors.

Voices could be heard from inside the hall. Aggie felt stupid then, for assuming she would have been the only one to come here. Jack had the same idea, after all. This led her to believe these people were also familiar with the place. So familiar, in fact, they'd entered from an entrance even she didn't know existed. Aggie sighed. That narrowed down the options significantly.

"What the zagging zag happened?" Rumi had just woken up.

Aggie watched Eliza place Rumi on her feet. "You passed out," said Eliza. "You were really tired."

"I knocked you out," Aggie added. "Unrested, you were useless."

Rumi pressed her finger against Aggie's chest. "You and I are going to have a talk about that, lady. But first, what did I miss?"

"Rumi?" Jack stepped forward, leaving behind the translucent man and a girl with thick glasses and buck teeth.

"Jack?" Rumi's eyes widened.

The two hugged.

"I'm so glad you're up!" he said, his voice cracking under the emotion. "I have so many things I need to say to you! I thought you were dead! I thought I let you die!"

"Oh please," said Rumi. "A dozen robots exploding over my broken body is just another Tuesday for Rumi Inyonara."

They hugged again.

"Oh!" Jack took Rumi by the arm and led her to his companions. "This is my brother Bobby and this is Anne. Oh and here's…"

Aggie turned her focus from that conversation, pushing back the feelings of jealousy and betrayal that came with it. They would not serve her well right now.

Eliza put her robot finger to her lips. "Shh! Could you all shut your food processors? We ain't alone up here."

Aggie walked away from all of them and entered the great hall. Her brothers followed, quietly. The space was massive; most of it was lost in shadow. Groups of huddled people (and other, stranger creatures) convened around single torchlights, chattering softly, their voices creating echoes that were swallowed by the cavernous space.

Nearest to Aggie were three men. They didn't need a torch as the tallest of them, a muscular warrior with a broadsword, emitted a soft yellow light. The warrior dwarfed the man beside him. He was small with a slight hunch, his face covered in wrinkles and a mustache. The third person, dressed in peasant's clothes with indigo skin and long black hair tied into a ponytail was someone all too familiar. Aemon turned to Aggie and offered a small smile.

"It's fine," she said to her brothers as Aemon bent down to kiss the old mustached man on the forehead. He shook the hand of the glowing man with the sword and then headed to Aggie.

It seemed like an eternity, the twenty or so steps Aemon took to reach her. "Agalfia Tirk," he began. "Is Mindy with you?" Aggie did her best to ignore the ache she saw in his eyes.

In a flash, Jack put himself between the two. To Aggie, he said, "What's going on? Are you okay?"

Aggie offered Jack her iciest glare and, with force and grace, pushed him aside. She closed the distance between herself and Aemon. "No." While Aggie had not examined each person who had come with Jack, she was certain Mindy would have immediately made herself known.

Aemon sighed. She did not fully trust him- she never would, most likely -but one could not feign the genuine melancholy in his body language. "I brought her people here, to be safe, because that's what she would have wanted," he said. As he searched for his next words, a dozen footsteps against marble sounded from behind her. Rumi and the rest were entering the hall. "Aggie," Aemon continued, "did you poison me?"

"No, my rage would not have been so subtle," she said, holding her brothers just a little tighter. "How are you faring?"

"Not perfect, but well enough." Aemon shook his head and waved his hand in front of him, as if wiping something away. "It doesn't matter. It doesn't. You were hurting. I have the face of your greatest enemy. I'm trying. I'm-" He paused, again, to think. "Mindy told me what happened to her. As a child. She told me about your fight. What I'm saying is, I banished the goblins. Even Peeps. I told them they had to find their own way. That their journey for peace didn't lie with us." He inhaled deeply, exhaled deeply. "I wanted to find you, to apologize, but we're past that. Reverie is broken. My friend there..." He gestured to the large muscular man with the sword. "Baldr, he's called. Apparently, a god of the north. He once worked for the enemy. He told us of a creature called Nihilo, the mastermind behind this chaos. It is almost too much to comprehend."

"Do you trust him?" Aggie asked.

Aemon shrugged, almost helpless. "He followed us here and we still live. That's the closest thing to trust I can conjure right now."

Aggie nodded. Then shouted, "You!" to Baldr. "Get over here." Those by the torchlights turned as well. Muffled whispers of Aggie's name speckled the still air. She had been part of their caravan once. Softer, Aggie called at once Eliza, Rumi, Jamal, and even Jack to her side.

Once they were together Baldr told them all he knew. He told them of Olokun and how she spared his life under the condition that she betray Nihilo, of the manifestations, of Arbitryx and his legion of black-clad yazata, of a baby destined to save everything, of Nihilo's master plan and how he twisted innocent creatures into horrifying monsters in his war to destroy all things.

"Baldr," said a voice, almost melodic. Aggie had not noticed until now that someone else had invited himself into her private circle. He was young and undeniably handsome, with thick locks of curly black hair and eyes deep and red. The clothing he wore was an eruption of colors and sharp design.

He kept his attention squarely on the god of the north. "The last time we met- the last hundred times, actually -you tried to kill me because, correct me if I'm wrong, it is easier to hate me than it is to hate yourself for killing your son."

Baldr's glacier-blue eyes narrowed and his face reddened. His hand tightened around the hilt of his broadsword.

"I am only saying this," he continued, "because in these end times I need to know you can put this history behind us. Bury it in the millennia where it belongs." To the others, he chimed, "I am Dion, by the way."

Baldr grunted. "I gave Olokun my word I would not hurt you."

Dion grinned a toothy grin and leaned to Rumi as if telling a secret. "Gotta love that Ollie, am I right?" He laughed. Aggie felt the strange and sudden urge to laugh, too, but stayed herself.

"You're Jason's guy, huh?" Rumi remarked. "He mentioned you a couple of times during the last battle."

Dion nodded. "I am indeed. But, alas, ever the hero, my beloved Lucid is off searching for his beloved Mindy."

Aggie saw relief wash over Aemon.

Just then another familiar face entered the circle. It was Pasqual, with his warm eyes and stern expression. He, Rumi, and Eliza had their heartfelt reunion. "I was examining the structural fortitude of this hall," he said. "It's good to see you all."

The translucent one (Jack's dead brother Bobby, apparently) and the girl with the glasses called Anne, joined as well.

"We are quite the motley cast of characters," said Dion. "And I should know. I am the god of theater, after all." He turned to Jamal for a reaction, but received none. "Jamal, where is the fire I have grown accustomed to from you?"

Jamal lowered his head. "Max is dead."

"Max, no." Dion looked to the others, to Aggie. Her eyes confirmed it. "I'm so, so sorry. I promise his death will not be in vain." Dion slipped into the center of the circle, addressing all with a sharp sense of urgency. "I am moved to believe that each of us is not the sort to stand by relying on some baby to save us from utter annihilation. Furthermore, Nihilo seems to have amassed quite the force of power. I submit to you all that it behooves us greatly to amplify our own-"

"Get to the point, man" said Eliza.

"Fair enough, dear talking robot." Dion cleared his throat. "The three realms are one. Human dreams on Earth create fantastical things in Reverie. But if Reverie is on Earth then humans, hypothetically, should be able to create fantastical things here. If Nihilo can terrify humans into becoming his servants, then we can empassion humans into becoming their own saviors. Fortunately for you, I am gifted with the ability to empassion, to make people open themselves to their dearest-"

"Enough," said Baldr.

"Okay, okay. Fine. Annabelle, if you please." Dion pulled Annabelle into the center of the circle with him. "Close your eyes and think about your best, most badass self. Your most powerful inner gladiator Amazon feminista warrior woman!"

"Uh...okay." Anne closed her eyes.

Aggie watched with much skepticism as Dion placed his forehead against hers and began to utter words she could not understand. The others also watched silently, lit only in Baldr's golden glow. It was subtle at first. Anne seemed a little taller. A little wider. And then the changes came quick. The gray, stony skin. The sharp-toothed underbite. The muscles upon muscles. The spiked club in her giant, rough, clawed hands. The burlap tunic and big bulging eyes.

Dion was pushed to the edge of the circle by her sheer girth. "Uh...maybe I need to recalculate…"

"No, this is perfect!" said a beastly Anne in a monstrous, garbled voice. "This is exactly what I wanted! It's the character I play in this online fantasy RPG. Glug the Troll: Ogre-Crusher. This is so so cool!"

Even after everything, Aggie could not believe what she had just seen. Judging by the others' expressions, including Dion's, she was not alone in that.

Dion stepped away from the circle and addressed the others in the hall. "Creatures of the Realms, line up! Become your best selves! Save the world!"

58

The centaur watched in quiet awe as Anza's crystal sword floated in the air in front of her. She was focusing hard on the item, taking in its texture, its every line, corner and curve. The centaur looked on as the sword began to change shape, elongating and in both directions, bending slightly, a thin strand connecting one end to another. What was once a sword had become a beautiful bow. The centaur gasped when one bow became two, two became four, four became eight. Each one floated to one of the centaur.

"Here you go," she said. "Tough, unbreakable. They should last forever. I'll get to work on some arrows next."

The patch of jungle Anza had found herself in offered excellent cover from the rest of Addley. She decided that if they were going to fight, she should use her abilities to arm them properly. She had come to the notion that she had not been overpowered so much as taken by surprise. This time she would be prepared for anything.

"My king," said a female centaur with copper fur golden hair in a hushed tone, clutching her new shiny weapon. "Someone is coming."

Anza turned in the direction the centaur had gestured. Someone had stepped out of the suburban neighborhood and into their jungle hideaway. A girl. In one hand she held a dagger made of- could it be? -Core Substance. In the other she held something silvery that gave off a powerful glow.

The grobi growled.

"What should we do, my king?" asked a centaur.

"Hold," Anza replied.

The girl stopped when she was close enough to notice Anza and the centaur. Anza then realized that the silvery item she was carrying was a head. A woman's head. Her shock was only abated by the fact that the head seemed to be alive, its eyes peering forward, its lips pursed.

Before Anza could speak, Nikkylos stepped forward on his thick horse legs and, with no small hint of adoration, said, "Mindy?"

Anza followed Nikkylos to Mindy. She had auburn hair and green eyes. Despite her torn clothes and the rank smell they gave off, she was beautiful. It was clear from their first exchanged words that Mindy and Nikkylos had a complicated relationship. As they spoke of battles, of an uncle lost to wounds of war, Anza's eyes met those of the severed head.

"Darling," said the head. "I must say I am surprised. I came here to find my family; my beloved manifestations. I followed the scent of their essence and, to my surprise, I am led to you." The head paused before saying, "Anza."

"Who are you?" Anza asked.

"Vita," the head replied. "Manifestation of existence; of all that is and will ever be. Guillelmina's absurd gambit paid off, I see. But what of my Initia and Somni?"

Mindy and Nikkylos had finished their reunion. Their attention turned to Vita and Anza.

"They're gone," Anza said, ashamed but she didn't quite know why. She had heard of Vita, of course. The oldest of the manifestations, Nihilo's counterpart. The toughest, according to many. "They offered themselves to me," she continued. "The world was ending and they gave me their power. They are a part of me. They sacrificed themselves."

Vita's face was unreadable. Her eyes that glistened like starlight darted one way. Then the next. She closed her eyes. "So be it," she said. "Bring me to your face, Anza. Let me have a clear look at the thing we created."

Anza willed Vita's head out of Mindy's arms. It floated to Anza so that Vita's line of sight was aligned with hers. Vita examined her. And in that moment she felt a wholeness like nothing she had felt before.

"You are the best parts of your father and mother," Vita said with a faint smile. "The best of all of us, I hope."

"Nihilo absorbed Mortem and Timor." The words practically leapt from Anza's mouth. "I tried to face him, but I failed! I wasn't enough!"

"Because you weren't complete, darling," Vita said. "Growth and desire cannot thrive in a vacuum. They cannot take hold of a soul that does not exist. I am Nihilo's counter, his foe, his greatest adversary. I am what he fears the most. Or, at least, I was." Vita began to glow, so brightly that Mindy and Nikkylos had to shield their eyes. Brighter, brighter, until everything was bathed in white. And, shortly after when the light faded, Vita was gone.

Anza felt a new power coursing through her. One that allowed her to feel the presence of every tree, every pebble, every thread and ant and cell and molecule around her as dearly as if they were her own. In this surge of realization, connecting to all that existed, she felt a great, expanding emptiness; a threat to the supreme glory of the world and the universe that housed it. Nihilo.

Anza turned to Mindy. "Queen Mindy Sparks, it's an honor to meet you. My name is Esperanza Ashford-Soto. Will you help us?"

59

There was darkness. It was warm and enticing, a welcome reprieve from the pain, the sting of failure. It was almost too much to bear. No, not almost. He was so tired. His final memories- at least that's how they felt -were of his best friend and his lost love.

And then a new sensation came. It was strange. He became aware of his teeth, his tongue, as something forced its way into his mouth. The unwanted discomfort of the invasion quickly gave way to something else. Life, but not in the bland, trivial, usual sense. This was life at its core, the building block of all things. Death, too. He tasted a trillion lifetimes at once.

It was then that he opened his eyes.

An endless sea of bent and broken cornstalks loomed over him. He caught a glance of his arm, drenched in blood. His blood. The bone was mending itself, accompanied by the expected agony. His leg twisted itself to its proper place. Wounds were closing.

A reddish-brown figure pulled its finger out of his mouth. Gross. The owner of the finger was a young woman; someone he'd never seen before. She had curious eyes and black hair. A jean jacket and T-shirt with a cartoon cat and penguin. In her other hand was an empty vial.

"I'm Satya," she said. "Sorry, but my finger was the only way I could get the stuff out of this bottle."

"I'm...I'm..." He couldn't quite get the words out.

"Jason Baker," she said, to his surprise. "It's working. You're healing. But while you do, let me tell you what's going on."

Jason listened to Satya's long and wild tale as he returned to full consciousness, to full health. And then, as the contents of Olokun's vial continued its work on him and the broken stalks of corn began to mend themselves around him and the sun filled him with more energy than he had felt before, Jason climbed to his feet.

Jason looked at his hands, the veins beneath his skin seemed to be coursing with light. He knew what he had to do.

60

The sun was beginning to set.

The giant, black sphere, had now grown to roughly the diameter of a basketball court. Everything that had once been in its way, the fountain, the statue of John Addley, and decent chunks of the brick post office and other shops, had been devoured; destroyed forever. The sphere was embedded in the ground, growing in all directions. Dark jagged arms reached out from it, stretching down roads and around corners, deleting anything they touched.

Surrounding the sphere were a few hundred creatures. They were literally the stuff of nightmares, all gray and ghastly, red-eyed and sharp-toothed.

This was the scene that Esperanza Ashford-Soto charged into on the back of the centaur, Nikkylos, crystalline sword held high above her head. She screamed something primal. The sort of sound someone could only produce when facing their destiny. The sound was emulated by Nikkylos and the seven other brave centaurs, all of whom wore armor crafted from the Core Substance. The same went for Mindy Sparks who rode atop a female centaur beside Anza.

"Stay close to me," said Anza. "I feel a dark power in the air. It's pressing toward us but my powers are holding it back."

"Understood. And remember the plan," barked Nikkylos just as the nightmares noticed them coming. The dark winged things had been watching them for some time already. "Maintain tight ranks but keep enough space to maneuver around the tentacles. Above all, protect Anza."

Anza turned to Mindy. "Are you scared, Queen Mindy?"

"Always," she said, then grinned and lifted her dagger. Anza, too, smiled then.

The seven centaurs changed formation, surrounding Anza and Nikkylos. They successfully dodged the swift, erratic intrusion of one of the sphere's many arms. The centaurs in front used their sheer strength to plow through the nightmares blocking their path as the ones on the side and behind let loose arrow after crystal arrow at the creatures on the ground and the ones coming in from above. Mindy produced them on the fly with the Core Substance they'd brought along.

It wasn't easy, but they did it. The centaur leading the charge broke off in either direction as the path had been cleared to the sphere. Nikkylos trotted forward and Anza leapt from his back.

Anza paused for a moment, in awe of the black shape before her. It was without texture or depth, just like the monster it had once been. She looked to the ground and saw how it was expanding, eating, eating away at reality itself. She stood about ten feet from it, but that distance was closing.

"Are you ready?" Nikkylos asked.

Anza shook her head. "I don't know. But that kinda doesn't matter at this point now, does it?" She faced the sphere and extended her arms toward it. "Just keep these things away from me."

"FOR PHOLOS!" cried Nikkylos as he turned and joined the rest in battle with the enemy.

...

Anza focused on the deep, terrifying void. She could feel her body reacting to it, every cell empowered by the beings who sacrificed themselves to her. Her entire being hungered for life, for completion, for the opportunity to combat this-

Ka-thunk!

A golden spear barely missed Anza's shoulder and landed a few feet in front of her, in the ground, between herself and the sphere. Her concentration was broken.

A scream, Mindy's, caused her to turn around just as she saw an orange-skinned monster with massive claws tackle the Queen and the centaur she rode on to the ground. She lost sight of both in the battle.

The other centaurs weren't faring well, either. It was less a matter of their skill, which was great, and more the fact that they were so vastly outnumbered. A yazata swooped down and lifted a centaur into the air, tossing it out of sight.

"Not again," Anza thought aloud.

A creature with a deep purple cape, pale skin, and bloodied fangs materialized before Anza in a cloud of smoke. As the creature opened its mouth, a translucent blur tackled the monster to the ground. Anza was filled with joy as her uncle Patrick sat atop it, punching it in the face until it returned to smoke and drifted toward a centaur.

"We have to get out of here!" said Patrick as he jumped to his feet. He pointed to the grobi. "Grab that thing and-"

"We can't," Anza replied. She looked to the centaur who were bruised and beaten, grunting and howling mere feet away from her as they created an ever-weakening wall between her and the monsters. "I can't run again."

"Better that than die!" he exclaimed.

A centaur went down and something purple and slimy creeped over it toward Anza and Patrick. The smoke creature reformed underneath another centaur. And, behind her, the sphere was almost at her back.

Anza lifted her sword from the ground with her mind and sent it flying, tearing through the slime and the smoke creature and the nearest yazata and anything else she could. She yelled as she did this- stabbing, slicing, slashing -but it was no use. The damage she caused wasn't enough. There was no victory. Not like this.

But she was enflamed with rage and guilt and would not run. She would not stop this time.

"GAAARAAAGHHHHH!"

A roar thundered from the distance; somewhere beyond the wall of monsters closing in on her.

Patrick picked the grobi from the ground and pressed it against Anza's chest. "Get her out of here!"

But Anza made herself intangible just as the grobi activated its gift and the grobi disappeared with Patrick, leaving her behind.

"GAARARAAASGHH" The roar was closer now.

Some of the nightmares turned away from Anza in response to the sound. Even the airborne yazata shifted their focus to something out of her line of sight. She heard voices shouting things she could not understand. Then fighting.

The green, slimy monster rolled closer to Anza and began to rise up and take humanoid shape. The smoke monster, too, reached its tangible form and moved in on her. Anza thrusted her sword into the smoke monsters' narrow head, but it didn't faze it.

"GAAARAUUGH!!" An enormous gray beast landed with a great quaking thud, between Anza and her attackers and the surviving centaur that still fought on. The beast grabbed the smoke monster in one hand and scooped up half of the slime monster with the other and tossed them far away. "THE HEROES HAVE ARRIVED!" it hollered in an awkward, deep voice.

Patrick and the grobi reappeared. "Anza! We have to-!"

"Patrick?" said the gray beast in a very female human way. Then it backhanded a yazata swooping in to attack. Patrick looked at it confused. "It's me. Anne," the beast said. "How are you here? Why are you here?! Claire said you were off with…" Then the beast looked to Anza. "Oh my God."

61

Jason Baker couldn't quite tell what was different about himself. All he knew was that he had almost died. Then some girl fed him some mystical god-blend with her finger-gross -and told him an insane tale about the end of the world. He was healed and very much alive. More than alive somehow. Even before he crossed the threshold back into the merged realms and got his Lucid powers back, there was something different about him and the way he experienced the world; like he had been viewing it in standard format and now everything was in 4K IMAX HD.

Jason pictured Ezekiel in his head and- poof -he found himself immediately hovering in the sky behind him this time, unnoticed. Jason was going to speak, but then observed Addley from above. Entire blocks had been destroyed, pulled into massive sunken pits. He could hear the agonizing cries even from his altitude. But it was more than that. He felt them, thousands of living things in pain, their very life essence slowly draining out of them. This was Ezekiel's doing.

"Hey!" Jason shouted, startling the mass murderer floating not eight feet in front of him. Ezekiel turned around, wearing a ghastly grin, cigar hanging from his mouth. "This ends now."

Ezekiel erupted into phlegmy laughter. "I couldn't agree more, kid." Ezekiel's eyes narrowed and Jason was suddenly overcome with excruciating pain.

Jason felt as if his entire body was being pulled apart. His head, his limbs, his muscles, his joints were all being yanked in different directions. It took everything Jason had just to hold himself together.

"I'm gonna do to you what you did to those gnomes," Ezekiel said. "And when I'm done collapsing you into a bloody lump." He turned his attention to the center of town, where a giant black ball was devouring the world and hundreds of people (and other things) fought. "I'm gonna do the same to all your little friends."

"N-no," Jason managed a single word through clenched teeth. His skin was beet-red. He was dripping with sweat. Jason had cheated death once before. He could do it again. He locked eyes with Ezekiel, furious at the man who manipulated him, taunted him, and took up too much of his damn time.

Then he noticed something; he could sense the life in Ezekiel. It was like an aura, an iridescent energy. And from that aura he saw a long thin cord made of the same stuff, reaching out into the distance.

Instinctively, Jason knew this was the strand of consciousness that connected this Ezekiel to the Ezekiel who was dreaming, hundreds of miles away. More than that, he could see and feel the anger and hate inside of him. The fear of his father, the gruesome things he had done...but there was no time to dwell on that.

With what little concentration he could spare, Jason focused on the cord. He applied a little pressure to it and, to his surprise, Ezekiel's form flickered. Ezekiel's grip on Jason weakened, allowing Jason to apply a little more pressure. And a little more. Another push and the cord broke and Ezekiel disappeared.

Exhausted and relieved, Jason Baker flew toward one of the sinkholes, following the aura of the dying. He had lives to save before Ezekiel's inevitable return.

Arbitryx, the solemn-faced leader of the shadow yazata, stood atop a parking garage, watching the world fall apart all around him. He looked upon the growing black sphere and its hungry arms as more and more joined the futile battle. He heard heavy footsteps approaching from behind. "He really did it," Arbitryx said.

"He did," said Baldr, moving to Arbitryx's side, both looking at the sphere. "If he succeeds, we're all dead."

"That we are," the yazata concurred. "I'll be the first to admit, I thought it was impossible. I was merely using the old shadow in the off-chance he'd sow enough chaos so that I might free my yazata from eternal servitude in Eternia. And there he was using my lack of confidence in his plan against me and my people. I must admit I am displeased."

"Hm." Baldr nodded, then added, "I betrayed him and took his plan to the humans."

"Ah." Arbitryx smiled. A little. "I was wondering where that army of colorful characters came from. Nice work. But will it be enough?"

"I cannot say. We have to believe Initia and the other manifestations had their own tricks...before he killed them all."

Arbitryx scoffed. "Like the baby?"

Baldr shrugged. "There is also Olokun who is more devious than all of them combined." Baldr scratched his chin. "But it would definitely help if you were to call back your men and have them fight for the other side."

Arbitryx placed his hands on his hips. "A life of eternal servitude to Eternia or no life at all."

"You can't rebel if you're dead," said Baldr. "Choose wisely." The god of truth and justice raised his sword and leapt from the rooftop toward the battle.

"Are you ready?" asked Victor as he listened to the cell phone ringing against his ear. He and Claire stood along a winding road surrounded by forest. Ironically, this was the road they'd taken to Addley after returning from Reverie.

Claire sat atop the hood of her mom's car. "For the last time, yes." She gestured for him to go on.

The phone continued to ring. Great. Victor had downloaded all the information he could think of for how this would go, but some things he couldn't control. Which is where Claire came in.

"He's ignoring the call," he said. "You're up. And remember: subtle, specific."

"Yeah, yeah." Claire thought for a second then said. "I need Elijah Peter Jones, the current warden of Monroe Valley Maximum Security Prison, to bring whatever stupid thing he's doing to a normal, natural close and answer his ringing desk phone as soon as he is able." She added, "Satisfied?"

Victor was going to respond but someone picked up the phone.

"This is Jones," said the gruff voice on the other end.

"Oh!" Victor collected himself. "Uh, hi, my name is Doctor Clive Clemmons, Chief of Psychology for the Federal Bureau of Prisons."

"Doctor?" the warden remarked, "You sound like you're twelve years old."

Victor panicked. He covered the speaker of the cell phone and whispered to Claire, "He's not buying it."

"No shit," said Claire. "I need Warden Elijah Peter Jones to feel slightly embarrassed that he would speak to Doctor Clemmons, as played by Victor Soto, in such a way."

"Aw, I apologize, sir," said the warden. "I'm letting this place get to me."

"Happens to the best of us," said Victor, trying to sound a bit more grown up. He gestured to Claire.

Claire rolled her eyes and continued. "Now fraught with embarrassment, I need the Warden to believe everything Victor Soto tells him for the duration of this phone call to make up for how rude he was."

"As I was saying," Victor continued, "the Bureau is conducting research on the, um, restorative properties of taking mass murderers out of solitary confinement and placing them into a room with four to five inmates they've disagreed with in the past to, uh, talk it out. After much research we've selected Ezekiel Christopher Clark to be one of our test subjects."

There was a pause. Then the warden said, "Some of the guys in here really want a piece of Ezekiel. He's pissed a lot of people off, inside and outside of this place."

Victor looked to Claire who only gestured for him to keep talking. "Yes. That's right. It's risky, but with great risk comes great reward, as they say!" Victor noticed Claire gesturing for him to wrap it up. "Anyway, yeah, take Ezekiel out of solitary and toss him in a room with his enemies. Let the healing begin, bye!"

Victor ended the call and handed the cell phone to Claire. "So, how'd I do?"

Claire kissed him on the cheek and, with a smile, said, "You are truly the worst."

"Thank you?" said Victor, blushing.

"So," Claire took him by the arm, "What's next? How do we help?"

Vic convulsed a little, his eyes rolling back into his head. Returning, most to normal, he rapidly said, "Well, there are hundreds of people trapped in sinkholes and seventeen buildings on the verge of collapse."

"Okay." Claire was already headed for the driver's seat. "Let's do it."

62

Mindy hit the ground hard after being knocked from the back of the centaur. Fortunately her armor protected her from the worst of it. There were at least a dozen bodies, most of them enemies, clawing and kicking and punching around her. Someone stepped on her. Then someone else. She rolled out of the way in time to avoid being crushed by a centaur hoof and scooted to her feet, just avoiding the falling centaur.

She had barely found her balance when she noticed a monster charging at her. It was like a giant blue centipede except it had the torso, head, and arms of a hideous woman with patches of wild black hair. "My babiessssss," hissed the monster.

Mindy touched her hand to her crystal chest plate. The hard object reacted, coming to life. The armor transformed into ten snake-like forms that leapt from Mindy's body and wrapped themselves around the centipede-thing, tripping up its many legs and sending it skidding across the ground. A single iridescent gauntlet was the only armor Mindy had left, but the beast had been stopped.

A closer look at the incapacitated monster and it was clear by its directed clawing and gnashing, even now, that it hadn't been aiming for Mindy at all, but Anza who struggled at the black sphere's edge with only a handful of centaur left to protect her. Mindy gasped when a giant gray monster soared through the air and landed with a thud near Anza.

"It's fine," said a voice, calm and familiar.

She turned and there he was, Aemon, standing behind her with his gentle smile. He had one hand outstretched as he used his formidable power to immobilize three winged creatures in the sky. "The troll is on our side," he said. Then he added, "It is good to see you." One of the deadly black arms projecting from the sphere zigzagged overhead and instantly destroyed two of the three winged creatures.

Mindy hugged Aemon tight, tears streaming down her cheeks. "Oh, Aemon. I thought I lost you."

"Never," he said. He wiped a tear from her cheek.

Mindy nodded. The gauntlet on her forearm changed shape, becoming a blade that stretched out over her hand. "Come with me. I have to introduce you to someone."

Jamal screamed out his rage, his sadness, as he unleashed a slew of exploding blue orbs from his massive gun. They embedded themselves in the enemies that surrounded him and exploded, one by one. A small part of him felt guilty. He knew that most of these nightmare creatures had been people who were warped by Nihilo into something else. But he didn't care. This release was just what he needed. There was peace in the chaos.

The armor Jamal wore offered him a great deal of protection from the attacking enemies. He pushed through something that looked like a zombie and rammed his gun into the head of what appeared to be a clown covered in blood.

"Gagh!" He felt a sharp pain in his side. He turned just enough to see a bronze-haired yazata snarling as he pushed the blade deeper, deeper into Jamal.

FWOOOOSH!

Jamal covered his face as a torrent of flame rushed over the yazata. It took the winged terror by surprise enough for it to stumble back and pull the knife out of Jamal with it.

"You okay, dude?"

Jamal could hardly believe it; Max had his arm around Jamal's waist, helping to hold him up. Max was was dressed in his basketball outfit. And he was translucent. Jamal could see right through him.

"Max?" Jamal's mouth hung open. "How...?"

Max let loose another powerful stream of fire at the yazata as he spoke. "I think I'm dead," he said with a calm certainty that only he could. "I felt myself go away, dude. And then I popped back, but you guys were gone. And my dead body was just laying there. It was freaky, man, but then I heard all this noise so I grabbed dead-Max's gun and followed it here and...here I am!"

Jamal was so happy he could cry. But instead he put his arm around his best friend and pumped that yazata full of about a dozen exploding orbs.

Aggie, Jack, and Bobby took on a number of nightmare creatures at once. With her little brothers safe and tucked away in Black Rock, Aggie was free to unleash her true fury on the enemy, slashing and stabbing with the daggers in her hand. Jack used his Lucid skills to make two yazata slam into each other at full speed in the air. Bobby had taken a sword and shield from Black Rock and held his own as best he could.

A dark spiral of smoke rose up between the three and from

it a pair of pale, clawed hands took hold of Aggie and Jack, lifting both into the air. They barely caught sight of the fanged smile in the smoke before they were spun around and launched into the air, away from the battle.

Jack altered his trajectory just enough to evade one of the black sphere's dark tendrils. He softened his fall so that when he crashed to the broken and abandoned street he was mostly unharmed. By the time he caught sight of Aggie, she had hit the concrete hard, her bones breaking as she rolled across the surface. She then stopped, motionless.

"No!" Jack ran to her, dropping to his knees. He cupped her head in his hands. "Aggie! Aggie, wake up! Aggie, are you okay?!"

They were blocks away from the battle.

Aggie's eyes eased open. She coughed a bit of blood.

"Oh thank God!" Jack exclaimed. "It's okay, Aggie. I'll heal you. I'll heal you, I just need a little time."

Jack watched as Aggie's eyes widened. She was trying to speak, but couldn't manage the words. "What is it?" Jack asked, then followed her gaze upward. One of those jagged black arms lashed above them. It jerked to the side, cutting through an office building about twelve stories tall. The entire building lurched forward, gradually collapsing onto the road, its shadow looming over the both of them.

With every ounce of concentration, with every fiber of his being, Jack held the building in mid-collapse. Hundreds of tons of stone and steel wanted nothing more than to crush them, but Jack kept it at bay. He clenched his teeth. A snake-like vein stretched across his forehead. His purple eyes flickered, then went dark.

"Aggie..." he said as his entire body shook. "I-I don't think I can hold it much longer."

The building creaked and cracked as his hold over it weakened.

"I'm sorry, I'm so sorry," he said.

A large stone fell beside them, leaving a hole in the road.

"All I wanted to do was be your hero."

Another stone. And another.

Then Aggie took Jack by his arm. "I do not need a hero," she said. "I need Jack."

A teardrop from Jack's eye landed on Aggie's cheek. He turned to the building as the death it promised drew closer to burying them both. He removed his hands from Aggie's face. He felt his biceps grew small, then soft. And with it the building became lighter. He felt his abs fade to a skinny little belly. And with that the falling building edged away. He felt the moment that his legs lost their mobility and as his body lurched to the side, he found the strength to move the entire building with a thought, so that when it collapsed, it missed them entirely.

Surrounded by a mountain of rubble, but safe and alive, Jack, skinny and barely able to move, lay flat against the ground beside Aggie. He was short of breath, but full of joy. He turned his body to the side so that he could place his hands on Aggie. And with power he did not know he had, power he had been using in the wrong way for so long, he began to heal her.

"Now head out of town," said Jason Baker as he placed a father and young daughter at the mouth of an enormous hole that had once been an entire residential block. "Keep walking and don't turn back, okay?" He waited for the father to nod in acknowledgement before he flew back down into the hole to gather and heal more survivors.

He'd been at it for a while now, with his newfound abilities acting as a detector for any signs of life. Jason would fly to a wrecked house and use his Lucid powers to dig through it until he found every man, woman, child (and in a few cases, puppy) trapped in the result of Ezekiel's senseless attacks.

With a thought he lifted a large slab of roof and tossed it to the side. Then some walls. Under a large mahogany table that had survived the attack quite well, was an older woman in a once-lovely, dust-covered dress. As Jason floated down to rescue her, she turned to him with her black eyes.

"It took you long enough." She climbed to her feet and was trying to wipe the filth from her clothing and hair. "A sinkhole is no place for a woman of my breeding."

"Mrs. Ashford?" Jason took her hand in his. "It's Jason."

"Obviously," she said. "I may be blind, Mr. Baker, but trust me when I say I see more than all of you. You're welcome, by the way," she added. "I allowed myself to be gulped up by the earth, not to mention ruin this one-of-a-kind dress from Bezzle's, so that you and I could have this chat. You owe me a lifetime of spa days."

Jason wasn't quite sure what to say. "Let me get you out of here." He lifted her up in his arms and flew her to the mouth of the hole. "I can fly you outside of town, if you'd like."

"No, no, that won't be necessary," she said. "I can get by just fine on my own from here."

Jason had no time to argue. "Sounds good. Well, I'm off to rescue more people. It was nice seeing you."

"Wait!" said Karen in a low tone. "Ezekiel. The red-headed devil I've seen in my dreams."

Jason paused. "How do you know-?"

"Keep up, Mr. Baker, I just know!" Karen crossed her arms. "We're both busy, so I'll only say this. You keep plucking these people out of their holes. Leave Ezekiel alone."

"Wait, is he back?!" Jason's heartbeat quickened. "Is he here?! I have to stop-!"

"No!" Karen barked. Then, in a cooler voice, continued, "You've distracted him enough. When he returns, he'll be taken care of. You have to stay away. You'll have your hero moment, but it doesn't involve him."

Ezekiel was his enemy. He hated him. "And if I don't listen to you?" he challenged.

Karen shrugged and, with an easy smile, said, "That's simple, Jason. You'll kill everyone."

63

Dion stood under one of the few remaining trees that lined the sidewalk near the battle. It was important that he kept an eye on things; that he stayed within range. Considering the proximity, he had been mostly left alone and, when a stray enemy would get too close, his very capable bodyguards would take care of them.

"I'd be lying if I said I was jealous I'm not part of the fight," said Eliza, burying her robotic fist into her brown, fleshy palm.

Rumi nodded. "Fortunately, our team is crushing the living zag out of the baddies."

Pasqual, ever quiet, offered no response.

FWIP!

"Gagh!" Dion keeled over. His colorful shirt was stained in a growing circle of blood caused by the knife that had lodged itself in his chest.

"What the-!" Eliza exclaimed. "Where'd that come from?!"

Rumi grabbed Dion by the shoulders. "It's okay. We're all trained in basic combat med-work. We'll remove the blade and-"

"No," Dion said. He'd gone pale, his body trembling. "I'm sorry. I'm so, so sorry..."

Rumi and the others didn't have much time to comprehend what Dion meant before the change began. Rumi and Pasqual's eyes went dead. They stood perfectly still, for only a moment, before both were overcome with a terror so complete it caused them to collapse. The change that that began to take over their bodies was almost immediate.

"Uhh..." Eliza looked to Dion for answers. "What is happening to them?"

"Nihilo's curse," was Dion's reply. "When that rogue knife stabbed me, my concentration broke. They belong to him now..."

"Him?" Eliza rolled her eyes. "What do you mean, h-?"

BZzZzZzzzzZZT!

Eliza convulsed as her body gave off sparks. Her glowing green robot eye went black and her brown human eye rolled into the back of her head. She dropped into a crumpled pile as the thing that had once been Rumi grinned. She had plugged some fork-shaped tool into Eliza's ankle.

Rumi rose to her feet. She was easily a foot taller now. Her skin was gray and shiny, as if it were metal pretending to be flesh. Her eyes glowed red. Pasqual, or what Dion assumed to be Pasqual, towered over Rumi, now a faceless robot; just a black hull with long mechanical legs. What appeared to be two large guns were affixed to the top of it.

Dion, with few options and significant pain, dislodged the knife and ran for it.

———

Before the backdrop of a setting sun, Arbitryx descended upon the battlefield on large silvery wings. He had arrived late, but with the best of intentions.

"My yazata!" he announced. "Spread the word! We are no longer at war! Nihilo's plan spells doom for us all so we must join forces and..."

It was then that Arbitryx realized his intervention had perhaps come too late. He watched in horror as hundreds of humans who fought against the blight of Nihilo began to transform before his eyes. Each became a twisted thing that wanted only to share its pain with the world.

Arbitryx felt the dark spell working its way into his own mind, but the yazata were stronger than that. It was a nuisance, an irksome voice in the back of his head, but nothing more.

"My shadow yazata!" Arbitryx called. "We must join forces with our sworn enemies so that we might find freedom another-"

"SHUT IT," boomed a guttural voice from above.

A large, calloused hand, roughly the size of the yazata himself, closed in a tight fist around him, snatching Arbitryx out of the sky. Before he could properly react, scheme an escape, the hand lifted higher and higher until it opened, tossing Arbitryx into a massive gaping mouth where he was chewed to mash by rotten yellow teeth.

Dion ran as fast as he could, knowing full well that it was futile. Twisted versions of Rumi and Pasqual pursued him as he moved into a crowd teeming with the enemy.

Rumi's cold, metallic hand grabbed Dion by his neck. He gagged, but only for a second, as the arm loosened and fell severed to the ground.

Baldr, Norse god of justice and one of Dion's oldest foes, appeared with his mighty sword covered in the oil spewing from Rumi's detached limb.

"You?" was all Dion could say. Baldr had always possessed a golden aura that protected him from most magic. Fortunately for him, that included Nihilo's.

"Me," said Baldr. "After this, we're even."

Dion nodded and Baldr fought as valiantly as any deity could. Even when a great shadow fell over them and a giant boot roughly the size of a pick-up truck collided with the earth, causing the ground to quake.

Jason handed a screaming newborn to her teenage brother. The mother was on the ground, suffering through a broken leg. As for the father they begged Jason to save, well, Jason hadn't sensed any other life coming from the rubble.

Jason was kneeling, healing the broken leg, when he noticed something expanding from the corner of his eye. Rising up over the trees and buildings in the distance, where he knew his friends were fighting for their lives, a man grew thirty, fifty, a hundred feet tall. But it wasn't just any man. Even from half a mile away he could recognize the crook in his nose, those long, frowning lips, the head of unkempt red hair.

"Ezekiel," Jason muttered to himself. It seemed as though his nemesis had learned a new trick.

Karen's words rung in his head. "You'll kill everyone."

Hmph. But what did she know? Jason was everyone's best hope; the most powerful Lucid there was made even more powerful by Olokun's god juice. Jason rose from the earth and, fueled by his conviction, flew toward the battle.

Ezekiel, a towering display of utter ruthlessness, looked down upon the battle at hand, the squabbling insects at his feet, and desired nothing more than their destruction. He looked mostly like himself, but his skin was grayer and he looked a little older. He had transformed into the only thing in his life he feared: his father.

He lifted his enormous leg and brought his foot down hard, crushing at least a dozen of them and sending deep fissures in all directions.

The great orb of Nihilo destroyed all it touched and Ezekiel, warped and empowered by the fear it exuded, wanted nothing more than to aid in that destruction.

A single thought is all it took and the entire battlefield was swallowed into a deep sinkhole.

"Mindy!" Aemon shouted as the ground disappeared beneath his feet. The unstable earth convulsed and he reached out toward his love, holding her in space with his mind as the earth collapsed around her.

"Thank you," she said, short of breath. "But save her!" Mindy pointed to Anza as she and Anne the troll, along with a floppy-eared creature and the ghost Patrick, were swallowed by the earth.

Aemon watched with great respect and relief as Anza summoned rocks and roots to rise up to meet her feet as she gracefully descended to the floor at the center of the crater. Anne the troll took hold of Patrick and the grobi, keeping them safely nestled in her arms as she landed hard on her back. Hundreds of others, foes mostly, tumbled down with the rocks.

"Stay close to me!" Anza commanded. "Or else you'll be transformed!"

As she spoke, Aemon noticed a centaur, one that had just been protecting Anza with her life, begin to shift and morph into something spiked and winged and ghastly. He and Mindy moved closer to Anza.

And there they stood at the lowest point of the crater, a storm of dust obscuring their view. Mindy, Aemon, Anza, Anne, Patrick. Amidst the barely visible shifting rocks, the sounds of rage-fueled creatures emerged. Above them the great black sphere hovered, ever-expanding, it's great reaching arms deadly as ever, drawing deep permanent scars in the earth.

"This is our best chance," said Anza. "Keep them back." She turned her attention upwards to the sphere and her body emitted a great, white light.

Dion's head banged against the side of a rock as he slid down the wall of the crater with hundreds of others. Being a god offered him a bit of resilience, otherwise that rock would have burst his skull open - or at least knocked him out. The avalanche continued to pull him downward as another rock pressed against his leg, breaking his femur. Above, through the veil of dust, he saw the silhouette of a gigantic man with his hands on his hips. Dion sensed the pride he felt for the destruction he had achieved.

A skeletal hand took Dion by his chest, right where he had been stabbed. The pain was intense. He was dragged up from the rocks and found himself looking into the sunken eyes of an undead pirate.

FWOOSH

A silver sword whipped by in a blur, lopping the pirate's head off.

Baldr had arrived with six nightmare creatures hanging on, trying their best to take him down.

Both the pirate's headless body, and Dion's broken one, collapsed back onto the rocks.

Baldr stood over Dion, fighting away the nightmares with all of his might. They kept coming.

And coming.

And coming.

Dion looked up as the dust settled. As a sword pierced through Baldr's armor. As a bullet drilled into his shoulder. As a furry, clawed hand bore into his neck. And Dion saw the gigantic man look down into the crater, pleased with himself.

The gigantic man bent his knees, as if preparing to jump. An axe shattered Baldr's knee and that same furry hand cut across his throat. Baldr looked to Dion, and Dion felt his final emotions, equal parts guilt and sorrow and relief.

As Baldr's corpse crumpled on top of Dion, Dion watched helplessly as the gigantic man leapt overhead. When he landed, Dion would be crushed. The ground would tremble once again. More would die.

But he never landed. The giant man simply disappeared. And at the same time, Jason appeared in the sky above like a superhero.

"J-Jason..." Dion could barely speak, Baldr's heavy body was crushing his lungs.

But it didn't matter.

Jason appeared next to Dion and sent all the nightmares flying away with a wave of his hand. With a simple glance, he moved Baldr's corpse to the side, got down on his hands and knees and placed a kiss on Dion's forehead.

"You stopped him," said Dion.

Jason shook his head. "That wasn't me. You're hurt."

"A mere inconvenience," said Dion, grinning through the pain. And then he realized something. Something more horrific than anything he had experienced so far. "You have to go, Jason."

Jason cocked an eyebrow, confused. "What are you talking about? I have to heal you."

"No," Dion was frantic now. "Jason, you're too strong. You have to go. Nihilo's magic-"

Dion stopped as he saw Jason's boyish features began to turn dark. His left eye shifted from blue to a fiery orange. His pinkish flesh turned gray.

"W-what's happening to me?" Jason asked, suddenly terrified.

Dion had to think fast. He hoisted himself up on his one good knee and placed his hands on Jason's head. He felt a powerful energy in his boyfriend. Something that had not been there before. Something...godlike.

"What's happening?" Jason repeated, his body trembling.

"Listen to me," Dion said urgently. "We are going to do this together, okay?" Jason nodded. "Just look into my eyes. Keep looking. Nihilo is trying to use your fears to turn you into a monster. But we cannot let that happen because you are too strong, too good, and we need you, Jason Baker, on our side. Do you understand?"

Jason nodded, tears streaming from his eyes. "I'm scared..."

"I know, my love." Dion focused with all of his might on Jason, pumping him with feelings of peace and joy and hope and calm, anything to combat the encroaching fear, as Nihilo's curse turned Jason's teeth sharp and his hair white.

Dion noticed one of the nightmares approaching them on all fours from the side. It was covered in green spikes and had bulging purple eyes. Its drool sizzled like boiling grease. Just before it would have attacked them, it stopped, looked to the sky, and ran toward the bottom of the crater. All of the nightmares stopped what they were doing to go to the same place.

Something had changed, but Dion had only had one concern: keeping Jason Baker from destroying everything.

64

Anza gazed up at Nihilo's sphere, so large that it was all she could see. She summoned all the power she had inside of her and focused every bit of it on the sphere, exerting the sheer force of her will to combat decline with growth, fear with hope, and nothingness with existence itself. She was the past, present, and future made manifest. She had quite literally been born for this moment. In order to fulfill her destiny, Esperanza Ashford-Soto allowed her perception of the world around her to melt away. Her safety, and by extension the safety of the realms, was in the hands of the few dedicated to protecting her.

Fortunately, this included Aemon. The indigo-skinned man with flowing black hair and peasant's clothes, stood with his arms outstretched in both directions holding back hundreds of nightmarish creatures. They snarled and howled and cursed and clawed but could not move a step further than the invisible wall Aemon had created around his allies.

"You're doing amazing," said Mindy. She readjusted the bladed gauntlet covering her right forearm and hand. "I may not even have to use this thing."

"Seriously, man, where were you, like, this whole time?" Patrick stood with his arms folded, visibly impressed. The grobi rubbed against his legs like a cat.

Anne, the twelve-foot tall troll, eyed the numerous enemies. Her guard was as high as ever; her club raised and battle-ready.

"Take position," said Aemon. The fatigue in his voice was clear. "I cannot hold them back forever. More of them are coming from all sides, weakening my defenses."

"We believe in you." Mindy took his hand in hers.

"And I appreciate that, my love," he replied. "But I am not a god and the poison still lives inside of me. Be ready."

***

Dion was trying his best not to dwell on how dire his situation was becoming. Jason had grown nearly twice in size. His right side was beastly, thick with muscle and hair. His left side was reptilian, covered in tough scales; lean, but just as strong. The fear in his eyes was all but gone. Succumbing to Nihilo's magic was only a matter of time.

"Stay with me, please, please," Dion pleaded. "I love you, I love you so much, and I came back from the dead and, gods, is it too much to ask for just one day where you and I can just be a pair of dumb wine-drunk teenagers in love instead of constantly, *constantly*, trying to stop the world from falling apart?!"

Dion maintained his grip on Jason's large, misshapen head, but looked up to the sky as if in desperate prayer. There was no response, but Dion did notice something interesting. The many jagged black arms reaching out from the sphere were growing thinner and retracting, pulling back toward their massive round floating source.

Dion pressed his forehead against Jason's and closed his eyes.

***

As Nihilo's sphere was suspended above, Aemon's protective circle was closing in around them.

"It's weakening," said Aemon, his outstretched hands shaking.

"Okay," Mindy addressed the others. "Form a tight circle around Anza. Take out anything that gets through."

As she said it, a moss-covered beast, like something from a swamp, lumbered toward Mindy.

"You got this?" asked Patrick.

Mindy smirked. She reached her arm forward and a rope-like shape stretched from her gauntlet and wrapped around the creature; a single thin ring around its chest and arms. It lost its balance and toppled to the ground. "I got this," she said.

More creatures were coming through, including a purple slime creature that Anne obliterated with her club.

Patrick took out a knight in rusty armor with a concentrated stab of his iridescent sword.

A monstrous centaur entered the circle. His horse body seemed as if it were carved from rock. His human half was engorged with muscle and he wore a crown atop his head from which blood poured endlessly. His features suggested that he may have been Nikkylos. He charged forward, evading Mindy's attack, then Patrick's. He picked up speed; its hooves leaving marks in the rocky earth.

By the time Anne heard him coming from behind, it was too late to react. The centaur would have ended Anza had the grobi not jumped on top of him and teleported them both away. A moment later the grobi returned alone, cleaning the centaur's blood from its paw.

"More of that!" said Patrick to the floppy-eared animal.

The battle continued this way, with more nightmares making their attempts at Anza as the heroes fended them off. Mindy immobilized them, Patrick hacked and slashed, the grobi teleported them away. Anne plucked a twisted yazata from the air and hurled it into the sphere. It was then that Anne realized that the sphere had gotten smaller. She could see the late-day sky again. Anza was doing it.

"We just need to hold out a little longer!" she said in her gruff troll's voice.

"YYYAAARRRRGGGHHHH!" Aemon released a gut-wrenching scream. His body rose from the ground and folded unnaturally, his bones crunching as his spine bent backwards twice. His neck turned almost completely around, snapping it. Yet through it all he remained alive.

"Aemon!" screamed Mindy.

His forcefield came down and hundreds of monsters barreled toward Anza; an unstoppable flood of nightmares. But their predatory joy was cut short as they all, every single one of them, rose up, suspended feet above the ground unable to move. Mindy, Patrick, and the others found themselves hanging in the air as well.

And then it appeared. A horrific monster that stood ten feet tall. Its right half was covered in thick, matted black fur and the left half, tough rust-colored scales. Its eyes were on fire, demonic. Its teeth were long and sharp and crooked. Every inch of it was engorged with muscle. It roared and all the other nightmares fell quiet.

"SILENCE," the monster snapped as slobber poured between its teeth. "YOU, ALL OF YOU THINK I'M CRAZY." Its voice was booming, but trembled with terror.

"NO, I AM NOT CRAZY. I AM POWERFUL! MOST POWERFUL. YOU ALL FIGHT AND FIGHT AND FAIL...BUT I WIN...I WILL DESTROY HER AND WIN...I AM NOT CRAZY. I AM IN CONTROL. YOU ARE ALL UNDER MY CONTROL..."

The beast stalked towards Anza.

"Monster standing at approximately ten feet tall," called Claire Ashford as she reached the bottom of the crater. "The one I'm walking toward right now that seems to be part gorilla, part crocodile, and all disgusting?"

"I think that's specific enough," said Victor, who was climbing down a chunk of stone that had once been the street. He made contact with solid ground and joined her.

Claire rolled her eyes, but maintained focus on the beast. "I need you to be incapable of using any additional superpowers."

The beast stopped and turned its furry, scaly head to them. "YOU TWO? YOU ARE JOKES," it growled. "WEAK. MEDIOCRE. COWARDS. HOW...HOW ARE YOU NOT BROKEN...?"

Claire frowned. "First of all, rude. Second of all, we had each-"

"DIE!" The beast charged toward Claire and Victor.

"I need you to stand still," Claire commanded. The beast did as it was told, though it wasn't happy about it. "And also focus quietly on my boyfriend and me until I snap my fingers." The beast stared blankly at the two of them, making not a sound. "That's a good boy."

"That's my sister!" cheered Patrick, stuck with the rest in the air.

"And my best friend!" roared Anne.

Victor had a stupid grin on his face. "Did you just say boyfriend?"

Everyone watched Anza in silent awe as a pure white light rose up from her body and enveloped the dark sphere, now no larger in diameter than an eighteen-wheeler. The light surrounded it completely and it shrunk, faster and faster, smaller and smaller, until it was no more.

Anza collapsed to her hands and feet, out of breath. She had missed much of the battle and was surprised when hundreds of humans and other creatures dropped to the ground all around her. No longer were they twisted, nightmarish perversions. Once more were they the confused, imperfect, yet complete creatures they had been before all this. Though, truly, many of them would never be the same again.

The ones unsure of what had happened wasted no time in making their way out of the crater. Most of them normal people who had lived normal lives before this catastrophe.

A normal life was something Anza had never known.

Just as the ones ignorant to the greater details of battle fled, those who were all too familiar gravitated toward the center. Some were people she had only heard of in Guillelmina's and Patrick's stories. Agalfia Tirk propped up someone who, aside from being a bit too skinny, looked like Jack. And, though missing a right arm, someone who could have only been Rumi Inyonara walked with a tall stern man in black. There were others as well, but none could compare to the two standing not fifteen feet away.

"Claire? Victor?" she said, unsure of where to go from there the moment they turned their attention to her. They looked exactly as Patrick and Guillelmina described. Despite all of this, they seemed so young.

"Uh...hey," said Victor, blushing. "You're..."

"Yeah," Anza replied. "How did you...?"

Victor just pointed to his head. "Superpowers."

They laughed awkwardly.

"And you look just like us," Claire said.

"Heh. I guess I do." Now Anza was blushing. "I guess I should thank you, for, you know, not getting me killed in my first year."

"It was our pleasure." Claire offered Anza a friendly, awkward punch to her arm.

"And look at you now," Victor added. "Saving the world."

"Yeah..." Anza gasped. "Wait, no. No. No. Oh no."

"What's wrong?" Victor asked.

"I stopped Nihilo, but-" Anza grabbed the sides of her head and began pacing. "When I was being raised in Origin Point, it wasn't Nihilo who destroyed the world. It was the realms collapsing. Something about unstable tectonic plates and the ozone layer then everyone died in space!"

"What!" Claire exclaimed.

Anza's pacing intensified, "Damnit, no." Then she turned to her parents. "I don't know what to do. We...we never really figured out that part. I don't have the power to undo entire realities...at least I don't think I do." She turned to her dad. "Do I?!"

Victor shook his head.

"Then what do we do?!"

Just then a dark swirling portal opened up just in front of them. Anza thought the worst: that Nihilo had found a way back, that she had failed again. But her fear lessened- a little - when a tall, beautiful woman with dark skin and a bald head, dressed impeccably in West African clothing and jewels, emerged.

"Olokun," Anza said in a way that was part awe, part gasp.

"That is correct, child," said the goddess. "And let's be clear. I decide what happens next."

65

Olokun first looked to the sky. It was streaked with purples and oranges and pinks, nature's most perfect sunset. One of the many gifts humanity had failed to appreciate. Measured, she allowed her attention to move to Claire and Victor who looked at her with reverence, sure, but not at a level befitting a goddess with the power to end them all.

"Victor and Claire," Olokun said, almost bored. "I must say I'm surprised you survived this whole thing." She opened wide her long, muscular arms, surveying the crater and all its wreckage. "And look at the mess you made." She found amusement in the statement. "Speaking of your messes..." She nodded her head toward Anza.

"This is on you," Victor said. "All of it."

Olokun honestly didn't think he had it in him to speak to her that way. She considered flinging him into the moon, but decided against it. "So I've heard, Mister Soto."

Olokun took a look around. Most of the remaining faces were familiar to her; people and things caught up in her...in Nihilo's...machinations. She frowned a bit when she saw that irritating girl Satya approach. She frowned even more when she locked eyes with Dion as he helped his beloved to his feet and removed his own shirt to cover his beloved's bruised and naked body.

Never mind all that.

"I am Olokun," she began, loud enough to be heard by all who needed to hear it. "Goddess of the unknown and the most capable mind in this or any realm. I hold mastery over destiny itself." She caught sight of Anne, returned to that buck-toothed fool that dared speak up to her. "What I do next comes down to a single choice: Do I use my power to save this world or do I let it be destroyed so that I might rebuild something better in its place?"

Olokun allowed her words to sink in as she surveyed her onlookers once more. Max and Jamal, despite the stakes, seemed more interested in each other than the current situation. Mindy was helping Aemon untangle his warped body. Olokun saw a strength in that Mindy girl that defied her mere humanity.

"I have reached my conclusion," Olokun said, adding, "and not without the counsel of a few obnoxious humans." She swallowed. Her face was unreadable. "My conclusion is that I am flawed. And in judging this existence I would be placing myself on a pedestal that I do not deserve. I would be emulating those who I hate the most: privileged, elitist monsters throughout history who thought themselves better; who thought themselves God, and in doing so, destroyed us all. I will be better than that. And I will hope to not regret it." She took a breath and continued, "If any of you were able to find joy in this disaster, revel in it one last time before I at last undo this mess I have made and return the realms, and their inhabitants, to their natural place."

Olokun closed her eyes and bowed her head. Her body maintained its shape, but turned to fluorescent blue light and a ring of energy burst outward from her.

Patrick took Claire in the biggest hug, lifting her off her feet. "I'm so proud of you, sis, and so happy I got to see you again." To Victor he added, "Thanks for taking care of her and my favorite niece." Patrick then turned to Anza and winked. "I have a feeling I'll be seeing you around."

"Time for Phase Two?" Anza said with a sly smile.

Patrick nodded. "Time for Phase Two. Guillelmina would be so proud."

Bobby and Jack pulled out of a teary embrace.

"I missed you so much," Jack said.

"Well, I'm always watching you, bro," said Bobby. "But right now, you've got other things to do." He gestured to Aggie and took a step back.

Aggie placed her hand on Jack's shoulder. "You were a hero today. I wish you well and I wish you love and happiness in your world. As yourself."

"I'll see you in my dreams," said Jack, sadness in his tone.

Aggie pursed her lips. "Perhaps. But they will only be dreams for you now, as you will be for me. Remember that. I must go to my brothers now. Goodbye, Jack." Aggie ran off, bounding up the crater's edge.

"She didn't even say goodbye to me. Rude." Rumi had sidled up next to Jack without him noticing. Pasqual was with her. She was missing an arm but the stump was contained by a translucent blue field.

"Are you okay?" Jack asked, examining the wound.

Rumi smirked. "Never better. You?"

Jack shrugged and looked to his brother. "Getting there." He faced Rumi and asked, "What are you going to do now?"

Rumi shrugged. "Great zagging question, kid. If my cloudy memories are any hint, first I'm gonna find Eliza and fix her up. Next," she bit her lip. "Futara's gone, so…I guess I'll do the most Rumi Inyonara thing possible and find another war to fight."

"Dude." Max clasped Jamal's shoulders. "Don't cry, dude, you'll make me cry!"

Jamal couldn't help it, he was heaving, barely able to look at his translucent best friend.

"Look, dude." Max's freckled face made way for a big, goofy smile. "At least I'm gonna be, like, somewhere, ya know? There's a somewhere that we'll both be someday. Better than nowhere. Better than never."

Jamal held him tight. "I love you so much, man."

"Me too you, dude. Me too you."

"My Queen," said Aemon as he kissed Mindy on the hand.

"Don't call me that," she said with a grin.

"It looks like you will finally be able to return home."

Mindy sighed. "Yeah. Back to the life of a teenage girl in a small town with no robots or centaurs or magic." She put her arm around Aemon's waist. "No you. So boring."

"A world with you in it is anything but boring, my love."

"Take care of them." She noticed many faces standing around; men and women and a spry young velociraptor who had faith in her even when she had little in herself.

Aemon nodded, "I will."

"We will," said Nikkylos as he trotted to them. "We will rebuild the Black Forest and your Valley of Hope into the refuge you envisioned."

Aemon searched the area. "Agalfia Tirk as well. It is as much her land as it is any of ours."

Mindy kissed Aemon on the neck. Then the cheek. Then the lips. "I'll visit often. You are the best man I've ever known."

Olokun could feel the raw power of life and death coursing through her and flooding the world. It was more than any body, man or myth, was meant to bear, but she would do it. She sensed the expanding perimeter where the realms had collapsed ceasing their destructive crawl, then reversing themselves, untangling and unfurling toward her from all directions. The tattered realms were healing, returning to their natural place.

She felt her flesh and bone give in to the power. The more power she summoned the more it ate away at her. Her muscles and organs, though bathed in light, were beginning to fail. As she used her might to restore the realms, her own body emptied itself of its essence, with every second growing closer and closer to a dried husk. She feared she would not survive long enough to stop the realms from collapsing.

And then she felt a hand interlace its fingers with her own.

She opened her eyes and saw Jason Baker in one of her colorful African shirts, connecting to her, sharing her burden with his power. And with him, Dion, bare-chested and eyes glowing wine-red, doing the same.

Olokun could not help but smile when Anza took her other hand, filling her with a rush of hope.

In the great chaos Olokun had caused, here, with her, beside her, were the ones who perhaps had the most reason to despise her. And yet, the most connected to her. The ones she was the proudest of. And as the realms returned to their rightful place and the friends and lovers with them, Olokun knew without a doubt, her decision to save them had been the right one.

Epilogue I:
2 months after Nihilo's War

Rumi watched with awe as a baby deer with butterfly wings fluttered awkwardly across a television screen. It was one of over a hundred screens she and her team had installed in her state-of-the-art surveillance facility.

"We've got a pack of goblins on the move," said Eliza, who had been repaired a few weeks earlier and given a fresh, new human skin. She turned a dial and her screen moved in closer on eight goblins making their way through a ruined mini-mall. "It's probably another day or two before they make contact with anyone. Sector 19-D."

"Got it," said Rumi. "Contact Black Rock and let Aggie's people know. I'm sure she'd love to deal with this one on her own."

"You got it, boss." Eliza turned away from the screens and began tinkering on an oversized silvery weapon.

"How are we doing, Pasqual?" Rumi shouted to the shadows above.

"Good enough," he responded. "We'll have eighty more cameras installed and functional within the next couple days."

The gentle "pop" heralded the arrival of Anza, with a grobi on her shoulder. Anza gave the creature a pat on the back. "Nice work, Pet."

"Ah, look who it is!" Rumi beamed. "How's the Guardian of the Realms, herself?"

Anza laughed. "We are all the guardians of the realms, Rumi. I just left a council in Eternia. We're discussing making significant reforms to the leveling system in the afterlife. Vacation days for the yazata. A half-way house system for well-behaved souls." She added with a sad smile, "We're calling it the Guillelmina Accord."

"Sounds like a lot," said Eliza.

"It's not easy." Anza moaned. "But I guess we knew that going in. Seriously though, Patrick and Bobby have been a big help organizing the lobbying committees and things. And Max, well, keeps things fun. I mean, Patrick literally killed Bobby in Cosmos and they argue less than these yazata do. But anyway, how are things in Reverie?"

"Crazy," said Rumi. "Just the way I like it. Come on, let's get some air." She led Anza from the surveillance room to the outside. They were standing on the balcony of a tall black building that stood in the middle of a flat, formless expanse of gray that stretched for miles in every direction.

"It's been months and I still can't believe that all of this used to be Futara," Rumi said. "My whole life. Just disappeared."

Anza placed her hand on Rumi's shoulder. "But you're here. And what you build in Futara's place will be a testament to the best of your city. Including your parents and everyone else who fought to keep it safe. And if you need anything, just let me know." Anza lifted the hair covering her neck, revealing a small tattoo. There were three horizontal lines and a silhouette of a tree that lay on top of them. "The Guardians of the Realms are here to listen, here to help."

Rumi nodded and brushed her neon-streaked hair from her own neck, revealing an identical tattoo. "No matter what."

Epilogue II:
3 months after Nihilo's War

Addley, as with portions of Reverie and Eternia, suffered greatly in the wake of the war. Three months had passed in the small town and the wounds were still healing. Homes and schools and bars and restaurants were still being rebuilt, made all the more difficult with the coming winter and most recently an early blizzard that brought most construction to a standstill. But on this quiet snowy night, with his parents off visiting family in Argentina, Victor decided to throw a party.

He plopped down on his old couch next to Claire and handed her a red drink that was most definitely just punch.

"Is your mom okay with you staying over?" Victor asked.

Claire shrugged. "She's at some singles resort in Mali showing off her new shoulders and returned gift of sight, so...who cares?"

They tapped their plastic cups together and took a sip, smiling at how normal this all was.

Mindy approached the two of them, with an expression more serious than this relaxing evening could possibly call for. "Hey, Claire, can I talk to you for a second?"

"Uh, sure." Claire stood up, kissed Victor on the forehead, and followed her to the stairs.

In the kitchen, Jamal took a shot of tequila as he and his basketball teammates shouted and howled in celebration. In Jamal's back pocket, folded in his wallet, was a picture of him and Max, together at the Spring Fling, before the world came undone.

Dion and Jason were in the dining room, each with a glass of wine, laughing as they recounted last night's episode of their favorite trashy reality show. They were explaining it to a seventeen-year-old transfer student. She had arrived weeks before from West Africa. She had dark skin and a bald head and had decided it was past time she reconnected with humanity. All three shared the same tattoo on their necks.

On the front porch, Anne and Jack sat side-by-side, warm in their coats and scarves and gloves. A mug of hot chocolate in each of their hands. Parties weren't really their thing so they decided to have a simple chat about video games and school and how much things had changed.

Upstairs, Mindy Sparks stood in Victor's parents' room behind a closed door. Claire sat anxiously at the edge of the bed.

"What's up, Mindy?" Claire asked. "Are you okay?"

Mindy shook her head, not able to find the words at first. Then she threw her arms into the air and dropped onto the bed beside Claire. "I don't know." She sat up, looked at Claire, and said, "I'm pregnant."

THE END

Author's note.

Thank you. *Thank* you. Thank *you*.

I hope you enjoyed following the twisting, turning tales of Claire, Victor, and the rest of the gang as much as I've enjoyed writing them. To be honest I'm a little sad to leave these kids behind, but I will be forever indebted to you (and to the citizens of Cosmos, Reverie, and Eternia) for going on this ride with me in the first place.

You haven't heard the last of me as my next series is already underway.

Keep in touch and see you on the next adventure!

-   Trystin S. Bailey

If you enjoyed the read, I would be beyond grateful if you:
- *Find me on Instagram and/or Twitter **@trystinbailey***
- *Leave a review on **Amazon** and **Goodreads***
- *Check out exclusive content at **trystinbailey.com***